Just Before
Dawn

NATIONAL BESTSELLING AUTHOR

ROCHELLE ALERS

Just Before Dawn

A HIDEAWAY NOVEL

ARABESQUE®

Recycling programs
for this product may
not exist in your area.

JUST BEFORE DAWN

ISBN-13: 978-0-373-53456-2

Copyright © 2011 by Rochelle Alers

First published by BET Publications, LLC in 2000

www.kimanipress.com

Printed in U.S.A.

Dear Reader,

Just Before Dawn, the second title in the Hideaway daughters and sisters trilogy, which is part of the larger series, won several Emma Awards at the Romance Slam Jam convention in 2001, including Favorite All-Nighter Romance, Best Killer, Thriller and Adventure Romance, and Favorite Heroine.

In the years since it was first published, *Just Before Dawn* has become a reader favorite and one of my personal favorites. Take a silent, sexy, clairvoyant hero, add a gun-toting heroine, a hybrid wolf-dog and a villain hell-bent on murder, and you have a recipe for a scintillating romantic thriller.

New Mexico is the setting for *Just Before Dawn*, and it lives up to the state's nickname, "the land of enchantment," with beautiful sunsets, colorful characters and authentic Native American and Spanish art. From the first page you become lost in a romance that draws you in and keeps you enthralled until the very last word.

As always, remember to read, love and live your romance.

Rochelle Alers

www.rochellealers.com

HIDEAWAY SERIES

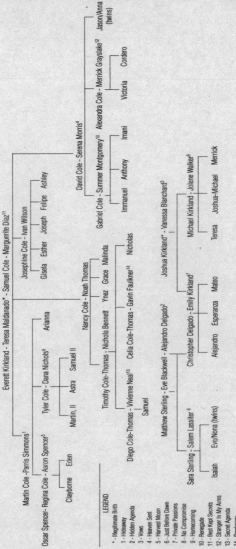

Everett Kirkland - Teresa Maldanado* - Samuel Cole - Marguerite Diaz[11]

Martin Cole -*Parris Simmons[1]

Oscar Spencer- Regina Cole - Aaron Spencer[5]

Claybourne   Eden

Tyler Cole - Dana Nichols[9]

Martin, II   Astra   Samuel II

Arianna

Josephine Cole - Ivan Wilson

Gisela   Esther   Joseph   Felipe   Ashley

Nancy Cole - Noah Thomas

Timothy Cole-Thomas - Nichola Bennett   Ynez   Grace   Malinda

Celia Cole-Thomas - Gavin Faulkner[14]

Nicholas

Diego Cole-Thomas - Vivienne Neal[13]

Samuel

Matthew Sterling - Eve Blackwell - Alejandro Delgado[7]

Christopher Delgado - Emily Kirkland[7]

Alejandro   Esperanza   Mateo

Joshua Kirkland* - Vanessa Blanchard[3]

Michael Kirkland - Jolene Walker[8]

Teresa   Joshua-Michael   Merrick

Sara Sterling - Salem Lassiter[6]

Isaiah   Eve/Nona (twins)

David Cole - Serena Morris[4]

Gabriel Cole - Summer Montgomery[10]

Immanuel   Anthony   Imani

Alexandra Cole - Merrick Grayslake[12]

Victoria   Cordero

Jason/Anna (twins)

LEGEND
* - Illegitimate Birth
1 - Hideaway
2 - Hidden Agenda
3 - Vows
4 - Heaven Sent
5 - Harvest Moon
6 - Just Before Dawn
7 - Private Passions
8 - No Compromise
9 - Homecoming
10 - Renegade
11 - Best Kept Secrets
12 - Stranger In My Arms
13 - Secret Agenda
14 - Breakaway

Chapter 1

Sara Sterling glanced at the delicate stainless-steel-and-gold watch on her wrist, frowning slightly. The nine-thirty meeting that should have ended half an hour ago continued without any indication of adjourning at noon.

She knew John Bohannon was waiting—she doubted patiently—outside the U.S. District Court building in Brooklyn to drive her to the airport. He had taken a day off from his coveted position as a securities broker to spend time with her before she began her planned three-month leave of absence. He'd offered his services to chauffeur her despite her objection that she could call a car service. They had argued, but in the end she'd relented.

As an assistant district attorney for New York's eastern district she had spent the past two years working diligently to alleviate the court's overloaded docket, and the result had been a string of victories coupled with the threat of impending career burnout.

She was now returning to her home state for the first time in twenty-six months. She had prepaid her rent for three months, disconnected her telephone and made arrangements to forward her mail to her parents' home in Las Cruces, New Mexico. She needed to reconnect with her mother, father, brother and the horses she had learned to ride a year after she had learned to walk.

Her gaze met the intense stare of the Brooklyn district attorney, and she nodded. He returned her nod as she stood up and pushed back her chair. All eyes were focused on the tall, slender woman who offered them a smile before she walked out of the conference room.

Her heels made distinctive clicking sounds as she made her way across the marble flooring to the small, cramped office she shared with another assistant district attorney. Barring a horrific traffic jam on the Brooklyn-Queens Expressway, John could make it to La Guardia Airport in time for her to check her luggage before she boarded her flight.

She retrieved her handbag, making certain it contained her ticket, and rushed out of the building, down the steps and around the corner, where John had promised to wait for her. She spied him leaning against the bumper of his late-model Lexus and waved. He straightened, returning her wave.

Sara had dated John half a dozen times over the past four months and, although she found herself the envy of many young black professional women who saw her and John as the perfect couple, she could not rouse any emotion deeper than friendship for the highly successful, very "together" brother.

Most times John looked as if he had just stepped off the cover of *GQ*. His professional curriculum vitae listed the best schools and professional affiliations, and his net worth was purported to approach seven figures.

He was perfect for any woman—except her. She did not know what it was, but there was something about John that would not permit her to completely relax in his presence.

John Bohannon watched Sara Sterling's approach, his dark eyes widening appreciatively behind the lenses of his sunglasses. She was ideal—his female counterpart.

She was a brilliant attorney who had come to the Brooklyn federal court at twenty-six, and had distinguished herself within less than three years as a tenacious, aggressive prosecutor. She figuratively devoured defense attorneys, relishing their decisions to go to trial rather than accept plea bargains. Sara had never discussed her work with him, and had warned him on their first date that she would no longer see him if he broached the subject.

He wanted to see her—every day, if possible. When he was first introduced to her through a mutual friend, he could not believe some man had not married her. It was only two days ago that he had realized he wanted to marry her. Not seeing her for three months had elicited an emotion he had not experienced in years—insecurity. He did not want her to leave New York and never return. He wanted her.

After an early-morning telephone call, he realized he had also needed her. Now he needed her to protect him from an impending legal entanglement that could destroy him and all that he had worked so hard to achieve over the past decade.

An admiring smile lifted the corners of his mobile mouth. Her stunning natural beauty was mesmerizing—especially her eyes. They were an odd shade of green with gold, which made him think of her as a lithe, graceful feline. Her naturally wavy black hair was cut in a becoming, sophisticated style that fell into layered precision when brushed off her high, intelligent forehead. Her delicate nose and lush mouth complemented a rich deep-brown coloring that made him wonder what bloodlines she claimed other than her obvious African ones. He had asked her once, and she had refused to discuss it.

If John found her face perfect, her body was even more so. She was tall for a woman, five-eight, slender without being thought of as too thin, and as physically fit as any professional female athlete. He knew she worked out five days a week at a local sports and health club. Her regimen included aerobics, thirty minutes on a treadmill and a vigorous game of racquetball. He had beaten her only twice on the racquetball court, feats which did little to assuage his bruised male ego.

His admiring gaze lingered on her long, shapely legs below the hem of a slim black linen skirt. Her conservative suit, ivory silk blouse, sheer black hose and two-inch black patent leather pumps did little to subdue the obvious sensuality she refused to openly acknowledge.

"I'm sorry I'm late," she said in apology, offering her cheek for a chaste kiss. "I thought it would have ended more than thirty minutes ago."

John flashed a warm smile he did not quite feel at that moment. He opened the passenger-side door of his car. "It's all right. We still have time to pick up your luggage from your apartment. I wanted to leave early because I thought perhaps we would have time to share lunch before you boarded."

Sara ducked her head and slipped onto the leather seat. *Impeccable manners,* she mused. Aside from his classic good looks and fastidious style of dressing, she silently admired John's manners. There was never a time when she was in his presence that she had not felt protected. John was the only man, other than her father, who had accomplished that.

Sara waited until he took his seat behind the wheel, then rewarded him with a warm smile. Her brilliant, jewel-like, slanting eyes tilted upward and caused him to catch his breath for several seconds before he let it out. Sara had no way of knowing how much of a turn-on it was for him whenever she smiled at him like that.

Reaching into her handbag, she withdrew a pair of sunglasses and perched them on the end of her short, straight nose. "Anything we'll eat in a restaurant in the terminal would have to be better than what I'll be served during the flight."

John returned her smile, then turned the key in the ignition. It caught immediately, and seconds later he maneuvered the luxury sedan through the narrow streets in the direction of her one-bedroom apartment in Brooklyn Heights.

He took a quick glance at Sara when she settled back on her seat and closed her eyes. "Tired?"

"Exhausted."

He wanted to talk, but decided against it. One thing he'd learned about Sara Sterling was that he could not persuade her to do anything she did not want to do. He had heard a rumor that she had been engaged to a fellow prelaw student when they were undergraduates, that it was she who had ended the relationship, and that they had decided to attend different law schools.

She attended a local New York City law school, making law review, and had come highly recommended to the district attorney's office. She always spent weeks preparing for her cases, and when she walked into the courtroom all eyes were riveted on the woman who never raised her voice above its normal tone. What caught everyone's attention immediately was that whenever she opened her mouth her words were layered with a distinctive Southwestern intonation. It had surprised John when she disclosed that she had grown up on a horse farm in New Mexico. But then, everything about the woman amazed him.

His jaw tightened as he clenched his teeth. She had picked the wrong time to take an extended leave. But then, maybe it wasn't. He quickly changed his mind. Her being away gave him three months. Three months to plan how he would make certain Sara never returned to New York.

Sara pushed her salad around on her plate with a fork, not hearing what John was saying. She was listening for the announcement that it was time for her to board her flight. It came, and she put down the fork and picked up her handbag. She waited until John dropped a large bill on the table, then stood up.

They walked side by side until they arrived at the gate where she would board the aircraft. Turning, she smiled up at him. "Thanks for everything."

He grasped her hands, pulling her closer. "I'm going to miss you."

She examined his even features and close-cropped hair, noted the exquisite quality of the fabric of a banded-collar, pale wheat linen shirt under his matching suit jacket.

"I'll send you a postcard," she teased.

"You *can* call me," he countered, successfully concealing his stinging annoyance regarding her apparent indifference to his feelings.

Moving closer, she curved her arms around his neck. "I'll do better than that. When I come back I promise I'll make more time for you."

His eyebrows shot up in surprise. "Are you saying you'll see me more than once every two weeks?"

"Yes."

Taking his cue from her apparent change of heart, he pulled her flush against his body, kissing her. Her lips parted slightly, giving him access to the sweet moistness of her lush mouth. The kiss only lasted seconds, but it signaled a promise of more to come—much more. And he would take the three months offered them to plan for their future.

Sara pushed gently against his chest. "I have to go. They're calling my row."

John released her, watching as she walked away. Then she disappeared completely from his line of vision. A satisfied smile curved his strong mouth under his neatly barbered mustache. *Everything is going to be okay. I will beat this.* The reassuring voice in his head comforted him; he had nothing to fear.

The jet touched down at the Las Cruces International Airport, and Sara adjusted her watch to reflect Mountain Time. She had gained two hours during the four-hour flight from New York to New Mexico.

Even before deplaning she felt the intense arid desert heat penetrating the glass. Removing her jacket, she inched along the aisle and made her way out of the aircraft to the baggage claim area.

A satisfied smile softened her mouth. *I'm home.*

She had grown to love the pulsing excitement of New York City, but there was never a time when she thought of it as home. She loved New Mexico: its color, cold, heat, mountain ranges and the colorful racial mixture of the people of the United States Southwest.

The blood of people who had built mighty empires before Europeans stepped foot in the Americas flowed through her veins. To the curious who met her for the first time and asked what she was, she always said African American. She did not add that her African blood had been blended with that of the Zapotec Indians from Mexico's southern region—a bloodline given her by her African-Mexican American father.

Her determined steps slowed when she saw a tall man leaning against a column in the baggage area, legs crossed at the ankles, holding up a sign bearing her name. It was impossible for him to see her clearly because of the wide, dark, straw Western-style hat he had pulled down over his face.

She tapped his forearm. "I'm Sara Sterling."

Salem Lassiter raised his head when he detected the touch on his arm and the haunting, seductive scent of a woman's perfume. Using a forefinger, he pushed back the brim of his hat so that he could see her face. He inhaled sharply, then let out his breath so slowly he felt light-headed. His neighbor had asked him to meet his daughter at the airport, and never had he been asked to perform a more pleasant task.

"Your father asked that I pick you up."

She arched a sweeping, curving eyebrow. "Who are you?"

He straightened from his leaning position. "Salem Lassiter, ma'am."

"Why isn't my father here?"

Salem felt a thread of annoyance at being questioned by a woman, especially one as haughty as the one confronting him. He had to admit, though, that Matthew and Eve Sterling had produced an exquisite child who had inherited the best features of her attractive parents.

"He and your mother had to fly to Switzerland to bring your brother back home."

Her eyes widened. "Chris?"

Salem nodded. "He broke his leg skiing."

Covering her mouth with one hand, she closed her eyes and successfully composed herself. She had not realized how loud her heart was pounding in her ears until she opened her eyes and saw Salem Lassiter's mouth moving with no sound coming from it.

She lowered her hand. "I'm sorry, Mr. Lassiter. I wasn't listening."

"How many bags do you have?"

"Just one."

"Show me." The words, though spoken softly, were a command. Taking her elbow, he led her over to the carousel. Various pieces of luggage were just beginning to slide along the conveyer belt.

Sara ignored the tall man standing beside her as she watched for her bag on the moving belt. She couldn't believe her half brother had broken his leg skiing. Thirty-three-year-old Christopher Delgado had taken to skiing the same way she had first sat on a horse—like an expert. There was a time when she thought he would become an Olympic skier, but once he'd entered college he'd changed his mind, deciding on a career in politics. He ran for the state senate and won by a very narrow margin on his first attempt. During his last trip to New York to visit her he had confided that he had his sights set on becoming governor of the state. Given his looks, intelligence and infectious charisma, she knew she would one day call her older brother Governor Delgado.

She turned her attention back to the man who had been instructed to meet her, her gaze fixed on the clearcut lines of his profile. It was difficult to tell Salem Lassiter's age, but she was transfixed by the smooth dark skin pulled taut over the elegant ridge of his high cheekbones. His nose was long and thin, his mouth firm and full enough to be thought of as sensual. She knew his large slanting eyes were very dark, but hadn't been able to detect the color or texture of his hair under the wide hat.

He was tall, not quite as tall as her six-foot, four-inch father, but he came close. But unlike her father's heavily muscled body, Salem Lassiter's was lean and slender. His pair of well-worn laundered jeans and matching pale blue denim shirt fit his tight body as if they'd been tailored expressly for him. Her gaze moved down to his dusty low-heeled boots. Her single piece of luggage neared them, and she pointed at the monogrammed leather bag.

Salem gave her a sidelong glance before he reached over and picked up the bag in one smooth motion. His dark eyes met hers for a brief second.

"I'm parked outside." Turning, he walked away, leaving her to stare at his broad shoulders.

Shrugging a shoulder, Sara stared at his slim hips and followed him. *Rude!* That was the only word she could come up with to categorize Salem Lassiter. When her parents returned she would talk to her father about his employee. There was no doubt the man was probably an expert when it came to horses—otherwise Matt Sterling would not have hired him—but it was apparent Salem spent too many hours with horses, and not enough time with women.

She was still smarting when he stopped beside a sport utility vehicle. She lingered in the hot sun while he placed her bag in the cargo area before he moved over to unlock the passenger door for her.

Salem waited for her to step up into the Navigator. He went completely still when he realized she couldn't get into the vehicle. The step was too high for her in her narrow skirt. Curving both hands around her narrow waist, he lifted her effortlessly. The sudden motion caused her to lose her balance, and she fell back against his chest. Tightening his grip, he steadied her, then settled her on the leather seat.

Sara stared down at Salem's smiling face, her own burning with humiliation. "Thank you." The two words were torn from the back of her throat.

He touched the brim of his hat with the thumb and forefinger of his left hand. "You're welcome, ma'am."

She felt a shiver of annoyance. "Please stop calling me that!"

"Ma'am?"

"Yes!"

He stood motionless, his expression impassive. "What do you want me to call you, ma'am?"

Her gaze narrowed, reminding him of a cat. "Sara will do."

He touched his hat again. "Then Sara it is." A slight smile touched his beautifully formed masculine mouth. He closed the door with a resounding thud. Without warning, his smile faded. *Spoiled minx,* he thought angrily. What was it with beautiful women? he continued in his silent tirade. What made them think men were supposed to genuflect before them just because they'd been blessed with extraordinary faces and bodies? He would deliver Sara Sterling to her father's ranch and then forget that he had ever met her.

Sara ignored the man sitting beside her as she stared out at the passing landscape. It was the beginning of June, and the blazing sun had already scorched the arid landscape. She had traveled New Mexico from north to south, and she always preferred the desertlike southern region best. The sight of cactus, mesquite, sagebrush and desert willow trees always evoked a feeling that she had come to another planet, one devoid of oxygen, water and other forms of life. However, she knew the desert was alive, alive and teeming with plants and animals whose numbers were astounding.

Her father, a native of West Texas, had purchased six hundred acres of land in Las Cruces before she was born, and subsequently established the most successful horse breeding farm west of the Mississippi River. He had bred a Kentucky Derby and Belmont Stakes winner, adding Sterling Farms to the celebrated annals of horse-racing history.

A flash of loneliness assailed her when Salem crossed the boundary to her family's property. She hadn't seen her parents and brother since Christmas, when they had flown to New York to celebrate the holidays with her, and not having them greet her return now elicited a feeling of disappointment. She wanted to ask Salem if he knew when her parents and brother would return to Las Cruces, then decided against it.

She would ask Marisa Hall, the live-in housekeeper who had come to the Sterling household nearly thirty years ago as a young divorced mother requesting work and a place to live. Even though her son, an only child, had graduated from Tulane University and moved to Chicago, where he and his wife had made Marisa a grandmother for the second time, she continued to maintain her residence at Sterling Farms.

Sara's gaze lingered on grazing horses as frisky young colts frolicked not far from the watchful eyes of their mothers; she recognized some of the offspring as potential champions. This was evident in the length of their elegant arched necks, strong muscular quarters, and high-set tails. Salem drove another quarter of a mile, slowing and stopping in front of an expansive one-story ranch house.

"I'll help you down," he announced quietly when she unsnapped her seat belt.

Her head came around slowly and she stared directly at him for the first time since getting into the truck. Sitting less than two feet away from him made her aware of his blatant masculine virility and beauty. The rich, deep red undertones of his sun-browned, clean-shaven face were similar to those in her own complexion.

She nodded, waiting for him to step out of the truck and come around to help her out. His hands curved around her waist for the second time, but instead of swinging her to the ground he held her aloft for several seconds. Her hands went to his shoulders as she attempted to maintain her balance. She felt the heat of his flesh through the denim fabric of his shirt.

"Put me down, Mr. Lassiter."

His near-black eyes narrowed slightly. "Say please."

Her delicate jaw dropped. "What!"

"I know you were taught the magic word." He pulled her closer, and she tightened her grip on his neck, bringing her breasts in contact with his hard chest.

"Please," she hissed between her teeth as her nipples hardened against a layer of lace under her silk blouse.

He set her on her feet and she flashed a saccharine grin. "Thank you—Salem."

A slight smile softened the firm lines around his mouth. "You're quite welcome, Sara."

Neither had noticed the open door or Marisa Hall standing on the loggia, hands on her hips, smiling. She had not changed much over the past thirty years except to put on an additional five pounds as well as claim a head of salt-and-pepper hair.

"Shame on you, Dr. Lassiter, teasing the girl like that."

Sara looked at Marisa, then Salem. She had called him

Dr. Lassiter. "Who are you?" Her voice was almost a whisper. It was the second time she had posed the question to him.

Removing his hat for the first time, Salem inclined his head. "I'm the resident veterinarian around these parts."

The fact that he was a veterinarian did not shock her as much as the curtain of silk flowing over his shoulders. The brilliant rays of the late-afternoon sun picked up glints of red in his jet-black hair. There was something so virile, so primitive, in Salem Lassiter's appearance that it made it impossible for Sara to draw a normal breath.

It can't be the hair, she told herself. That was only a single characteristic that made the man who he was. She watched him watching her, and suddenly she wanted to be anywhere but in his presence. There was something in his midnight gaze that made her feel that he could see inside her, see the real Sara Ellen Sterling, not the woman everyone thought they knew.

"Thank you for picking me up," she said. She smiled when she realized the pun.

Salem nodded. He placed his hat on his head, not bothering to tuck his shoulder-length hair under the wide circle of black straw.

Sara turned and walked over to Marisa. Extending her arms, she hugged her tightly.

Marisa returned the embrace. "Welcome home, Sara."

"Thank you, Miss Marisa. It's good to be home."

A questioning frown furrowed the housekeeper's nut-brown forehead. "How long you staying for?"

"Three months."

Marisa's smile mirrored approval. "That will give me enough time to fatten you up before you go back to New York."

"If I gain too much weight I'll have to buy a new wardrobe. Don't forget I'm a public servant, which means I don't earn a lot of money."

Marisa gave her a skeptical look that spoke volumes. One thing Sara Sterling never had to worry about was money—unlike herself, who had married young and found herself alone with a son of eighteen months. Her husband had abandoned her once he decided he did not want the responsibility of being a husband or a father.

"I fixed up your cabin for you."

Sara nodded. Once she entered college she had moved out of the main house and into one of the cabins usually occupied by the live-in employees at the horse ranch. The joke was that she had moved away from home without ever leaving the Sterling property.

"I think I'm going to spend a few days in my old room. It won't feel as if I've come home if I stay in the cabin."

"Why don't you change into something more comfortable while I fix you a plate?"

Leaning over, Sara kissed her smooth cheek. "Thank you."

Marisa watched her, her gaze softening, as she made her way to the wing of the house that held the bedroom she had occupied during her childhood. She had watched Christopher Delgado and Sara Sterling grow up with her William, the two children treating him as an equal rather than the offspring of one of their parents' employees. They rode horses together, learned to swim, argued and sometimes fought like normal siblings. William Hall never saw his biological father after his mother relocated from California to New Mexico, yet had grown up protected and secure at Sterling Farms.

Salem walked into the entryway and placed Sara's leather bag near a drop-leaf table. He'd turned on his heel and was striding through the door when Marisa's voice stopped him.

"Don't forget she's the boss's daughter."

Salem went completely still. He did not turn around. A muscle in his lean jaw tightened, and his eyes narrowed. "Have you forgotten who I am?"

The older woman stared at his broad shoulders, shaking her head. There was a swollen silence, only the sound of soft breathing, punctuating the space. "No, Salem. I did not forget."

He touched the brim of his hat with his thumb and forefinger. "Good evening, Miss Marisa."

A knowing smile touched her mouth. "Good evening, Dr. Lassiter."

Salem made his way to his vehicle, the twitching muscle in his lean jaw signaling his annoyance with Marisa and himself. He didn't know what had made him tease Sara Sterling. And he did not know what it was about Sara that had made him forget how a beautiful woman had nearly destroyed him when she took the flesh of his flesh with her when she sought to escape their marriage, destroying herself and his son in the attempt.

Marisa had no need to worry about him and Sara. One thing he had become, and that was an expert when it came to shutting women out of his life.

Chapter 2

Sara stood in the middle of the room where she had spent her youth sleeping, dreaming and entertaining herself whenever she idled away the hours. Those were the times when she had left a world of reality behind to enter one of sheer fantasy.

Her mother had called her Dream Weaver. Eve Sterling had teased her daughter, saying if she did not take her head out of the clouds she would grow up to become a recluse. Sara's preference for spending hours alone and interacting with horses rather than other children her age had become a source of great concern to her mother until she turned seventeen. It was then that she showed a marked interest in the opposite sex. She began dating a boy who was also a high school junior, and their involvement escalated when they decided to attend the same college as prelaw majors.

Eric Thompson proposed marriage during their last year in college, and she accepted. However, before the spring

semester ended Sara had returned his ring. Eric had tearfully confessed an increasing unrest with his own sexual
identity. He claimed he loved her, but he was also in love
with a male student.

The days that followed were the darkest she had ever
experienced in her young life, and after she graduated she
decided to spend the summer in Santa Fe with her best
friend, Emily Kirkland. She and Emily were only a year
apart, but Emily had always seemed much older. Emily
suggested she attend a law school on the east coast, and she
did. Living thousands of miles away had helped her heal
more quickly than if she had remained in New Mexico.

Spending the five weeks of that summer with the
Kirklands had also uncovered another secret: Emily had
confessed that she was in love with Sara's half brother,
Christopher Delgado. This disclosure hadn't surprised
Sara, because she suspected Christopher was in love with
Emily. However, his fascination with politics had taken
precedence over any affair of the heart.

This three-month leave of absence would give her time
to reconnect with her family and her friend. She removed
her clothes, then walked into an adjoining bathroom to
shower. After she ate dinner she planned to call Emily to
schedule a time when she would drive up to Santa Fe for
a reunion.

Sara made her way into a spacious kitchen, stopping and
inhaling the mouth-watering aroma of baked chicken. A
slight frown marred her smooth forehead as she watched
Marisa set the table in an alcove with one place setting.

"Aren't you going to join me?" she asked.

Marisa turned, shaking her head. "No. I'm going to
eat later. I promised Joe Russell that I would share dinner
with him."

Sara shifted an eyebrow. What she had suspected years ago was still evident. Joseph Russell had come to Sterling Farms from Kentucky with the reputation of being the best horse trainer in the racing business. Joe had come west to start over after his wife died, and for many years did not seem remotely interested in any woman until William Hall, Jr. decided not to return to New Mexico and had settled permanently in Chicago. Joe had waited for Marisa to fulfill her maternal responsibilities before he made his feelings known.

"How is Mr. Russell?"

Marisa ducked her head, unsuccessfully concealing a shy smile. "He's well. Like all of us he's bothered with the usual aches and pains that go along with aging, but other than that he's still the best horse trainer in the Southwest."

"I wasn't talking about his horse training abilities."

Marisa pulled herself up to her full five-foot, three-inch height and tilted her chin in a haughty gesture. At fifty-six, she could easily pass for a woman ten years younger. Her skin was smooth, her large round eyes were bright and alert, while her short nose and pouty mouth gave her an extremely sultry look for a middle-aged woman.

"We've decided not to marry. It would spoil everything."

Sara shrugged her shoulders under the white cotton blouse she had paired with her soft faded jeans. "I'm sorry if you thought I was prying, but I had no way of knowing that you were *that* involved with Mr. Russell."

Wincing, Marisa realized she had made a *faux pas*. She had forgotten Sara Sterling had not been home in more than two years. Within that time she had let down her guard to let the man into her life. The scars from her ex-husband's deception hadn't faded completely, but she did let go of the pain the first time she accepted Joseph Russell's invitation to share dinner and a movie.

"I'll serve myself," Sara informed the housekeeper and cook as she picked up the plate and walked over to the stove.

"Are you sure?"

"Of course I'm sure. I'm not completely helpless. I've even learned to cook." She registered the other woman's dubious expression. "And quite well."

Marisa arched her eyebrows, then shook her head. The only thing she remembered Sara Sterling doing well was riding horses and bringing home good grades. Her father had spoiled her. He had sheltered her and seen to her every need, and she had been as surprised as everyone else who knew Sara Sterling when Sara decided to leave home to attend law school in the East. The move had changed her. She had become quite successful, and apparently a very independent woman.

"When are my parents and brother coming home?"

Marisa crossed her arms under her breasts. "They didn't say. I spoke to them last night and your mother said she'll call you tonight or early tomorrow morning. They're still trying to recover from jet lag."

"When did my father hire Dr. Lassiter?" Sara questioned, smoothly changing the topic of conversation.

Marisa's gaze narrowed at the mention of Salem's name. "Dr. Lassiter doesn't work directly for your father. He has a private practice. He's on call for most of the big ranchers and farmers in the state."

Sara registered the change in Marisa's tone. She gave her a quick glance as she spooned a small portion of roasted potatoes and steamed carrots onto her plate. "Where does he live?"

"On the other side of the stream."

Turning, Sara stared directly at her. "He's our neighbor?"

Marisa nodded slowly. "He bought the land over two

years ago, and built one of the finest houses in the valley for his wife and son."

"Wife and son?" She did not know why, but she hadn't thought he was married.

Marisa's dark brown gaze fused with Sara's brilliant, jewel-colored eyes. "They lived together as a family for exactly one month before she left him, taking the little boy with her."

"What happened? Why did she leave?"

"I don't know, Sara. No one knows. She left the house with the boy just before dawn, drove down to the railroad tracks and waited for the five-seventeen. There was nothing left to bury, so Salem had them cremated."

Closing her eyes, Sara bit down on her lower lip when she felt a band tighten around her chest, making it difficult for her to draw a normal breath. "Oh, sweet heaven."

"Stay away from him, Sara," Marisa warned in a quiet voice. "He doesn't have the nicest reputation when it comes to women."

Going completely still, she opened her eyes. "Are you saying that he drove his wife to suicide?"

"No, I'm not."

"What are you saying?"

"What I should do is mind my own business." Turning on her heel, the housekeeper walked across the kitchen.

"Miss Marisa!"

She stopped her retreat, but did not turn around. "I've said more than I should have. Leave your dishes in the sink. I'll clean up everything later."

Staring at the space where Marisa had been long after she walked out of the kitchen, Sara recalled the sensual image of Salem Lassiter. She did not know why, but he intrigued her—made her want to know more about the Sterlings' closest neighbor.

* * *

Sara spent the next forty-five minutes going through the motions of eating while staring out the window at the setting sun firing the pipelike spires and pinnacles of the Organ Mountains and showering the western slopes with a dazzling spectacle of flaming red. Her eyelids drooped slightly, then she shook herself awake. Her body's circadian rhythms still had not adjusted to the change in time zones.

Standing, she cleared the table and rinsed her dishes before she stacked them in the dishwasher. She then picked up the telephone and dialed Emily Kirkland's number. Waiting until she heard an answering machine switch on after four rings, she said, "Emmie, this is Sara. I'm back. Call me the first chance you get so you can clear your calendar and we can hang out together. Give me until the weekend to get used to the heat and recover from jet lag. Talk to you later."

She wanted to go to the stables to see her favorite mare, then decided against it. Even though the stables were equipped with telephones, she did not want to miss her parents' or Emily's call en route. Glancing at her watch, she noted the time. It was nearly eight-thirty, which meant it was ten-thirty in New York and early morning in Europe.

Sara realized it wasn't only the two-hour time difference and the heat that fatigued her, but more than two years of nonstop legal work that had drained her mentally and physically. Despite recommendations from her boss to take a break, she had not taken a vacation because she feared any interruption would snap her continuous string of convictions for the state.

She was finally forced to stop. After her last conviction she had fled the courthouse through a side door with a trio of court officers. They escorted her to an unmarked police car, and two New York City police officers escorted her to her apartment. She had waited three days after the trial ended to answer her telephone or her doorbell. The strain of convicting a high-profile businessman with alleged ties to an organized crime family had taken its toll on her. Even though she had received two death threats prior to the trial, she had refused to relinquish the case to another prosecutor. She asked for and was given a police escort, and when the jury rendered a guilty verdict she stared across the courtroom at the defendant. The man had smiled, then motioned across his throat with his forefinger. The blood ran cold in her veins. It was then that she knew she had to get away from New York, even if only for a few months.

Now she was away from New York and the threats. She was home and she was safe. Walking out of the kitchen, she made her way down a wide hallway to her bedroom.

It seemed as if she had just taken off her blouse, jeans and underwear, pulled a nightgown over her head, brushed her teeth and had gotten into bed when the telephone on the bedside table rang. She reached for the lamp, flooding the space with soft golden light.

"Hello." Her voice was heavy with sleep.

"I'm sorry to wake you, baby."

Sara suddenly became alert when she heard her father's West Texas drawl. "Hi, Dad."

"Did you get in okay?" Matt Sterling asked.

"Yes." She combed her fingers through her hair, smiling. "How're Mom and Chris?"

"Your mother's still asleep, and Chris is resting comfortably in a hospital. The doctors set his left leg and shoulder, which means we'll be leaving here within a week."

"He broke his shoulder, too?"

"He dislocated it."

"What happened, Dad? Chris is an expert skier."

"He says some guy was clowning around on the slopes and plowed right into him. He's lucky he only broke a leg. It could've been his neck. I don't think he wants to see a pair of skis for a long time."

"I always told him riding a horse was safer than skiing."

Matt's deep laugh came through the telephone wire as if he were around the corner instead of on the other side of the world. "Maybe now he'll listen to you."

Sara chatted with her father for another three minutes, then rang off. Her brother was not seriously injured, and her parents were safe. And she was safe, safe from death threats from people who operated outside the law. She flicked off the lamp, closed her eyes, then went back to sleep.

"Where are you calling me from?"

"A pay phone."

"At least you know how to do something right."

"There's no need to talk to me like that!"

"I'll talk to you any way I want, you spineless little turd. If it wasn't for you I wouldn't be in this mess."

"You got yourself into this, as you say, mess. And if I'd known what you were going to do with the information I gave you I never would've had my friend fax you those advance copies—"

"Shut up! Just shut the hell up! What I want to know is, did you say anything to that assistant district attorney?"

"No. I didn't tell Miss Sterling anything."

"And you'd better not, or I'll—"

"Don't threaten me."

"Listen, turd, and listen good. I'm going to say this only once. You'd better keep your mouth shut or your mama will be signing your little sister into a rehab center instead

of a college dorm. A syringe filled with pure heroin and a little crack cocaine can do wonders for mind expansion. She should make the dean's list without opening a book."

"Leave my sister alone! She has nothing to do with this."

"Keep your mouth shut—"

"Not when you threaten my family. This call is over."

"Don't you hang up on me! Well, I'll be damned. The sniveling little punk hung up!"

Chapter 3

Sara woke up at dawn and sat up quickly, totally disoriented. Instead of staring at floor-to-ceiling windows with a view of the Brooklyn Bridge, she found herself gazing at the peaks of the Organ Mountains. She had traded the hustling, bustling, nonstop electricity of the Big Apple for the colorful picturesque solitude of the Land of Enchantment.

Combing her fingers through her hair, she slumped back against the pillows, cradling her shoulders, realizing she did not have to get up to ready herself to go into her office. She wasn't in her small one-bedroom apartment in a Brooklyn Heights brownstone building, but in an expansive one in the wing of a ranch house built in the sprawling Mesilla Valley only an hour north of the Mexican border.

Instead of showering and putting on a conservative suit, functional blouse and practical footwear, she would now wear jeans, cotton shirts and boots. She would not work out as usual at the health and sports club after she left the office where vigorous exercise helped alleviate her tension and stress, but she would go down to the stables and ride her favorite horse and watch the rays of the rising sunlight warm the New Mexico landscape. Pushing back the sheet, she swung her legs over the side of the bed and headed for the adjoining bathroom.

The sight of Marisa Hall and Joseph Russell and the distinctive aroma of brewing coffee greeted Sara as she walked into the kitchen. A warm smile crinkled her eyes when she studied the man who had become the horse guru of Sterling Farms. His experience with horses spanned more than five decades. He had grown up in a rural area of Kentucky, one of four children whose parents picked tobacco for a living. He dropped out of high school three months before he graduated, and took odd jobs to support himself until he found a position as a stable boy at a horse farm near Lexington. He had never been very talkative, but he had always been very observant, and a good listener. By the time he'd turned twenty he was promoted to groom, and before he was thirty he had become a head trainer.

He married a local woman, knowing she had been diagnosed with a terminal, debilitating disease. It took her twelve years to die, and a week after burying his wife he handed in his resignation, put all of his possessions in a pickup truck and headed west. Matthew Sterling could not believe his good fortune when Joseph Russell came to him asking for work. Matt hired him on sight and Joe moved into one of the three cabins built on the Sterling property for resident employees. It took only two years for Joe to train a spectacular horse that made Sterling Farms a winner in its first major horse race—the Belmont Stakes.

Sara watched the tenderness in his touch as Joe laid his large, gnarled hand against the velvety softness of Marisa's brown cheek. Lowering his liberally streaked, graying red head, he kissed her gently on the lips.

Taking a step backward, Sara felt the heat flame in her face from observing the intimacy between the couple. She felt as if she were a spy in her own home. Waiting a full minute, she cleared her throat, smiled brightly, and walked back into the kitchen.

Marisa and Joe sprang apart, exchanging guilty glances. Neither had expected to see Sara Sterling until at least noon. Whenever she had returned home between semesters when she attended law school, it had usually taken her a week before she established a routine of rising before the noon hour.

"Good morning." Her greeting was filled with obvious amusement.

Joe's bright eyes sparkled like polished blue topaz. Crossing muscular arms over his wide, thick chest, he angled his head and smiled. "Well, well, well. You look pretty good for a city girl, Missy."

Closing the distance between her and the horse trainer, Sara found herself in a smothering bear hug. "You won't call me that once I'm back on Blaze."

"It's good to have you home." Joe chuckled, pulling back and holding her at arm's length.

Her smile was dazzling. "It's good to be here, Mr. Russell."

His fair skin bore the result of working outdoors in the dry Southwest heat. Small lines fanned out around his eyes, deep grooves creased his forehead, and a spray of freckles across his nose and cheeks afforded additional color in what would have been a pallid complexion.

"That little filly of yours has been pinin' somethin'

fierce since the last time you left her. The funny thing is, she won't let anyone ride her."

"That's because I told her not to," Sara teased.

Marisa clucked her tongue against her teeth, mumbling under her breath about people talking to horses as she walked over to a counter and filled two large mugs with freshly brewed coffee. She added milk and sugar, then covered them with matching tops.

She handed the mugs to Joe and Sara. "Take your coffees. Now, if the two of you can take all of your talk about horses out of my kitchen I'll begin breakfast."

Joe gave her a lingering stare. "If you'd ever learn to ride a horse you'd know what Sara and I are talking about."

"I've gotten along just fine all of these years without riding, thank you," Marisa retorted.

Sara looped her arm through Joe's. "It think that's our cue to leave," she whispered conspiratorially.

Side by side, they made their way out of the house and to the stables, each taking sips of coffee as they covered the distance. The rising sun bathed the landscape in a pink-gold, and prompted Sara to stop and catch her breath.

"It's beautiful, ain't it?" Joe asked, a reverent quality softening his normally gravely voice.

She smiled. "Yes, it is. This is what I've missed the most, not counting the horses. The sunrises and sunsets." There had been times when she rose early as a young girl just to shoot an entire roll of film, hoping to capture the awesome sight of the rising sun.

Joe stared at her delicate profile, silently admiring the woman she had become. When he first came to Sterling Farms Sara had been on the threshold of womanhood. She had been a quiet young girl, hanging around the stables and watching intently whenever he put the horses through their pacing exercises. There were times when he forgot his employer had a daughter—until she sat a horse. Seeing her perched atop the back of a thoroughbred always made his pulse beat a little faster. It was as if she had been born to ride.

Sara watched Joe punch in a code, allowing them access to the stables. Her father had installed the sophisticated security system after someone broke into the structure and stole one of his prized breeding mares.

The thief made the mistake of stealing the property of Matthew Sterling, totally unaware that the man had at one time lived a double life as an independent operative for a U.S. intelligence agency. Not waiting for law enforcement officials to apprehend the criminal, Matt had found the thief and his mare before it was shipped out of the state. Sara heard whispered rumors that the man was arrested and sent to prison, and that his injuries were so severe that he would never regain the use of his right hand.

The familiar smells of the stable wafted in Sara's nostrils like a powerful aphrodisiac. Placing her half-empty mug of coffee on a shelf, she walked down the length of the broad path, peering into the stalls for her favorite horse. She spotted the roan-colored mare and whistled softly. The horse's ears flicked alertly. She neared the stall and came face-to-face with Blaze. The horse backed up, her head moving up and down as she whinnied softly in response to the familiar whistling sound.

"Hey, girl," Sara crooned, reaching out and rubbing the mare's nose. "I'm back." Blaze whinnied again.

Joe came up behind Sara. "Let me get her out and saddle her up for you."

"I want the English saddle and bridle with a snaffle bit."

"You plan on putting her through a few jumps this morning?"

"Only if she feels up to it."

"I have several of the young kids from the university come and walk her around the track at least four times a week. She got downright ornery when any of them tried getting up on her back."

Sara followed the trainer, watching as he quickly and expertly saddled the patient horse. Her gaze shifted to the number of saddles resting on built-in shelves along a wall, and she ran her fingers over the exquisite leather of a saddle her parents had given her for her sixteenth birthday. Her forefinger traced the initials SES branded into the leather. It had been her first Western saddle. She had always preferred the lighter-weight English type. Her brother and William favored the Western saddle, with its horn for anchoring a lariat. Both boys had perfected throwing and roping any object they aimed for.

Joe stood back, holding the reins. "Check the stirrups for length." He bent down, lacing his fingers together, and Sara placed her booted left foot on his hand. In one continuous motion she sat atop the horse, easing her feet into the stirrups.

"Perfect," she said, smiling. The horse sidestepped, anxious to be out of the barn. She felt the power of a half a ton of muscle and flesh between her knees, reveling in the familiar bond of horse and rider. "I'll see you later."

Those were the last four words Joe Russell heard as he stood, shielding his gaze against the rising sun, and watched horse and rider race across the land before disappearing from his line of vision.

Sara felt the warm breeze ruffle her short hair as she placed her cheek against Blaze's neck, giving the horse her lead. Woman and beast became one, the pumping of their hearts keeping rhythm with the sound of pounding hoofs. She felt safe. Safer than she had been in weeks.

Sitting astride Blaze she forgot about indictments,

search warrants, opening and closing arguments, cross-examinations. She was able to forget the death threat that had temporarily made her a prisoner in her own apartment; able to forget that she had taken to carrying a licensed gun whenever she left home.

Blaze did not slow her gait when she raced across the narrow stream ending the Sterling property line. Sara's head jerked up when she felt the mare break her stride. The horse whinnied, rearing, her hoofs slicing the air. A large wolf stood less than thirty feet away, poised to attack.

Struggling to maintain her balance as the rearing horse threatened to unseat her, she could not pull her gaze away from the wolf. "Easy, Blaze," she crooned, tightening the reins and hoping to settle the horse. "Easy, girl."

She did not understand how a wolf had gotten so far south without someone putting up notices. There were still a lot of sheep farmers in the region who deliberately ignored the fact that the wolf was an endangered species, and would shoot it on sight.

The wolf took a step forward and Blaze bucked again, all four hooves leaving the ground, and Sara slipped off the saddle. She managed to free her feet from the stirrups and let go of the reins before the horse took off in the opposite direction. She lay motionless, gritting her teeth against the pain radiating at the base of her skull.

She could not get up and she could not run. The wolf would be on her before she sat up, so she decided to stay where she lay. Closing her eyes, she said all of the prayers she had learned as a child.

A slight shiver shook her at the moment she felt warm, moist breath against her cheek. Then a shadow blocked out the heat of the early-morning sun. Opening her eyes, she stared up at Salem Lassiter standing over her, hands resting on his hips. He motioned with his left hand and the wolf moved away, panting and sitting on its haunches.

Salem went to his knees, staring at her eyes filled with unshed tears. The moisture turned them into shimmering emerald pools. "Don't move," he urged when she attempted to sit up.

"Blaze," she whispered.

"She'll find her way back home."

Sara swallowed painfully, trying to slow down her runaway pulse. "If she comes back without me—"

"I'll call Joe and let him know where you are," Salem interrupted. "Where does it hurt?"

"My head," she whispered.

Closing her eyes, she felt his fingers inch up her neck. His touch was like a whisper of the wind moving over her scalp. His thumb grazed a slight swelling behind her right ear, and she jerked her head away from him.

"I said don't move." He hadn't shouted at her, but the no-nonsense tone in his voice warned her not to challenge him again.

"Am I bleeding?"

Withdrawing his hand, Salem looked at his fingertips. "No. But you're going to have a lump the size of an egg if you don't put some ice on it."

"That wolf spooked my horse."

"He's not a wolf."

"He looks like one," she insisted.

"He's only half wolf. His mother is a shepherd."

"I thought he was going to attack me."

"Shadow would not attack you unless I ordered him to do so. I'm going to help you stand up, and I want you to tell me if you feel any dizziness." Curving an arm around her waist he eased her gently to her feet. "Are you dizzy?"

"No," she breathed out slowly. She swayed slightly, but

he caught her easily and cradled her against his taller stronger body.

Staring up at him she noticed he looked different this morning. He had secured his hair in a ponytail, allowing her an unobstructed view of his beautifully formed male face. His forehead was high, his thick black hair growing from a widow's peak. Surveying his features, she wondered if he had ever been mistaken for someone of Asian descent. She wasn't given time to admire her rescuer. He swung her up into his arms.

"I can walk," she protested.

"Where? You certainly can't walk back home."

"Where are you taking me?"

"I'm taking you to my place. I'll call Miss Marisa and tell her that I'm bringing you home."

Sara tightened her grip on his neck, noticing his pierced lobes for the first time, wondering what type of earrings he favored. Did he wear small hoops or decorative ones in silver and turquoise?

She felt the power in his upper body as he shifted her to a more comfortable position, felt the heat emanating from him, and inhaled his clean masculine scent mingling with his cologne. She felt a stirring of desire that she had not felt since her liaison with Eric ended. It had been a long time, too long, since she had been turned-on by a man. And Dr. Salem Lassiter definitely turned her on. She had to get away from him before she embarrassed herself.

"Please, put me down. I can walk." He tightened his grip under her knees and began walking. "Now!" she shouted in his ear.

Stopping, Salem stared at her, unblinking. "Yell in my ear again, and I will hand you over to Shadow."

Her gaze widened. "You wouldn't!"

As he lowered his head, his mouth was only inches

from hers. "Care to test me?" She shook her head, eliciting a smile from him. "I thought not."

"Bully," she whispered under her breath.

"Don't you know when to give up, Sara?"

Her gaze lingered on his mouth before moving up to his eyes. A sensual smile curved her lush lips. "Not giving up comes with the job."

"And that is?"

"Federal prosecutor."

Salem shifted his eyebrows and whistled softly. "You must be one tough lawyer, lady."

"When I have to be," she confirmed.

A bright smile softened his stern features, making him look like a different man. He did not know what it was about Sara Sterling that made him want to hold her in his arms and not let her go—at least not yet, not until he uncovered what drew him to her.

"Consider yourself overruled, Counselor. You are not walking."

There was a maddening arrogance about Salem Lassiter that she found very attractive. Most men she met were usually intimidated when she revealed what she did for a living, but it was apparent Salem would not join those ranks.

"You win, Dr. Lassiter, but only because I let you."

He slowed his pace. "Are you always so competitive?"

"I don't like to lose."

"How many cases have you lost?"

"None."

His grin widened. "So, not only are you competitive, but you also have to have *naighiz*."

A slight frown furrowed her forehead. "What?"

"It's a Navajo word for *control*."

"You're *Diné?*"

Salem nodded. "Navajo and African American."

"Who's *Diné?*"

"My father's people."

"Which clan?"

"How do you know so much about the *Diné?*"

"My undergraduate minor was ethnology. Which clan?" she repeated.

"*Tabaaha.* The Water's Edge People."

He smiled, shifting Sara's slender form as he climbed a rise where he had erected a spacious two-story structure overlooking the stream separating his property from the Sterlings'. It wasn't until he pushed open the door and stepped into the foyer that he realized Sara was only the second woman to cross the threshold of the house he had built for a woman he'd loved unconditionally.

He'd loved Grace, and she loved another. And in the end everyone in the love triangle had been a loser.

But it would be different with Sara Sterling. He would invite her into his home, but never into his heart. And, like Sara, he did not like losing.

Chapter 4

Sara forgot the throbbing pain in her head as she stared up at the towering interior of a structure designed to take advantage of all the panoramic vistas. Reminiscent of a museum hall, the immense foyer showcased primitive-looking pieces of sculpture, each placed on its own free-standing block of wood. An artfully designed dramatic lighting technique cast shadows on the carved figures, which appeared to dance playfully along the smooth white backdrop of the walls. Recessed lights and polished hardwood floors contributed to the entry's streamlined look, while a neutral palette imbued the space with elegant sophistication.

She was only able to catch a glimpse of white walls, expansive windows which went from the highly polished wood floors to the towering cathedral-style ceiling, and a staircase constructed in a style made popular by the Frank Lloyd Wright School.

Salem carried her through the foyer, past a living room and formal dining room, then into a room where she instinctively knew he spent most of his time. Even if she knew nothing about the man, his personality was reflected in the colors and furnishings. A massive, potted saguaro cactus rising more than six feet was the room's focal point, competing only with an antique mahogany desk and three walls of built-in shelves crowded with books on subjects from anthropology to zoology.

Her gaze caressed and lingered on the colorful and fading woven Navajo rugs stacked on tables, racks and over the back of a loveseat of white Haitian cotton. An assortment of eagle feathers dangled from the long decorative handle of a pipe hanging over a fireplace. Pieces of broken and intact pottery, several arrowheads and black-and-white and color photographs were displayed over a mantelpiece.

He set her down on a cushioned chair with a matching footstool. She felt instantly bereft—of his comforting protection, strong arms, body heat, and the haunting fragrance of his lime-scented cologne.

Fluidly, gently, he bent down and raised her booted feet. His head came up slowly as he met her direct stare. "Are you in pain?"

Her eyes widened at the same time that she shook her head. She couldn't believe it. It was the first time in her memory that she was at a loss for words. She, who earned her living by verbal exchange, was rendered mute by the presence of a man. She knew he was real, yet he appeared not to be who he was.

There was something about him that made her think he was born too late; that he belonged to a bygone era when his ancestors roamed the rugged splendor of the American

Southwest without the threat that their lands, language, and culture would be wrested from them by force.

"A little," she lied smoothly. She wanted to tell Salem that the pain was excruciating. It radiated from her neck up to her temple, and tightened like a band around her forehead. She prayed she had not suffered a concussion when Blaze unseated her.

A smile played at the corners of Salem's strong mouth, and he straightened. Sara watched him as he walked over to the desk and picked up a cordless phone. Pressing two buttons, he turned and stared at her. Staring intently back at him, she shivered as if a cool breeze had swept over the back of her neck when she felt a mysterious sensual energy pass between them.

She wanted to glance away, but did not. She saw his fingers tighten on the telephone as his gaze widened, and he pulled her into a force field from which she could not and did not want to escape. Who was he? What power did Salem Lassiter possess to make her feel as if she had stepped outside of herself, to see herself as a stranger?

"Miss Marisa, this is Salem."

The sound of his soft controlled voice broke the spell, and Sara glanced away.

"Yes, I know," Salem continued, still staring at Sara's enchanting profile. "Tell Joe to put Blaze in her stall. I'll bring Sara back in a little while." A gentle smile crinkled his eyes. "Yes, Miss Marisa, I'm sure. She's not seriously injured, just a little shook up. Stop worrying. I'll see you later." Depressing a button, he ended the call. Taking half a dozen steps, he moved over to the chair and hunkered down beside Sara, his head level with hers.

"I suppose Miss Marisa is having a fit," she remarked, her gaze shifting to meet his.

Salem nodded, his expression impassive. He noted that

the gold in her eyes had disappeared, leaving them a brilliant emerald-green. He successfully forced back a knowing smile. It was apparent that Sara Sterling was truly Matthew Sterling's daughter. She had inherited not only his eye color, but the fact that it changed with a shift in mood. Heightened excitement or anger had now turned them a deep green. And he wondered which emotion was coursing through her at that moment.

"She admitted that she was ready to call the sheriff when Blaze came back without you."

"She can be quite melodramatic at times."

"If that's the case, then I'd better get some ice for your head."

Lowering her feet to the floor, Sara used the padded arms of the chair for support when she attempted to stand up. Salem curved an arm around her waist, anchoring most of her weight against his thigh.

She waved him off. "Let me try to walk by myself."

Ignoring her, he swung her up in his arms, tightening his grip when she struggled to free herself. "I told you before that you're not walking—at least not on my property. What you do once you're back on Sterling land is your business."

Her temper flared and her right fist pounded his hard chest, shocking him though she did not hurt him. He went completely still.

"Put me down—*now!*" The words were forced from between clenched teeth.

He complied with her request, easing her back down to the chair. Placing a large hand on her shoulder, he leaned in closer.

"Don't move."

She glared up at him, her eyes a verdant green, her breasts rising and falling heavily under her blouse. What she failed to notice was that Salem's own heaving chest kept the same rhythm as hers.

"It's apparent you've been around animals so long that you've begun to act like some of them," she spat out in rapid Spanish.

He stared at her, then burst out laughing. The sound was deep, warm and rich. "Do you care to tell me which animal I resemble?" he questioned in the same language.

Her mouth dropped open when she realized he understood Spanish. Her shock was short-lived, replaced with embarrassment, and there was no way she could stop the heat flooding her face.

"Pig!" she whispered angrily.

Salem arched an eyebrow and cocked his head at an angle. "Bacon, pork chops, ribs, ham. Good choice. Thank you, ma'am."

He was still smiling when he knelt and curved a hand around her neck, his fingertips grazing the swelling lump on her tender scalp. As he eased her head forward with a minimum of effort, his smile faded. Their faces were only inches apart, each feeling the other's breath whispering over their lips.

His eyes darkened dangerously. "This will be the first and last time you will ever call me out of my name, Sara Sterling," he warned in a soft, lethal tone. "The name is Salem Lassiter, not *pig*. I trust you can remember that."

A shiver of panic rippled through her, and she felt the same foreign fear she had experienced when the defendant in her last case drew his finger across his throat in a threatening motion.

Her catlike eyes narrowed as she struggled to not let Salem know how much he had unnerved her. "Are you threatening me?" Her sultry voice had dropped an octave.

He did not move, not even his eyes. "A man would have

to be either a fool or a complete idiot to threaten anything Matt Sterling claims as his. No, Sara, I'm not threatening you. I am warning you, that's all."

She felt a return of confidence. She had forgotten that she wasn't in New York City, but in Las Cruces, New Mexico. And she was home—a place where she had grown up secure and protected.

Lowering her chin, her mouth mere inches from his, she flashed a sensual smile. "And if I did call you out of your name again, what would you do, *Dr. Lassiter?*"

There was something in her tone that triggered a flashback for Salem. Sara Sterling looked nothing like Grace Clark, but her query echoed his late wife's when he discovered she was sleeping with another man. He had confronted her and she challenged him: *If I continue to see him, what are you going to do about it, Dr. Lassiter?*

What he had done was to go to their bedroom and pack a bag with a week's change of clothes, then walk out of the apartment they'd shared for the first six months of their marriage. He'd lived with his elderly grandmother until Grace came to him with the revelation that she was pregnant. He wasn't certain whose child she carried, but he took her back; he took her back because he had loved her in spite of her infidelity. And when Grace delivered a son there was no doubt who the father was. The child was his.

"I'm going to do this," he whispered, moving closer. He watched her eyes widen, her lids flutter and then close, when he moved his mouth over hers, devouring its lush softness.

Sara felt the press of his lips against hers, silently demanding a response. His kiss sent shivers of desire racing down her body, reigniting a desire she thought had died years ago. As she gasped for breath her lips parted, giving

Salem total access to the honeyed sweetness of her intoxicating mouth.

Everything about him seeped into her, making them one from the moment of contact. She felt the rapid pumping of his heart keeping pace with her own, inhaled his masculine heat, which intensified the citrus scent of his aftershave, registered the strength of his long slender fingers around the column of her neck and gloried in the dizzying passion racing headlong through her body and settling in the moist secret place between her thighs.

I am a woman, a silent voice crooned in her. It had been more than six years since she felt like a woman, totally female. Men had kissed her, but she did not and could not respond. Most times they never got to the part where they would attempt to touch her body. She always rejected them before they were given the opportunity to reject her—for being frigid.

Her right hand moved up and she placed trembling fingers alongside Salem's smooth-shaven jaw. Her touching him broke the spell. He pulled back as if she had branded him with a red-hot poker.

Salem's shock was as apparent as Sara's. He did not know why he had kissed her, except to rationalize that she had challenged his male ego. That was the only asinine justification he could come up with to explain his impulsive behavior.

His obsidian gaze was fixed on her moist, thoroughly kissed, parted lips, then inched down to her full breasts, which rose and fell under her white man-tailored shirt. The outlines of her prominent nipples were clearly visible through the delicate fabric of a white lace bra. It was his turn to gasp inaudibly when he felt a rush of desire settle in his groin. It had been a long time since the mere presence of a woman had elicited a rush of desire within him.

And he never would have thought that it would be with his neighbor's incredibly beautiful daughter.

He released her, his mouth curving into a mocking sneer. "I am judge and jury on *my* property, so consider yourself overruled and in contempt, *Counselor.*"

Sara had not recovered from his sensual assault on her senses when she found herself smarting from his comeback. She sat motionless, watching him stalk out of the room. Folding her arms under her breasts, she stared at the fireplace, pouting. It had been a long time since she had pouted, and even though she found it childish this was one of those times when it was warranted.

She was still pouting when Salem returned carrying a small plastic bag filled with ice. He handed it to her, frowning when she practically snatched it from his fingers. He waited until she had positioned it against the lump over her ear before he leaned down and swept her up in his arms.

Sara's free arm curved around his neck. She stared at his impassive expression. She did not know what it was, but something seemed to whisper to her to kiss his ear. A slow smile softened her mouth.

"What are you smiling about?"

Her smile faded. Salem's deep, soothing voice had shattered her erotic musings. "Your ears."

Turning his head slightly, he arched an eyebrow. "What about them?"

"They're very sexy," she replied softly. "You should always wear earrings."

Much to her surprise, he smiled, softening his stoic expression. "Perhaps I'll ask you to lend me a pair."

"Hoops or studs?"

The corners of his mouth inched higher. "It doesn't matter."

Running her tongue over her lower lip, she gave him a direct stare. "I'll see what I can find for you."

Salem walked across the floor of his study and made his way to the rear of the house. Shifting Sara slightly in his arms, he pushed open a door and walked out to where his truck was parked.

He opened the passenger-side door of the Navigator and deposited her on the leather seat. Moments later he took his seat behind the wheel, turned on the ignition, and headed in the direction of Sterling Farms.

She did not glance at him again until he crossed the shallow stream marking the boundaries between Sterling and Lassiter properties and pulled up in front of the house, where Marisa and Joe were waiting for her.

"Don't move," he said in a quiet voice. "I'll help you down."

Her head came around, her gaze narrowing, reminding Salem of a cat poised for attack. He pitied any man foolish enough to become involved with her.

Forcing a saccharine smile, she nodded. "Yes, sir, *Dr. Lassiter.*"

He shot her a warning look, but decided it was not worth it to engage in a verbal exchange with Sara. It was more than obvious that she was spoiling for an argument, and that was one thing he detested—hostile verbal exchanges. He and Grace had argued enough for two lifetimes.

A muscle twitched noticeably in his lean jaw as he stepped out of the Navigator and came around to help her down. His sharp gaze had not missed Joe Russell holding on to Marisa's arm as she started toward them.

Opening the door, Salem scooped Sara off the seat as if she were a small child. Again, he felt the changes in his body when she curved her arms around his neck and pressed her breast to his chest.

What was it about her that tested his normally iron-willed control? Was it Sara Sterling, or had he just allowed too much time to elapse between women?

Joe released Marisa and she raced forward to meet them, her eyes filled with unshed tears and apprehension. "Why are you carrying her?" she shouted at Salem.

He stopped and offered the older woman a comforting smile. "She has a nasty bump on her head. Only time will tell if she has a concussion. Call a doctor if she complains of dizziness and nausea."

Marisa's jaw dropped. "What was she doing on your property?"

He stared down at Sara. "Why don't you ask Sara?"

Joe strolled over to the trio, knowing he had to diffuse what could become a volatile situation. "Risa, let Salem be." His tone was soft, yet layered with a no-nonsense edge. "Son, take Sara in the house. I'll be waiting for you in the stables." Reaching out, he held Marisa's arm when she turned to follow the young couple. "Don't," he warned her quietly.

Marisa rounded on him. "You know we should keep her away from him."

"*We* know nothing of the sort. In case you haven't noticed, Sara Sterling is a grown woman. I'm certain she can take care of herself when it comes to men, and that includes Salem Lassiter."

"But…but you know what he did to his poor wife."

"What went on between that man and his wife was their business, and only their business."

Resting her hands on her narrow hips, Marisa Hall glared up at Joseph Russell. "Are you telling me to mind my business? Because if you are—"

Her words were cut off abruptly when Joe lowered his head and moved his mouth over hers. "Enough, sweetheart," he breathed into her slightly open mouth. Raising his head, he glanced over her shoulder and saw Salem coming out of the house. "Why don't you finish with breakfast while Dr. Lassiter examines Blaze?"

Marisa's temper cooled quickly. "Okay."

Joe released Marisa, smiling at Salem and falling in step with him as they headed for the stables. "Have you had breakfast?" he questioned in an unusually loud voice.

Salem ran a large well-formed hand over his hair, which was pulled off his face and secured in a black elastic band on the nape of his neck. "Not yet."

Joe patted his shoulder. "How about joining us? Marisa made her fabulous biscuits this morning."

"Thanks for the invitation."

Joe did not turn around to see Marisa's thunderous expression. He had been on the receiving end of the woman's volatile temper before, and he had survived. But he did not want to press his luck—at least not too much. He had been in love with Marisa Hall for more years than he could count, and within the past month he had come to the realization that he wanted to share not only his love but also his life with her.

Marisa sat down on a plush armchair in Sara's bedroom, watching her as she settled herself on an antique iron bed. Sara had managed to change out of her blouse and jeans without her help. She had slipped into a pair of pale blue loose-fitting drawstring cotton pants with a matching overblouse.

"I can't remember the last time you fell off a horse."

"I was thirteen," she admitted, a frown turning her mouth downward. "Remember when I tried jumping the fence Dad put up to keep Mr. Saunders's sheep from wandering onto his property?"

"You almost broke your neck that time."

"I *was* lucky I didn't break something, and it took more than a month for the bruises on my face and body to fade completely." She had been thrown headfirst over the horse.

"What fence were you jumping this time?"

Closing her eyes, Sara settled back on the pillow cradling her shoulders. "It wasn't a fence that spooked Blaze, but a dog. Or more accurately, a wolf-dog."

"Shadow," Marisa mumbled under her breath. "You crossed the stream?"

Opening her eyes, she stared at the stunned expression on the housekeeper's face. "I hadn't planned to cross it. Blaze just took off in that direction." She gave Marisa a questioning look. "Was I in danger of being shot for trespassing?"

Rising to her feet, Marisa shook her head. "No. Salem would never shoot anyone, but you did take a chance with that wolf-dog. He won't let anyone cross the stream unless Salem is with him. I heard he attacked a couple of guys who tried burglarizing Salem's house several months back. The police reported they were looking for drugs."

Sara sat up. "Drugs?"

Marisa nodded. "Some people abuse the drug veterinarians use to sedate horses."

"Ketamine," Sara confirmed. "What happened to the burglars?"

"Let's say they were more than ready for the police when they arrived."

"What did the dog do to them?"

"I'm certain Shadow would have had them for dinner if Salem had not returned when he did. I hope you'll know better the next time, because Salem may not be home to call the dog off if he attacks you. Now, you just lie there and relax. I have to finish cooking. We're having company for breakfast."

Marisa walked out of the bedroom, biting down on her lower lip. She had not said that she feared Sara had sought out the veterinarian, or that if she had she would not be the first woman who wanted to get to know the enigmatic man. But what most did not know was that he was not interested in women—at least not the ones who flirted openly and shamelessly with him. Once she had observed a very beautiful young woman's smile fade quickly after Salem looked through her—despite her fluttering lashes and seductive glances. And over the past two years it had appeared he much preferred the company of mares, cows and ewes to the females of his own species. If Sara could spend her three-month leave of absence in Las Cruces without becoming involved with Salem, she would be guaranteed a long and happy life.

Lying back down, Sara recalled Salem saying Shadow would not have attacked her unless he ordered it. She could say she was lucky he was nearby.

Shifting slightly, she turned her head, wincing when she felt a dull ache with the motion. "Damn," she cursed softly. Then she mumbled several other colorful expletives under her breath. After that she cursed Salem Lassiter *and* his dog. She had returned to New Mexico to see her family and ride her favorite horse, but she had fallen and nearly cracked her skull. It seemed as if Matthew and Eve Sterling's offspring were competing with each other to see who was the clumsiest.

Chapter 5

Sara woke to lengthening afternoon shadows and a dull throbbing over her ear. After eating half of the monstrous portions of food Marisa had placed on a tray, she had settled down to a comfortable position to take a nap. What she had not known when she closed her eyes was that the nap would become nearly eleven hours of deep uninterrupted sleep.

Leaning over, she peered at the clock on the bedside table. It was five-thirty. If she had been in New York she would have felt guilty about lazing in bed because she always felt the need to fill her days and nights with nonstop activity. Her life revolved around a strict schedule: preparing cases, shopping for groceries, working out at the health club, going to the movies, taking in a play or attending a concert, sharing dinner with John or her colleagues, visiting the many museums dotting the boroughs of New York City. There was never a time when she was bored or lonely. If she kept busy, she would not have to acknowl-edge her inability to summon up desire for a man.

She dated several men while she attended law school—fellow students. Most of them preferred discussing torts to becoming emotionally or physically involved, and by the time she joined the D.A.'s office she had decided to never date another lawyer. She hadn't wanted to spend her free time analyzing judges or the cases they had won or lost.

A slow smile parted her lips when she thought about John Bohannon. She had met him at a celebration at a popular restaurant in the Wall Street area when the people in her office feted a prosecutor who had been promoted to head an office in an upstate county. The man, with whom she shared cramped office space within the Brook-lyn courthouse, had grown up with John, and introduced them only minutes after he walked into the restaurant.

John Bohannon had it all: looks, impeccable manners and an enviable position with one of the leading Wall Street investment firms. She'd offered him her telephone number at the court, and it wasn't until a month later that she gave him the number of her apartment. She did not see John as often as he would like, and he complained that he had yet to see the inside of her apartment. He teased her, saying perhaps she was hiding a husband or live-in lover. When she gently reminded him that they could stop seeing each other, he apologized.

What John or other men did not know was that she would never invite them into her apartment, nor would she go to theirs. She refused to put herself in a situation where her sexuality would be put to the test. After Eric Thompson confessed that he derived more pleasure from watching a fully clothed male than actually sharing her body, she had begun to doubt her femininity. Something within her died at Eric's disclosure, and she had come to believe that she could not please a man.

On those occasions when men pressed their aroused bodies against hers, or tried kissing her passionately, she felt nothing. There was no warming desire or rush of arousal—except now, with Salem Lassiter.

His kiss had been a shock to her senses, reminding her that she had been born female, that there had been a time when she had experienced sexual fulfillment. When he kissed her she hadn't gone stiff in his embrace or pushed him away. Maybe she had been wrong when she told herself that she was frigid. Perhaps she just had not met the man who would be able to shatter the shield she had erected to keep all men out of her bed.

Moving slowly, she made her way gingerly to the bathroom to fill the tub. She forced herself to forget about her headache as she recalled the sexual magnetism that made her want to see Salem again.

Salem Lassiter stood under the spray of cold water that beat down on his head and body. He clenched his teeth against the sting of icy needles penetrating his flesh. In the past, taking a cold shower had helped him repress the sexual urges that occurred whenever his body reminded him that his prolonged periods of celibacy were usually followed by prolonged bouts of tension and frustration.

This time a cold shower had done little to relieve the throbbing hardness that had awakened him in the middle of the night. He had lain in bed waiting for it to subside, but to no avail. He had wanted to pick up the telephone and call the one person who understood his waking her up before sunrise. He would listen for her breathless voice inviting him to come to her home and her bed. It had been more than two months since he called her. He had resisted the urge, opting instead for the shower.

Pressing his back to the cold tiles, he closed his eyes, his chest rising and falling heavily. It was clear who had prompted his craving for a woman—Sara Sterling. A powerful shudder racked his tall body and he pounded his fists against a wall of the shower stall.

"Damn her!" he whispered savagely. There was something about Sara that reminded him of Grace. Something that said if he became involved with her, his life would change, he would change—forever.

Opening his eyes, he reached for the lever, turned off the water and pushed open the door. He left the imprint of his wet feet on the marble floor as he walked to a window and stared at the nighttime sky. There were still another three hours before dawn would pierce the thick, dark cover of night to herald the beginning of a new day—a new day that would serve to remind him that at thirty-six he had achieved all of the goals he had set for his future, but he had lost the most profound one with the death of his wife and son. It was not the first time that Salem had asked himself what hadn't he done to make Grace a complete and fulfilled woman. What was it he'd withheld from her to make her love a man who never wanted to claim her as his wife?

Waiting until most of the moisture was absorbed by his body's heat, he returned to his bedroom and lay facedown on the twisted sheets. Closing his eyes, he willed himself to go back to sleep. In another three hours he would leave Las Cruces for Carlsbad. He was scheduled to go to the Living Desert Zoological and Botanical State Park to join a surgical team of veterinarians who were scheduled to operate on an injured female gray wolf. The doctors at the zoo were excited because X-rays indicated that the female was carrying a litter of five pups. Concentrating on saving the pups—and also the mother, if they were lucky—would temporarily garner enough excitement for him to forget about his neighbor's daughter.

"I'm in."

"Good. When did it happen?"

"Yesterday. The trainer hired me on the spot. I knew growing up on a farm would come in handy one of these days."

"Where's her old man?"

"He's out of the country for a while."

"Have you seen her?"

"Yeah. I gotta admit she's quite an eyeful."

"Don't let her beauty fool you. Just remember what you're being paid to do."

"Don't worry. I'll take care of her."

"It's not me who has to worry. Mess up, and it's your ass."

"Look, pal. You came looking for me, not the other way around."

"Just do it!"

"Consider it done."

Sara woke up two days later, just before dawn, to the soft chiming of the telephone. Reaching for the instrument, she mumbled a groggy greeting.

"Wake up, sleepyhead. If you were in New York you would've been up hours ago."

"Emily! Where have you been?"

A sultry contralto laugh came through the receiver. "I'm in D.C. The network had me filling in for the regular political analyst, who's on family leave."

"When are you coming back to Santa Fe?"

"Wednesday. Why don't you drive up Friday and spend the weekend with me?"

Sara smiled in the darkened space. "You're on." A slight frown replaced her smile, and she wondered if Emily knew of her brother's skiing accident. If her friend did not mention Chris Delgado, then she wouldn't.

"I have to go," Emily continued. "I'm scheduled to attend a White House breakfast for the press corps."

"Look for me Friday afternoon."

"You're on," Emily replied. *"Adiós."*

"Adiós," Sara repeated, depressing a button and ending the call.

Her childhood friend was right. If she had been in New York she would have been up and stirring with the rising sun. But what Emily Kirkland did not know was that she had taken to swallowing aspirins at least twice a day because of a lingering headache.

Pushing back the sheet, she swung her legs over the side of the bed and made her way to the adjoining bathroom. Emily would return to New Mexico in another three days, and her mother, father and brother were scheduled to return to the States a week later. Her parents had decided to spend a few days in Venice and Florence before returning to Switzerland to pick up Christopher.

Dressed in a pair of jeans, T-shirt and boots, Sara made her way to the stables. The colors of gold, sage and pink fired the fenced paddocks. In a few hours two dozen mares, stallions and foals would be turned out into the well-tended fields covering more than two hundred acres set aside for the year's grazing. Matthew Sterling was as meticulous about the land on which his horses grazed as their overall general health. He used good rot-and-weather-resistant lumber with nontoxic preservatives for his posts and rails;

he planted tall hedges at the rounded corners, providing shelter and extra security for the horses, along with several sheds positioned where the horses could not get trapped between them and the fence. The grass was cut to uniform height and free of weeds, while several water troughs were always filled with fresh drinking water.

It was common knowledge in Las Cruces that Matthew Sterling's obsessions were his wife, son, daughter and his horses. Some doubted the order, but never admitted their speculations publicly.

She punched in the code and opened the door to the familiar sounds of whinnying and stomping. She passed the stall of a magnificent stallion who snorted and shook his noble head as she whistled softly. Slowing her pace, she stopped and patted Blaze's nose before making her way to a stall where a mare had birthed a foal three days ago.

She found the mare standing over her foal, nudging it with her nose. The tiny colt lay on its side, abdomen distended, as it quivered with each breath it struggled to take. She had grown up around horses all of her life and she knew a medical emergency when she saw it. Racing back to the entrance to the stable, she picked up the phone and punched in the programmed number before the word VET. The telephone rang three times before there was a break in the connection.

"Lassiter."

"Salem, this is Sara Sterling. There's a foal who can't breathe!" she screamed into the receiver.

"Calm down, Sara. I'll be right there."

She was still holding the receiver when a dial tone buzzed noisily in her ear. She had not realized how fast her heart was pumping until she replaced the receiver on its cradle. Lacing her fingers together, she tried to stop them from shaking. Something told her to go back to the stall to check on the foal, but she did not want to see the tiny horse shaking uncontrollably, or its dam standing help-lessly over her baby.

Somehow she managed to pick up the telephone again and punch in Joe Russell's number. His voice was grav-elly when he greeted her, and when she quickly explained what she had discovered all vestiges of sleep vanished and he told her that he would be there as soon as he put his clothes on.

Salem raced into the stable a full thirty seconds before Joe arrived. His damp black hair hung over his shoulders like thick, moist, silk threads. He wore his usual battered boots and a stark white T-shirt he had tucked into the waistband of a pair of low-riding jeans.

"Get the dam out of the stall," he ordered Joe as he walked in, placing a large, black, leather medical bag on the floor.

Sara backpedaled, giving the two men space to tend to the foal. Joe led the straining mare out of the stall, lock-ing her in an empty one opposite the one where her foal still lay convulsing on the hay-littered floor.

Sara inched forward, her gaze fixed on the expanse of white cotton stretched over Salem's broad back. She was transfixed as she watched him listen to the foal's heart with a stethoscope, his long, brown fingers stroking the tiny horse's bloated side. It was the first time that she had noticed the narrow circle of silver threaded with tiny beads of turquoise and coral around his left wrist.

He murmured softly to the horse as he inserted a ther-mometer into his rectum. He continued to talk to the animal until it was calm and motionless.

Joe leaned in closer. "What do you think, Doc?"

Salem shook his head. "I'm not certain. But I suspect

that the little fella has a ruptured bladder. It can only be verified by performing a paracentesis."

"What's that?" Sara asked, speaking for the first time.

Glancing over his shoulder, Salem stared up at her. "The procedure involves tapping the fluid in the abdomen. The presence of urine can be recognized by its smell and chemical constitution. Then an ultrasound examination will demonstrate the quantity of fluid in the abdomen."

"Can you do that here?"

"No." He turned his attention back to the foal. "I'm going to have to take him up to Santa Fe."

Sara felt a shiver of panic. "Santa Fe is four hours away. He'll never make it."

"Get me a blanket, Joe," Salem ordered. "I'm going to give him something to settle him down until I get him to the hospital."

Standing helplessly by, Sara watched Salem shake a bottle, then clean the plastic seal with an antiseptic swab. He drew a small amount of injectable fluid into the syringe before thumping the foal's hindquarters twice with the side of his right hand. He performed the next motion quicker than the eye could follow as he inserted the needle, then reattached the syringe. Checking carefully that no blood flowed back into the syringe, he depressed the plunger until the syringe was empty, and within a minute the foal was resting comfortably due to the tranquilizer. He replaced his instruments in the black bag and snapped it closed.

Joe returned with the blanket and handed it to Salem, who tucked it around the sedated animal's distended middle. With a minimum of effort, he picked up the foal and carried it out of the stable to his truck. Sara picked up the medical bag and followed the two men.

"I'm going with you," she announced, not relinquishing the bag when Salem extended his hand.

His obsidian gaze shifted to Joe, who nodded. "Get in."

Handing Salem his bag, she opened the passenger-side door and pulled herself up into the truck. Salem slid onto the driver's seat beside her, closed the door, and turned on the ignition in one smooth motion. He drove quickly, expertly, along a local road, leaving the boundaries of Sterling Farms behind him as he headed for the interstate. The semi-arid desert air flowed into the open windows, lifting his unbound hair from his shoulders.

Sara managed a surreptitious glance at his profile, her breath catching in her chest. His black, flowing, blunt-cut hair, chiseled features in a mahogany-brown face, and the power of his muscled upper body blatantly displayed by a mere T-shirt were hypnotically mesmerizing.

Turning her head, she closed her eyes to shut out the sight of the virile man sitting beside her. A small smile played at the corners of her mouth when she realized that there was something about Salem Lassiter that reminded her of her father. He possessed the same quiet dangerousness that shrouded Matthew Sterling's large stalking presence.

"How's your head?" he asked, breaking into her musings.

"It's a lot better."

"Any pain?"

"Only a little. The area is still a little sensitive to touch. Don't forget I'm a Sterling, and we have very hard heads."

Salem gave her a quick glance. "My father always said that a hard head is an open invitation for a sore behind."

"I wouldn't know about that, because I was never spanked."

"Neither was I," Salem confirmed.

"You remind me of my father," she stated, staring at his perfect profile.

It was Salem's turn to smile. "Then you approve of me?"

"Should I not?"

He shrugged a broad shoulder. "That will probably depend on who you talk to."

"I haven't spoken to anyone about you. I won't judge you harshly unless you give me reason."

His smile was dazzling. "Why thank you, Counselor."

She sat silently, watching the countryside whiz by as Salem followed the signs pointing the way to the Las Cruces airport. She listened intently as he pressed several buttons on his car phone, switched over to the speaker, and alerted the animal hospital that he was bringing in a three-day-old colt with a suspected ruptured bladder.

Twenty minutes later Sara sat beside Salem in his twin-engine plane, the sedated foal on a blanket in the cargo area, waiting for clearance from the air traffic controllers so that they could take off. They were given the signal, and she closed her eyes as the small aircraft taxied down a runway in preparation for liftoff. Within minutes they were airborne.

"You can open your eyes now."

She did and flashed a smile of relief. The amusement in his midnight gaze was apparent. He must have been laughing at her when she had voiced her concern that the two hundred seventy–mile drive between Las Cruces and Santa Fe would take at least four hours.

"Don't you dare say anything," she hissed between clenched teeth.

"You owe me, Sara Sterling," he crooned, his soft voice lowering to a seductive growl.

Affecting a haughty expression, she looked away. "How much?"

"Dinner."

Her head came around, and she stared numbly at him. "Is that all?"

"That's enough for *now*," he replied in Navajo.

"What did you say?"

He translated it into English, and burst out laughing when she rolled her eyes at him.

"You wish," she countered, laughing softly.

"You've got that right, Sara," he replied. Then, much to his surprise, her laughter joined his. It was the first time in a very long time a woman had shared her laughter with him. It was something he had missed and could get used to—again.

Chapter 6

Sara alternated pacing the floor with sitting and flipping through magazines in a waiting room at Santa Fe's largest animal hospital. Salem had touched down at the airport at exactly six fifty-five, and by seven-thirty the foal had undergone an ultrasound and was prepped for surgery. She stopped pacing and stared at the clock on the wall. She had now been waiting three hours.

A breath of warm air swept over her neck and she went completely still. She felt it—him. Feeling his presence even before she turned, Sara sucked in her breath and then let it out slowly. Her pulse was racing when she finally turned around and stared at Salem. He was dressed in pale blue scrubs, his long hair hidden by a matching cap.

Salem saw a myriad of emotions cross Sara's lovely face—fear, apprehension and hope. The operation had gone well, taking a little more than ninety minutes to drain the foal's abdomen of urine and repair the tear in his bladder. He had waited in the recovery room, monitoring the horse's vital signs as it struggled to come out from under the anesthesia.

Taking long strides, he closed the distance between them. "He's going to be okay. That little guy is a survivor."

Sara did not know whether she wanted to laugh or cry. She leaned against Salem's chest, her arms going around his neck, feeding on his strength.

"Thank you."

His arms came up and he cradled her waist, feeling her warmth, savoring the soft curves of her feminine body and inhaling what had become the familiar fragrance of her sensual perfume.

Shifting his head, he buried his face in the jasmine-scented strands of her waving hair. What he wanted was to comb his fingers through her hair and hold it off her face while he devoured her mouth. He wanted to brand her with his kisses until she begged him to stop. He wanted her to feel what he was feeling at that moment—an unbridled passion that totally swept away all of his excuses for not becoming involved with a woman, all his reasons why that woman should not be a neighbor's beautiful daughter.

It had been weeks since he had lain with a woman, and holding Sara Sterling confirmed that he had been waiting for her. Why her, and not some other woman? He did not know why, and at that moment he did not care.

Pulling back, he stared down at her upturned face. All of the gold in her eyes had vanished, leaving them a shimmering jade-green. He gave her a gentle smile.

"I called Joe before they took the little guy into recovery to let him know everything went well."

"When can we take him home?"

"He'll be here for at least a week. The doctors need to

monitor him closely to make certain his bladder is functioning correctly. Right now I need to shower and change my clothes." Lowering his head, he kissed the tip of her nose. "I'll be right back, kitten."

Nodding, Sara lowered her arms and stepped back. "I'll be here."

Their return to Las Cruces was much more relaxed than their departure, and Sara was surprised when Salem maneuvered his vehicle into the driveway leading to his house instead of the one at Sterling Farms.

"I don't know about you, Miss Sterling, but I'm starved. Will you join me for what will become an early dinner?"

"Is this the dinner I owe you?"

He wagged a finger. "Oh, no, you don't. You won't get off that easily. The dinner you owe me will be on your terms. You decide—the time and the place."

A secret smile curved her lush mouth, enchanting Salem with the seductive expression. "Here, tomorrow night, eight o'clock."

His expressive eyebrows lifted. "My place?"

"You said it could be on my terms. And I've selected your place."

Placing his right arm over the back of her seat, he curved his fingers around her slender neck. "I suppose you want me to do the cooking?"

"Bingo, Dr. Lassiter. I can make an exception if you can't cook. And if that's the case then I'll take you out to your favorite restaurant."

But he could cook. And very well. "I think I've just been had."

Unbuckling her seat belt, she smiled at him. "I told you I don't like to lose."

But one of these days you're going to lose, Sara, Salem

countered silently. And when she did, he would make certain it would be the sweetest surrender she had ever experienced.

Sara set a table in a dining alcove as she examined the large, ultra-modern kitchen while Salem went to change out of the T-shirt and jeans he had hastily thrown on when she called him earlier that morning. The enormous space was equipped with the most up-to-date state-of-the-art appliances: compactor, walk-in freezer, double refrigerator, dishwasher, eye-level microwave oven, cooking island with a stove-top grill, built-in convection oven and several television screens placed at strategic viewing places.

She recalled Marisa's statement: *He bought the land over two years ago and built one of the finest houses in the valley for his wife and son. They lived together as a family for exactly one month before she left him, taking the little boy with her.*

Closing her eyes, Sara tried to imagine why a woman would leave Salem Lassiter. What had he done to drive a woman to take her own life and their child's? Was he such a monster that she had not wanted to leave the little boy with his father?

Opening her eyes, she saw the object of her musings standing only a few feet from her. He had entered the kitchen without making a sound, and she realized it was his stalking silence that reminded her of Matthew Sterling. Her father's ability to enter a room without being detected always astounded her.

She stared numbly at Salem, wondering how he could be labeled a monster when he was so gentle with animals. And how had he summoned up a passion in her that she had repressed for years?

Her eyes widened and she instinctively took a backward

step when he moved closer. He had exchanged his white T-shirt and jeans for black ones, the color making him appear darker and sinister. He had secured his long hair in a ponytail, giving her an unobstructed view of his strong face with each distinctly defined feature. Small silver hoops hung from his lobes, answering her question as to what type of earrings he favored.

"I suppose you won't need earrings from me."

Shaking his head slowly, Salem raised his right hand, startling her when his fingers curved under her delicate chin. His gaze was hypnotic as he lowered his head, drawing her into a spell from which there was no escape. A flicker of apprehension coursed through her and a panic she had never known welled up in her chest, making it difficult for her to draw a normal breath.

Lowering his head, their mouths separated by inches, he smiled, and the gesture softened the stern lines in his face. "Are you afraid of me, Sara Sterling?"

The sound of his voice broke the spell, and Sara felt a return of self-confidence even though she found his nearness disturbing and exciting. "Should I be, Salem Lassiter?" she challenged.

Curving his free hand around her waist, he pulled her flush against his middle. "No, you shouldn't."

"That's good," she murmured seconds before his mouth descended on hers, staking a slow, persuasive claim.

She forgot who she was, and that she did not know the man who held her to his heart; she forgot her fear and dread that she would never desire a man again as he tightened his hold on her body.

He deepened the kiss, his tongue probing her mouth until her lips parted. A soft groan escaped him as Sara relaxed in his arms, sinking into his cushioning embrace.

Her tongue met his, retreated, then tentatively darted out again, testing how far she would allow herself to go.

Sara felt a dizzying rush, then a jolt as if her emotions had been short-circuited. She had to stop herself before she went over the edge, had to stop before she found herself begging Salem to make love to her.

Pushing against his chest, she struggled in his strong embrace. "No! Please, no more." She did not recognize her own voice as she buried her face against his solid shoulder, inhaling the fragrance of antiseptic soap mingling with the clean scent of laundry products that clung to the cotton T-shirt.

"I'll stop," he gasped, trying to slow his own runaway pulse, "but don't ask me to apologize for kissing you."

She looked up at him, unable to believe his arrogance. "Did I ask you to apologize?"

He went completely still, visibly stunned, his features frozen in an expression of amazement. "No," he said after an interminable silence.

"Then don't presume to think for me," she chastised softly.

Her retort shattered the sensual spell, bringing with it an icy chill and a realization that they were more alike than dissimilar. Each recognized in the other an unyielding will not to submit at any cost—even if that meant denying what it was they refused to acknowledge—an increasing awareness of each other.

A muscle throbbed in his lean jaw, mirroring his annoyance. Forcing a tight smile, he asked, "May I offer you something to drink?"

"I'll have water, thank you."

Salem brought his open hand down on the countertop. "Dammit, Sara! Don't—"

"Don't what?" she shot back, interrupting him.

Closing his eyes, he bit down hard on his lower lip. Again, she had reminded him of Grace—this time with her accommodating demeanor.

He opened his eyes and stared at her. "I'm sorry. I didn't mean to yell at you. But, please don't ever attempt to placate me again. If there's something I've done or said that you didn't like, just let me know."

Crossing her arms under her breasts, she turned her back. "I don't know what you want from me, Salem, but whatever it is it can only be temporary. I will be in New Mexico for three months, then I'm going back to New York. My life *and* my career are there, not here."

There was a swollen silence, only the sound of their breathing keeping perfect tempo. Salem nodded. "Point taken, *Counselor.*"

She turned to face him, her direct gaze meeting his steady one while she registered his sarcasm. "Thank you, *Dr. Lassiter.*"

He inclined his head, bowing slightly from the waist; the gesture was incredibly graceful and elegant for a man so tall.

"Can I help you with something else? I've already set the table." Crossing his muscular arms over his chest, he gave her a questioning look. "Yes, Salem, I do cook."

He held up both hands. "I didn't say anything."

"You didn't have to. Your expression said it all."

"Have you perfected reading minds?"

Sara flashed a saucy smile. "Not yet."

He extended his left hand. "Come with me."

She placed her smaller hand in his, permitting him to lead her across the kitchen to the freezer. He opened the door, and a wave of frigid air escaped into the climate-controlled kitchen.

"What do you want to eat?"

She stared at shelves filled with packaged and labeled meats, bagged fruits and vegetables and differing varieties of fish. It was apparent that Salem was not one to make weekly visits to the supermarket.

"I'll have steak." Since she had relocated to New York she rarely ate beef. However, she knew that her diet during her stay in the Southwest would include much more red meat, not only because of the quantity, but because of the quality.

Releasing her hand, Salem entered the walk-in freezer and took two steaks from a shelf. He lingered long enough to withdraw two plastic freezer bags filled with single-size portions of broccoli, cauliflower, carrots, green and red peppers and red onion.

He handed her the bags of vegetables and closed the door to the freezer with his shoulder. "Potato or rice?"

Her professionally waxed eyebrows lifted slightly. "Oh? I have a choice?"

He gave her a sidelong glance. "I will always offer you a choice, Sara."

She nodded, knowing that there was an obscure purport behind his acquiescence.

"Potato."

"Mashed, baked or fried?"

"I'd like mine baked."

"At least we can agree on how we prefer our potatoes."

"Even though we didn't get off on the best footing, I believe we have a lot more in common than not," she stated confidently.

Salem's deep-set, penetrating eyes crinkled in a smile, transforming his solemn expression into one that literally took Sara's breath away. She could not believe that he looked like such an entirely different person whenever he smiled. It was not that she did not find him attractive when he didn't. It was just that his smile was slow in coming, reminding her of the rays of the rising sun breaking through the cover of darkness to light the sky for a new day.

She made her way over to the sink, Salem following, and placed the bags of vegetables on the countertop while he deposited the frozen steaks in one of the double, oversize stainless-steel sinks.

"I take it you were also born in New Mexico?" she queried.

"Albuquerque," he confirmed.

"So, we're both native New Mexicans."

"What type of music do you like?" he asked close to her ear.

"I like pop and jazz. You?"

"I'm somewhat partial to classical music."

Turning slightly, she stared up at him. She assumed he played the magnificent concert piano she had caught a glimpse of in a corner of the large living room. "Do you play the piano well?"

He smiled, nodded and made his way over to the refrigerator. He returned to the sink with a decanter filled with cold water and lemon slices. "My instrument of choice is the cello."

"Cello?" There was no mistaking her surprise as she glanced at his large, well-formed hands. Again she was intrigued by the silver bracelet on his left wrist.

"I'll play for you one of these days. How about yourself?"

"I also play piano," Sara confirmed.

"Great. We can play duets."

"I'm going to hold you to that."

"We can play tomorrow, either before or after dinner." He continued with his questioning. "Are you into sports?"

"I'm a willing spectator for most sports, with the exception of racquetball."

"Your father mentioned you were quite the equestrienne when you were growing up."

"Any hope I had of becoming a professional equestrienne ended at age thirteen. I was thrown after I attempted to jump a neighbor's fence. My face made contact with the ground before any other part of my body, and my mother went temporarily insane after I managed to stagger back to the house bruised and bloodied. She threatened to divorce my father if he continued to let me compete. Mom can be quite formidable when she doesn't get her way."

Reaching into an overhead cabinet, Salem withdrew two glasses and filled them with water. "Like mama, like daughter?" he teased, handing her a glass.

Sara shook her head. "I don't think so." What she did not say was that her temperament was more like her father's than her mother's. She was slower to anger, and less demonstrative. Ignoring Salem's expression, which mirrored his skepticism, she took a sip of water. Lowering her glass, she asked, "Why did you become a vet?"

"It wasn't my first career choice. I had studied the cello for years with the hope that I would eventually play with a symphony orchestra. That ended during my last year in high school. I broke my wrist playing basketball, and all my hopes were shattered, along with a bone in my left hand. Instead of going to New York to attend the Crane School of Music at the State University at Potsdam I made a slight detour to Ithaca for preveterinary studies."

"Where did you do your graduate studies?"

"Cornell University, New York State College of Veterinary Medicine. I'd applied to Tufts and Tuskegee, but Cornell offered me a full scholarship so I decided to save my parents a few bucks and accepted their offer. My folks rewarded me for graduating at the top of my class by investing the money they had put aside for veterinary school in a high-yield, tax-free bond. I used the proceeds to build this house."

"Did they do the same for your brothers or sisters?"

"They didn't have to. I'm an only child."

"Where do your parents live?"

"Up north in Taos. They own an art gallery."

Sara's mouth displayed a knowing smile. "So that explains the incredible sculpture in your foyer."

"I purchased all of the pieces in the foyer from my parents' gallery, while most of the other artifacts scattered around the house were passed down to my father from his relatives. The woven rugs, arrowheads and pottery are Navajo."

She was fascinated with the man standing less than a foot away. There was something about him that said he was dangerous and able to disappear inside of characters. He was a veterinarian, but he was also a shaman. He had touched the foal and murmured a language she did not understand. Apparently the horse had, because it had quieted and stilled even before it had been sedated.

Salem Lassiter claimed African and Navajo blood, and spoke fluent English, Navajo and Spanish. The characteristics attributed to his racial blending with the shape of his eyes, skin color, height and hair texture were a visually intoxicating exotic combination. She found him to be the most breathtakingly beautiful man she had ever encountered.

She knew she had asked him a lot of questions, some she deemed quite personal, but she wanted and needed to know as much about him as he was willing to impart.

"How did your parents meet?"

This question elicited a quick smile from Salem. "My

paternal grandmother introduced them. Nona Jennings had no way of knowing—when she accepted a research project to learn the intricacies of rug weaving—that she would meet, fall in love with, and eventually marry a sculptor named Vance Lassiter. My mother was born and raised on one of the South Carolina sea islands. There she learned the art of basket weaving from her mother, who had learned it from her mother. The tradition had been passed down for generations from the first Africans who had come to the New World in chains. Nona grew up knowing she wanted to draw and weave, so she decided to attend a college in the Southwest where she would be surrounded by people who were expert weavers. She spent a summer on the reservation with my grandmother, who not so subtly introduced her to my father when he came for a visit."

"Your father didn't live on the reservation?"

"No. He left to attend college, and decided not to return. With the old ones, it's hard for them to leave. They feel a special kinship when they're able to practice their language and religion and keep the laws and customs of their ancestors.

"My grandmother did not have to play matchmaker for long, because Dad took one look at Mom and before the summer was over they spent all of their free time together. They married two years later and waited five years before starting a family. What they did not know at the time was that Nona would only have one child. Doctors discovered a malignant growth in her uterus less than a year after she delivered me. They removed her uterus, and now, after more than thirty-five years, there has been no evidence that the disease has returned."

"Good for her," Sara said softly. "Who taught you to speak Navajo and Spanish?"

"My grandmother taught me the Navajo language, while my father is fluent in Navajo and Spanish." Curving an arm around Sara's waist, he steered her over to a tall stool at the cooking island. "Let me get you something to nibble on before we begin cooking, and then I'll take you on a tour of the house."

Sara thought of Salem's house as a jewel in the desert. He told her the style was Southwest Contemporary, and had been designed by a woman who had graduated from college with his mother. She was transfixed as he related that his mother and Dorothea Evans-Reid were the first two African American women to graduate with degrees— in fine arts and architecture, respectively—from a small, private, newly integrated college in northern Arizona that had only admitted white males in the past.

A gorgeous, sand-colored, flagstone walk, rare cacti and native plantings adorned a unique center atrium that welcomed visitors before they walked through massive carved doors into the grand foyer. She was overwhelmed by more than nine thousand square feet of uncompromising quality and a meticulous attention to detail expressed in the gleaming walnut floor, latilla ceilings and stained-glass accents.

Sara had already concluded that the kitchen was a chef's dream with the cozy dining area looking out onto a view of a garden filled with cacti and fauna indigenous to the Southwest. The family room was extraordinary in its extensive use of custom walnut built-in shelves, including an entertainment center and floor-to-ceiling bookcases.

The formal dining room featured custom cabinets with leaded glass, granite counters, and massive double doors and windows that opened to the patio, which offered a spectacular view of the landscape and the narrow, meandering stream dividing Salem's property from her family's.

Salem led the way to the upper level, explaining that he had decided on a two-story structure with an air-conditioning unit with temperature sensors in each room. She noticed that all of the rooms were constructed with romantic fireplaces. The bedroom in the master wing beckoned her with every luxury imaginable, including his and her baths, separate dressing areas, cedar closets and an environmental sauna. There were two additional bedrooms, each with marble floor baths and walk-in closets.

"Your home is exquisite," Sara stated reverently when they returned to the kitchen. "I pray that you'll spend many long and happy years here."

A muscle quivered in his lean jaw while twin emotions of pride and anger battled each other. Sara liked his home, while Grace had hated it. His late wife had complained that the house he had purchased after the birth of their son was too small, so he had spent his life savings to build one for her in the Mesilla Valley. He did not know then that Grace would not have been happy if he had erected a castle for her, because she was in love with another man—a man whose child she was carrying when she decided to end her life.

"Thank you, Sara," he murmured quietly, his voice echoing in his ears as if it had come from an empty tomb.

Chapter 7

Familiar landmarks identifying Sterling Farms came into view as Salem crossed the stream and drove slowly down a narrow paved road. The trip from his house, which would have normally taken only five minutes, had become ten. He had no way of knowing that Sara was as reluctant for their time together to end as he was.

He could not remember when he had enjoyed a woman's company as much as he had when sharing the day with Sara. She had fired questions at him, giving him a glimpse of what she would be like if he were under cross-examination, and he had answered all of her questions, though he would have been averse to divulging the information to most people.

During dinner he had asked her why she had elected to attend a law school in the East. There was a slight hesitation before she admitted that she had ended a long-term relationship with a fellow student and felt she needed a change of scene. Her voice was calm, controlled, but she had not been able to successfully hide the pain which had briefly filled her luminous eyes, a pain he was familiar with—the pain of loving and losing.

The conversation then shifted smoothly to impersonal topics: sports, national political campaigning and the ongoing gossip surrounding a popular actress who disclosed that she had been born male. Salem also found himself laughing at Sara's attempt to tell a joke without revealing the punch line. After a while she confessed that she was never good at remembering any of the legal jokes bandied about at the social clubs where many upwardly mobile African Americans gathered at the end of the work week.

She did admit to having a full and varied social life, and he wanted to ask her whether she was involved with a man. The words were poised on the tip of his tongue, and he swallowed them back when he recalled her curt reprimand: *I don't know what you want from me, but whatever it is, it can only be temporary. I will be in New Mexico for three months, then I'm going back to New York. My life and my career are there, not here.*

What Sara did not know was that he was really interested in her. He wanted to know her in the most intimate way possible, and the realization shocked him that after only three days he not only wanted her in his bed but also in his life—even if it was only for three months.

Spending nearly ten consecutive hours with Sara was a reminder of how sterile his life had become. He had become an authority in his field on the North American gray wolf and his professional calendar was usually filled with lectures, conferences and symposiums. He was also on call for ranchers and many zoos throughout the Southwest. After his decision to dissolve his private practice partnership with another veterinarian, he had become as solitary as his pet. He had declined so many invitations to social engagements over the past two years that most people had removed him from their mailing lists. He had not wanted to attend unaccompanied, and if he did invite a woman he did not want to invite gossip about their association. Therefore, he had stayed away.

He maneuvered into the driveway to the expansive ranch house and put the vehicle in Park. Shifting slightly, he stared at Sara as she sat motionless, staring through the windshield.

"I'll pick you up tomorrow night at eight," he stated in a low, composed tone.

Her head came around slowly and she looked directly at him. "You don't have to pick me up."

"Why not?"

"I think I can find your place without getting lost." There was a trace of laughter in her voice.

"It has nothing to do with you getting lost. Whenever I date a woman I usually pick her up and make certain she returns home safely."

Her gaze widened. "Date?"

He smiled. "Would you prefer we go into town to a restaurant?"

"No," she said quickly. She had not been back a week, and she did not want to elicit gossip about her and Salem before she was given the opportunity to talk to her father about him. "You can pick me up at my place."

Vertical lines appeared between his eyes. "Your place?"

"I'll be staying in the cabin on the eastern end of the property."

Salem's expression did not change when he registered this information. If Sara had elected to stay in that particular cabin during her visit, then she lived less than three minutes away.

"What would you like to eat?"

Placing her hand on the door handle, she said flippantly, "Surprise me."

Reaching over, Salem caught her free hand, stopping her from getting out of the truck. "I'll help you down."

She nodded and waited for him to leave the vehicle and open the door for her. Extending her arms, she grasped his shoulders as he lowered her to the ground. "Thank you."

He flashed a half smile, inclining his head. "I'll see you tomorrow night."

Sara turned and made her way toward the stables, feeling the heat of his gaze on her back. She glanced over her shoulder, looking at Salem as he stared back at her. Raising her hand, she waved, smiling when he returned it. Opening the door, she walked into the stable and bumped into a young man she had never seen before. She felt the raw power in his hands when he reached out to steady her.

"I'm sorry, miss."

"Excuse me."

They had spoken at the same time.

Sara stepped back, her eyes crinkling in a friendly smile. "Do you work here?"

Wiping his right hand down the side of his jeans, he extended it. "Kareem Daniels. Mr. Russell hired me to muck out the stalls."

She took the offered hand, registering the calluses covering his palm. "Sara Sterling. Welcome to Sterling Farms."

Kareem wasn't much taller than she was, but what he lacked in height he made up for in musculature. The girth of his neck and shoulders were blatantly revealed by a shirt that appeared a size too small. A low stubble of hair covered what she knew had been a clean-shaven, well-shaped head. His features were pleasant in a smooth face the color of rich, dark milk chocolate. It was difficult to tell his age, and she placed him anywhere between twenty-one and twenty-five.

"Do you have a hat, Mr. Daniels?"

He stared at her, complete surprise on his face. "No, I don't, Miss Sterling."

"I suggest you get one to keep the sun off your face and head. I don't think you'd want to come down with heat stroke."

His head bobbed up and down as he flashed a perfect white smile. "No way. I'll buy one tomorrow."

Sara returned his smile with a friendly one of her own. "It's nice meeting you."

"My pleasure, Miss Sterling."

Kareem watched Sara as she walked the length of the barn, stopping to pat and talk to the horses who had been put through their pacing exercises earlier that afternoon.

He had made a mistake. How had he forgotten to wear a hat? He had worked his grandfather's watermelon farm in Alabama, but that was when he was a kid. He wasn't a kid anymore. He was a thirty-eight-year-old man, but with his boyish-looking face and soft voice he could easily pass for twenty-five. There were times when he cursed his youthful appearance, but this was not one of those times.

He had received half of a very generous bounty to eliminate Sara Sterling, and he intended to collect the balance. What he had to do was make her death look like an accident, and the clock was ticking. He had less than three months to complete his assignment. The man who had hired him had given explicit instructions that Sara Sterling was never to return to New York.

Sara rose early the next morning and went to the stables to see the horses, lingering at the stall of the dam whose foal had undergone surgery the day before. The mare appeared forlorn, staring and sniffing the space where her baby should have been.

She whistled softly, garnering the horse's attention. "Don't worry about your baby, Ginger. He's going to be all right. And one day, even if he doesn't race, he's going to sire a line of winners," she crooned. "I know he hasn't been named, but I'm thinking he should be called Survivor, because that's what he is."

She knew if she had not happened upon the foal when she did he might not have survived the day. Salem had revealed that every hour the tiny horse's condition had gone undetected had lessened his chances for survival by thirty percent. That meant if she had come into the stables an hour later the horse would have been close to death or probably would have drowned in his own urine.

The mare bobbed her head up and down, as if she understood the comforting words. Moving forward in the stall, she nudged Sara's shoulder gently, whinnying and snorting.

"I knew you'd understand," she continued, laughing softly. "Dr. Lassiter says he's going to bring your baby back next week." Patting the mare's nose, she moved down the path to Blaze's stall.

She lingered with her favorite horse, then greeted and talked to the others one by one, giving each equal time. Of the two dozen horses stabled in the large structure, there were at least eight she had not seen before. These had been born after her last visit to New Mexico.

The summer sun was blazing in the eastern sky when she made her way back to the house. She would change her clothes, pick up a car from the garage, drive into Las

Cruces and eat breakfast at her favorite restaurant, then stroll the streets of downtown Las Cruces to reconnect with her youth and college days.

All that was Las Cruces enveloped Sara the moment she entered the centuries-old hub in the sprawling Mesilla Valley. The city's population had swelled to nearly sixty-five thousand in the early nineties, up from about forty-five thousand only a decade earlier. Many had come for the region's vastness, mountain ranges, weather and natural beauty. Modern Las Cruces was home to both fascinating historic districts and brand-new malls, poverty-stricken Mexicans and Ralph Lauren—clad college students, bustling street corners and indomitable mountain peaks just minutes from town.

Maneuvering and parking an updated model of a sapphire-blue Volkswagen Beetle behind a row of stores, she sat staring through the windshield for a full minute before attempting to alight, trying to analyze the rush of emotions making it temporarily impossible for her to get out of the car.

She had not been in her home state for more than two years. Whenever she had returned in the past, she had not felt the surge of loneliness and confusion melding, merging into one dizzying emotion of insecurity; and in that moment she did not know fully who she actually was.

She knew she was Sara Ellen Sterling, the only daughter of Matthew and Eve Sterling, twenty-nine years old and a U.S. prosecuting attorney. However, even though she had it all, she continued to deny herself a social requisite.

She and her brother were heirs to a horse-breeding enterprise in which the cost of buying and selling a single horse was sometimes six figures; she was also heir to half of more than six hundred acres of prime grazing land. She had achieved the success she had planned for her career. Her days were filled with legal machinations, and her nights with a physical and social flurry that was the perfect justification to offset her not committing to a relationship with a man.

She used the excuse that she was not quite where she wanted to be in her life to vindicate her whenever anyone asked her when she was going to embark on marriage and motherhood. Rumors were also circulating that no man in her social circle had ever seen the inside of her Brooklyn Heights apartment. She had ignored them, and had come to accept the pattern and her decision not to enter into a physical liaison with a man as normal for a woman her age.

But it was not normal when she rejected the advances of men, not normal when she refused to seek professional advice to help overcome her belief that she was frigid. And it was not normal for her to continue to substitute strenuous physical activity to offset the sexual frustration that occasionally kept her awake for hours after she had retied to bed.

A slow smile parted her lips as she recalled Salem's kiss. When he had kissed her it seemed as if he had reached inside of her to grab and harness the fear that kept her from submitting to what she had known was the strong passion within her. Kissing him made her recognize her own needs, and those needs had to be assuaged.

She dismissed the sensual image of Salem Lassiter once she stepped out of the car and walked the short distance to Annie Mae's Kitchen—a family-owned restaurant that had occupied the same location for nearly fifty years.

Warm memories assailed her as she pulled open the door and stepped into the air-cooled space. Waiting until her vision adjusted to the darkened interior, she walked over to the counter and sat down. She was early. There was only one other customer—an elderly man who sat in a booth sipping coffee while he concentrated intently on a newspaper spread out on the table in front of him.

A young woman came from the direction of the kitchen, balancing several plates along her arm. She offered Sara a friendly smile. "I'll be right with you, miss."

Sara returned her smile, recognizing the woman. They had gone to high school together. However, she hadn't seen Patricia Mayfield in more than ten years, so she doubted whether Patty would recognize her at first glance.

The waitress served the elderly man, then returned to the counter to take Sara's order. "Would you like to see a menu?"

A mysterious smile inched up the corners of Sara's mouth as she stared at the other woman, seemingly daring her to recognize her. "Has it really been that long, Patty?"

Vertical lines appeared between Patricia's liquid brown eyes before recognition dawned. Her lush rosebud mouth opened, closed, then opened again. "Sara? Sara Sterling?"

"Bingo."

Patricia screamed, rounding the counter, arms outstretched. Within seconds the two women were hugging, talking excitedly.

"I can't believe it," Patricia exclaimed as a flush of excitement darkened her peaches and cream complexion. "I can't believe you're back."

"Only for three months."

Patricia sat down on the stool next to Sara, squeezing her fingers. "Every time I see your parents I ask them about you. They usually come in here for Sunday brunch after church services. How's New York? You know everyone missed you at the ten-year reunion," she continued without taking a breath.

"New York is wonderful."

"Is it as exciting as everyone says?"

"It is," Sara confirmed. "I love it."

Releasing her hands, Patricia jumped up. "What do you want to eat? It's still early, so we can sit and talk awhile before the regulars come in."

Ten minutes later Sara sat in a booth with Patricia, bringing her up-to-date on how her life had changed since they last saw each other between bites of buttered toast, crisp broiled bacon and fluffy scrambled eggs.

Patricia hadn't changed much in eleven years. She still wore her naturally curly red hair in a short stylish cut, even though there was a light sprinkle of gray in the bright curls.

"Didn't you move up to Alamogordo after graduation?" Sara asked Patricia.

"I still live there, but I come down every summer to help my parents out. My mother's varicose veins won't permit her to stand for long periods of time. I look forward to getting a break from Wayne and the kids, even if I'm on my feet for twelve hours a day."

Sara arched a delicate eyebrow. "It's nice to hear that you and Wayne are still together." Patricia had dated the high school football team quarterback, who had put his engagement ring on her finger minutes after he walked across the stage to accept his diploma.

A soft blush swept over her cheeks. "Thanks. I work very hard at staying married. If you had come back for the reunion you would have been amazed at the number of people who are now on their second and third marriages. The only ones who seem to have solid marriages are the ones who moved away. How about yourself? Have you found that special guy?"

Staring down at her ringless fingers, Sara shook her head. "Not yet." Her head came up and she smiled at Patricia.

"What are you waiting for?"

Shrugging her shoulders, she picked up her coffee cup. "I still have time. My biological clock hasn't begun to tick too loudly. How many children do you have?" she asked, shifting the topic of conversation back to the other woman.

"Two. One of each." The front door opened and closed, and Patricia rose to her feet. "I'll be back as soon as I serve these guys."

Sara glanced at the two men who had walked into Annie Mae's, her eyes widening when she recognized the man to whom she had given her love and her innocence. Everything she had remembered about Eric Thompson came rushing back as if it had been only days instead of years. His posture was still ramrod straight, his chin tilted slightly upward as he appeared to peer down on anyone who did not match his impressive six-foot-two-inch height. She also recognized the exquisite cut of the suit jacket draping his broad shoulders. Judging from his outward appearance, Eric had attained the success he'd always craved.

Reaching into her handbag, she withdrew her sunglasses and perched them on her nose. Then she removed several bills from her wallet. Waiting until Eric and the man accompanying him walked past her booth, she stood up and walked over to the counter and placed the money near the cash register.

Without bidding Patty goodbye, she turned and made her way out of the restaurant. And it wasn't until the door closed after her that Eric Thompson turned and stared at her departing figure. He had only caught a glimpse of her profile, but he was certain he knew her from somewhere.

Waiting until Patty walked over with a menu, he gave her his practiced, winning smile. "Who was that woman?"

Patty handed the two men menus. "Shame on you, Eric. How can you forget your high school sweetheart?"

"Sara Sterling?"

Patty flashed a smug grin. "She's the one."

Recovering quickly, Eric swallowed, hoping to relieve the dryness in his constricted throat. "When did she get back?"

"I don't know. But she says she'll be here for three months."

"How about that," he crooned softly, his handsome mouth curving into a wide grin.

Chapter 8

Sara made her way to the parking lot, slowing her stride. She was quite pleased with herself. She had not fallen apart when she saw Eric. She had remained as calm as she had been during their last encounter, when she had twisted the ring off her finger, handed it to him and silently cursed him in English and Spanish. She had not wanted to believe him—not when the passion between them had been so intense.

When Eric introduced her to passion, he had come to her very experienced with the opposite sex. Both of them were twenty-two when she offered him her virginal body, and from their first encounter she had believed they were the perfect combination—in and out of bed.

It wasn't until after she had left New Mexico for New York that she finally realized that she would and could never become Mrs. Eric Thompson. She had thrown herself into her courses, spending long hours in the law school library. She was rewarded for her diligence when she graduated top of her class and made the law review. Several prestigious New York law firms had courted her with lucrative salary offers, but she'd declined in favor of a position with the United States District Court of the Eastern District, in Brooklyn.

There was no doubt she would see Eric again during her three-month stay, and she would be prepared for him. This time emotions would not come into play. Even though she no longer loved him, she also did not hate him. After she had recovered from his startling revelation, she was grateful he had revealed his sexual unrest before she had married him.

Slipping into her car, she started it up and drove slowly up and down the avenues of downtown Las Cruces. She had been away so long that she felt more like a tourist than a native. The buildings comprising New Mexico State University came into view. She had cheered her teams as fervently as the next student. As an Aggie alumna, she felt warm memories flooding her mind, and she promised herself that she would revisit the University Museum in Ken Hall to view the exhibits that usually focused on historic and prehistoric Native American culture. She also planned to take advantage of the Olympic-size swimming pool. Swimming laps would replace her aerobic and treadmill workouts.

She drove southward for a quarter of an hour, and when she saw the signs indicating the distance to El Paso, Texas, she reversed her direction. The city was wide-awake and bustling when she maneuvered into the parking lot of a brand-new mall. Three hours later she emerged, her hands clutching shopping bags and plastic-covered garments. After loading the trunk of the Volkswagen, she headed for a supermarket. She had to buy groceries to stock her refrigerator and freezer.

* * *

Sara parked in the back of her cabin, which was a smaller but close replica of the ranch-style home where she had grown up. The one-bedroom structure claimed a loggia and more than two thousand square feet of living space. The other two cabins on the Sterling property each claimed two bedrooms. Marisa and her son had lived in one, and Joe Russell in the other. A slight smile crinkled her eyes when she thought of Marisa and Joe. It was good that they had found each other after being single for so many years.

She unlocked the front door, pushing it open. She stepped into the entry and spotted an envelope on the floor. Someone had slipped it under the door. Placing her purchases on a drop-leaf table in the entryway, she bent over, picked up the envelope and withdrew a single sheet of paper.

Her gaze raced quickly over the bold writing with large sweeping loops: *Sara—I've been called up to the Alamo Navaho Indian Reservation to vaccinate sheep. I expect to be back in time for dinner. Be prepared to eat out. SL*

"Whatever happened to *please* be prepared, Salem?" she whispered, tossing the note on the table. Gathering her bundles, she headed for the L-shaped living/dining room and deposited them on a sofa covered in a dove-gray-and-white-striped cotton chintz and on the two armchairs facing the sofa—one in the matching striped fabric and the other in white linen, cradling a striped throw pillow. Picking up the bags with the perishable items, she headed for the narrow efficiency kitchen.

When she had moved into the cabin, her first decision was to redecorate it entirely in shades of white. It had taken her more than two years to find antique tablecloths, linens, crockery and just the right fabrics to cover the chairs, sofa and pillows. Her mother had been a staunch assistant, accompanying her when she drove or flew to estate sales or auction houses to bid on a table, chair or bed. She had pleaded with her father to add a back porch, and since he had conceded she had used it as a sheltered escape, a perfect getaway space, with an oversized hammock she used for lounging once the intense daytime heat dissipated.

The cabin had been her sanctuary, a place where she studied, a place where she and Eric had spent hours in bed together formulating plans for their future. However, Eric and everything she had shared with him was her past. Now it was time for her to plan her future. If given the opportunity, she knew John Bohannon could become a part of that.

She emptied the bags from the supermarket, then filled a kettle with water for a cup of herbal tea. Moments later she dialed the number of the main house and left a message on the answering machine for Marisa, informing her that she had moved into the cabin.

Sara pumped a small amount of mousse onto her fingers, combing the rich, scented foam into her freshly shampooed, blow-dried hair. Using a small round brush, she arranged her hair off her face, lifting the strands on the crown, affecting a sophisticated style.

Satisfied with the results, she began the ritual of making up her face. Within minutes a smoky-gray shadow, mascara, plum-tinted blush, a matching lipstick and a light cover of loose, shimmering powder transformed her face into one that made her look seductive and mysterious. It had been weeks since she had worn makeup. Usually when she went to work she opted only for mascara and a muted shade of lipstick.

The doorbell chimed melodiously throughout the cabin

and she stared at her reflection before she stood up and went to answer the door. The sensual fragrance of Asian sandalwood, peony petals and everlasting trailed in her wake.

Her pulses raced a little faster as she neared the door. She did not know why, but she wanted to see Salem again. She felt comfortable with him and enjoyed his company. His manners were not as impeccable as John's, yet he was as intelligent and charming.

Opening the door, her gaze widened when she saw Kareem Daniels standing where she had expected to see Salem Lassiter. He appeared as surprised as she when his eyes swept over her face and body.

"I…I'm sorry, Miss Sterling," he stammered. His fingers curled nervously around the crown of a wide straw hat.

A soft smile parted Sara's lips. "Yes?"

Reaching into a pocket of his jeans, he pulled out an envelope and thrust it at her. "Miss Marisa asked me to give this to you before I went home."

She took a quick glance at the return address on the letter. It was from John. "Why, thank you, Kareem." A slight frown creased her smooth forehead when she glanced over his shoulder. "How did you get here?"

He ducked his head, staring down at his dusty work boots. "I walked, miss."

"Why didn't you ask Mr. Russell to drop you off?"

Kareem gave her a shy smile. "He offered, but I told him that I don't mind walking."

"You intend to walk back?"

"I'll drive him back."

Kareem and Sara jumped at the sound of the male voice that seemed to come out of nowhere. Salem had come up so silently that neither of them had heard or noticed him.

Sara's heart stopped, then started up in a staccato rhythm that forced her to breathe through her open mouth. He was dressed entirely in black: shirt, double-pleated linen slacks and imported loafers. His thick black hair was brushed off his forehead and secured at the nape of his neck. His expression was impassive, hiding his innermost emotions from her and the world.

Kareem looked at the man towering over him by at least eight inches. "That's okay."

Crossing his arms over the silk fabric of his banded-collar shirt, Salem motioned with his head. "Let's go." His voice, though quiet, had an ominous quality. Not waiting for Kareem's response, he turned and walked back to his car.

"Good evening, miss," Kareem mumbled as he followed Salem.

Sara stood on the loggia, watching the two men as they slipped into a gleaming black Jaguar convertible. She could not understand what would make Kareem walk a mile in the heat, and she also could not fathom how Salem had driven up without her hearing him.

Waiting until the car had disappeared from her line of vision, she returned to the house to retrieve her purse and keys. After turning on a lamp in her bedroom and one in the living room, she locked up the cabin, then sat down on a chair on the loggia to await Salem's return.

Salem's expression was a mask of stone when he drove back to the cabin. Not even the sight of the delicate fabric of a flowing organza skirt in a soft plum shade floating around Sara's long shapely legs, or the matching silk shell displaying her silken shoulders, could dispel the uneasiness he had felt when he drove up and found the strange man at her door. He could not explain it, but a wave of cold had swept over him. The feeling was similar to the one he experienced the morning he woke up to find that Grace had left the house and had taken Jacob with her. And it wasn't until after the sheriff had come to his house asking him to identify the bodies of his wife and son that he knew what he felt had been the icy fingers of death.

He stopped the car and put it in Park, but did not turn off the engine. Stepping out of the car, he watched Sara warily as she rose to her feet. His gaze swept over her, admiring her startling beauty. He took half a dozen steps and stood in front of her, a slight smile crinkling his eyes.

"You look beautiful." There was no mistaking the reverence in his voice.

Tilting her chin, she returned his smile, bringing his gaze to linger on the plum color outlining her sensual mouth. "Thank you. You also look very nice."

Inclining his head in acknowledgment, he reached for her hand and tucked it into the bend of his elbow. Leaning closer, he inhaled her scented body. "Should I be jealous?" he whispered.

She stared up at him, unblinking. "Of whom?"

"Your young admirer."

Vertical lines appeared between her eyes. "Who are you talking about?"

"The muscled jock I just drove back to your folks' place."

"Kareem?"

"Oh, is that his name?"

She nodded. "His name is Kareem Daniels. Mr. Russell hired him to muck out the stables."

"Your cabin is a long way from the stables."

Suddenly, Sara was annoyed with his sarcasm. "Are we going to stand here and discuss Kareem Daniels, or are we going out for dinner?"

His gaze narrowed as he glared at her. It was apparent she did not mind men stopping by her cabin. "If you're looking for an excuse not to go out with me tonight, then think again," he warned softly, leading toward his car.

"Did I say I didn't want to go out with you?"

Opening the passenger-side door, he helped her into the low-slung sports car, then waited for her to settle her skirt around her knees before he closed the door firmly.

Leaning over, he winked at her. "No, you didn't."

"Then don't presume to think for me," they said in unison.

Shaking her head, Sara forced back a smile. By the time she pulled the seat belt over her chest, Salem had folded his tall frame down beside her and had secured her own belt.

"Should I put up the top?" he asked before he shifted into gear.

"No. Please leave it down."

He stared at her enchanting profile. "The wind will muss your hair."

Turning, she smiled at him. "There are worse things in life."

Throwing back his head, he laughed. It was apparent there wasn't a vain bone in Sara Sterling's perfect body. Shifting into gear, he drove across the stream and headed in a southward direction.

Sara saw the sign indicating the number of miles to El Paso. Salem had been driving for nearly an hour, and within minutes they would leave New Mexico and cross the state line into Texas.

"Where are you taking me?"

Concentrating on the road in front of him, he drawled, "Mexico."

"You're taking me to Juárez?"

"*We* are going to Juárez."

"We don't have to go to Mexico to get good Mexican food," she argued softly. "We could've gone to La Posta in Mesilla."

"You're right about that, but it's usually too crowded."

"We could've also eaten at El Patio Restaurante y Cantina."

"You're right again, but the food isn't as good as where I'm going to take you."

Resigned to the fact that she was going to eat dinner in another country, Sara relaxed against the leather seat and stared at the passing landscape. The sun had set beyond the horizon, leaving a blush of orange in the darkening sky.

Going to Mexico brought back memories she did not want. She and Eric had spent a week in Mexico, and on their return trip he had proposed marriage and she had accepted. She had come back to the States literally glowing when she told her parents that she was to become Mrs. Eric Thompson a month after she graduated college. Then the plan she and Eric had made to attend the same law school as a married couple was shattered with his unexpected confession.

This was to be her second trip to Mexico with a man—a man who directly or indirectly was responsible for his wife taking her own life and that of their child. A man who was as breathtakingly sensual as he was virile; a man who disturbed and intrigued her; and a man who was not who he appeared to be. There was something so incredibly mysterious about Salem Lassiter that she felt that he could will himself to change shape and form, to pass through time and space.

They crossed the bridge over the Rio Grande River into

Ciudad Juárez, Mexico, and the fact that they had left the United States behind was evident in the overt poverty in the border city.

"Did you drive up to the Navajo reservation earlier this morning?" she asked him after an extended comfortable silence.

Salem had not sought to initiate conversation because he was content to savor her presence, take furtive glances at her enchanting profile, and watch the wind ruffle her short hair.

"No. I flew up."

"When did you learn to fly?"

Slowing to avoid hitting an emaciated dog ambling along a dusty street, he gave her a quick glance. "My cousin taught me the summer I turned twenty-three. He's an air force fighter pilot."

"Is he a career officer?"

He nodded. "His father was one of the original Navajo code talkers during the Second World War. My uncle was seventeen when he enlisted in the Marine Corps at Fort Wingate, New Mexico, in 1942. After he was signed up he underwent basic boot camp training at the San Diego Marine Corps Recruit Depot. Following boot camp, he was transferred to the Field Signal Battalion Training Center at Camp Pendleton in California. After he was honorably discharged he confessed that it had been a traumatic experience for him because he had never been off tribal land.

"He saw action in Guam and Guadalcanal. Once he was even captured by American troops who mistook him for a Japanese soldier. An army unit sent a message to his command saying they had captured a Japanese soldier in a Marine uniform wearing identification tags. A Marine officer was sent to see if the prisoner was indeed a Japanese soldier, and was startled to find that he was a Navajo code talker."

"Where is your uncle now?"

"He returned to the reservation. It was ironic—when he was going to the boarding school on the reservation the Anglo teacher told him not to speak Navajo, but during the war the government wanted him to speak it. After the war he came back and became a Navajo language teacher."

As Sara had studied the history and culture of the Native Americans of the Southwest, she knew that the Navajos had become America's secret weapon during the war. They had used their own language to encrypt codes that Japanese cryptographers were unable to break.

"Will you teach me the language, Salem?"

He maneuvered the car into the parking lot of a building ringed with tiny red lights. Pressing a button, he raised the convertible top, then turned and stared at her.

"It's not that easy," he replied softly.

"Why not?"

"There is no written alphabet, no other symbols. There are dialect variations among the different clans, and sometimes within the clans themselves."

"Teach me the dialect of the *Tabaaaha*."

The light from the dashboard cast enough light in the car's interior for him to see the expression of determination on Sara's face.

"Why, Sara? Why do you want me to begin something with you that you know we cannot possibly finish? It would take more than three months for you to learn enough to communicate effectively. And don't tell me you'll have someone tutor you once you return to New York."

"Maybe I won't go back," she countered. "Maybe I'll stay and join a local law firm or set up my own practice."

His lids came down slowly, concealing the satisfied

light that had filled his eyes, and when he looked at her again he had successfully concealed the deep longing he was beginning to feel for her.

He raised his right hand, and his forefinger touched the single pearly stud in her delicate lobe. "We'll begin with a word that sounds like *nehemah*."

"What does it mean?"

Leaning closer, he pressed his mouth to her ear, eliciting a slight shiver from her. "Our mother. Our homeland is our mother."

Turning her head slightly, she inhaled his warm, moist breath before his lips touched hers. *"Nehemah,"* she whispered.

His hand curved around her neck, increasing the pressure and deepening the kiss. She pushed against his shoulder and he eased back, releasing her.

Sara sat motionless, her chest rising and falling heavily, and stared straight ahead as Salem turned off the ignition, stepped out of the car, retrieved his unconstructed, black linen jacket from the space behind the seats, and then came around to open the passenger side door for her. She placed her hand in his, feeling the power in his strong fingers as he pulled her gently to her feet.

He did not let go of her hand when he led the way to the restaurant. The door opened at their approach, and they were greeted with a cacophony of sights and sounds. Several musicians were seated on stools in a corner, strumming on acoustic guitars while half a dozen waitresses moved sensually over the sawdust-strewn floor in traditional Mexican blouses and colorful skirts. They flirted with the men who were dining alone, but were overly polite to those accompanied by a woman.

What drew Sara in immediately were the tempting smells wafting from the trays of food coming from the kitchen. She spied a platter filled with green chile stew, black beans with Mexican cream and tomato salsa, and gorditas. A bottle of tequila and a pitcher of margaritas graced every table that claimed a diner.

Salem stared at the awe lighting up her face. "Did I not tell you?"

"Yes, you did." Pressing closer to his side, she smiled up at him. "I'll never doubt you again."

He flashed a sensual smile. "Thanks."

A waitress beckoned them, and they crossed the room and sat down at a scarred wooden table in a corner where they were permitted a modicum of privacy. A minute after they were seated a bottle of tequila appeared, along with two glasses and a pitcher of icy-cold margaritas.

Salem picked up the pitcher, his eyes crinkling in a smile. "May I pour you a drink?"

Sara returned his warm smile. "Yes, please."

He half filled both glasses with the pale yellow-green liquid. He handed her a glass, then raised his own in a toast. "To friendship. *¡Salud!*"

She touched her glass to his. *"¡Salud!"* she repeated, putting it to her lips. First there was an icy coldness, then a burning that brought tears to her eyes and set her entire body aflame.

"¡Viva México!" she gasped.

Salem swallowed a mouthful of his own drink, grimacing. "Amen," he gasped, shaking his head.

They stared at each other, blinking back tears, then dissolved into a fit of laughter.

Chapter 9

Salem was still smiling when he rose to his feet, extending his right hand. "May I have this dance, Ms. Sterling?"

Sara placed her slender hand in his larger one, returning his smile. "Why, yes, Dr. Lassiter."

Tightening his grip on her fingers, he pulled her gently to her feet and curved an arm around her narrow waist. The feminine heat and sweetness assailed him with feelings he had thought long dead. It was the first time in more than two years that he had taken a woman into his embrace for more than just a quick release of pent-up sexual frustration. He could remember the last time he had danced with a woman—it had been with Grace at their wedding reception. He had dated her, married her and had gotten her pregnant while she had been in love with another man. And he had loved her enough to believe she would eventually return his love.

His arm tightened around Sara's body as he drew her

closer. She went stiff in his arms and he went completely still, staring down at her.

"Relax," he whispered.

She nodded, unable to meet his direct stare. "I'll try."

He pulled her closer, feeling the rigidness in her limbs, then the slight trembling. He had asked her if she was afraid of him and she had denied it. What had she heard about him? Who had told her that she should fear him?

Lowering his head, he pressed his mouth to her ear and murmured softly in a language she could not understand. The low chanting was similar to what he had said to Ginger's foal to calm him. The strange language had an Asian sound to it, and she realized he was speaking a Navajo dialect.

Sara felt as if she were floating outside of herself, watching herself rise higher and higher until the ethereal image disappeared. The stiffness left her arms, her legs; she was melting against Salem's taller and stronger body. She registered the press of the metal of his buckle on the belt around his waist, the solid wall of muscles in his back when her arms curved around his waist inside his jacket, and the unyielding hardness of his chest against her breasts. Without warning, her breasts swelled, growing heavier, the nipples springing into prominence against the delicate silk covering the heated mounds of flesh. Salem stopped chanting, gasping for breath, and she knew she had aroused him because he had aroused her.

Moving like someone in a hypnotic trance, she relaxed against his frame, following his expert lead as he executed intricate steps in tempo with the crisp notes coming from the acoustic guitars. At least half a dozen couples were on the dance floor and the lights were dimmed, adding to the sensual, romantic atmosphere enveloping the rustic structure.

Closing her eyes, Sara smiled and rested her head on Salem's hard shoulder, reveling in the newfound freedom she discovered in his embrace. It was as if she had suddenly been liberated from a self-imposed exile. It had been more than six years since she had permitted a man to hold her close. If they'd made the attempt she'd usually panicked, experiencing temporary paralysis.

She felt the strong pumping of his heart against her breasts, the power in his upper body that made it so easy for him to lift a foal without straining. And not for the first time she wondered, *Who are you, Salem Lassiter? Are you doctor or shaman? Real or apparition?*

Her thoughts went unspoken as she lost herself in the man and the spell he had woven around her to make her at times question her own sanity. The musicians ended their vibrant guitar strumming, taking their bows for the soft applause coming from the diners and dancers, and Sara and Salem returned to their table, smiling at each other.

He seated her, lingering over her head longer than necessary before he returned to his own chair. He did not realize how fast his pulse was racing until he picked up a menu laminated in plastic and discovered his hands were shaking.

His gaze swept over the selections, seeing and not seeing. He had come to the restaurant often enough to know everything they offered. However, he needed time, time to bring his runaway emotions under control. Dancing with Sara had elicited a rush of desire, reminding him of the night he had left his bed to stand under the spray of an icy shower, the night that the cold water had failed to relieve the heaviness in his lower body. He had thought it was because he had been too long without a woman, but after their dancing he realized it had nothing to do with a prolonged period of abstinence and everything to do with Sara Sterling.

He had to uncover what there was about her that shattered the barrier he had set up to keep his distance from women, and why she had come into his life when he was at peace with himself for the first time in years.

Raising his head, he stared across the table at her bowed head. The wind had rearranged her carefully coiffed hair, and soft waves fell over her forehead in seductive disarray. She looked less sophisticated with her hair mussed. He had noticed that even though he had only seen her wearing jeans and boots there was something very staid and proper about her, and he realized it had come with her profession. Seeing her dressed in silk, with the wispy fabric of her skirt floating around her long legs, made her appear softer, more feminine. He knew she was very secure about her height because she had chosen to wear a pair of three-inch black patent leather pumps, which put her close to the six-foot mark.

"Would you like an appetizer?" he asked in a quiet voice.

Her head came up and she smiled at him. "You can order for me tonight."

Salem nodded to a waitress who stood a short distance from their table. He gave her their order in Spanish, the young woman offering him a sensual smirk before she walked away to put in their selections.

"When are your parents and brother coming home?" he asked, still speaking Spanish.

"Next Wednesday," Sara replied in the same language.

She could never thank her parents enough for teaching her her paternal grandmother's native tongue. Her father had grown up completely bilingual, and her mother had learned enough Spanish during a three-month stay in

Mexico to facilitate an adequate grasp of the language. After Eve Blackwell-Sterling returned to the States she had continued to study the language, and eventually became fully bilingual.

The older Sterlings had established a house rule: only Spanish was to be spoken whenever the family sat down to share a meal. The ability to speak Spanish had become an asset for her brother when he campaigned for his state senate seat. Christopher's political platform was based on inclusion for all New Mexicans, no exclusion, and it was the first African American and Latino vote that had made him a winner by the narrowest of margins. He defeated the incumbent by a mere sixty-four votes, establishing a rivalry that would eventually be played out at a later date, because both men had announced that they planned to seek the gubernatorial seat in the upcoming election. However, Christopher's opponent had a distinct advantage: his father was the current governor of the state—the most popular governor in New Mexico's history.

"Have you ever met my brother?" she asked.

Salem nodded. "Twice," he acknowledged. "Once when he took a break from campaigning, and another time at your folks' place when they gave a celebratory party after he'd won the senate seat. And yes, I did vote for him."

She grimaced. "I have to admit that my very mild-mannered brother threatened me with bodily harm if he lost the election by one vote."

"I take it you did not come back to vote in the election?"

Sara shook her head. "I am legally a New Yorker."

Salem arched an eyebrow with this disclosure. "You prefer New York to New Mexico?"

"It's not about preferring one state over the other." There was no mistaking the annoyance in her voice. "New York is where I have chosen to work, and therefore live. I've established a lifestyle that is completely different from one I would have here."

"How different?"

"Everything. Especially my social life."

"You're involved with someone." The statement should have been a question. His stare drilled into her, not permitting her to move or draw a normal breath.

"I am seeing a man," she confirmed, refusing to wither under his dark hypnotic gaze.

"A man who lets you stay away from him for three months?"

Sara's eyes widened, permitting him to see the now dark jade-green depths of her golden eyes. "I do not have to ask a man to *let* me do anything."

"I'm not talking about you, Sara. I'm just saying that things would be very different between *us* if *I* were your *man*."

"But you're *not* my man!" she countered.

"You're right about that," he retorted in a voice so quiet she had to lean forward to hear what he was saying. "Because if I were, I would never permit you to stay away from me that long."

"What would you do?" she challenged.

"Come after you."

The three words told her everything she wanted and needed to know about Salem Lassiter. He was possessive and territorial. Pulling her gaze away, she glanced at her hands atop the table, the fringe of her lashes casting a seductive shadow on her high cheekbones.

"What if *my* man could not come after me?" She looked up at him through her lashes, realizing his eyes were as dark and powerful as the rest of his face and body.

A small smile played at the corners of Salem's strong mouth. There was no doubt he had put Sara on the defensive. Reaching across the table, he held her hands firmly within his strong grasp.

"Then he cannot be in love with you. Because if he were, then he would not permit time or space to keep you apart."

"I said I was seeing a man. I don't recall saying I was in love with him."

Releasing her fingers, he leaned back on his chair. "Good." The single word came out in a hushed whisper.

Her delicate eyebrows lifted. "Good?"

Again he affected the hypnotic stare, pulling her in, and she felt what he was feeling—a silent expectation, an increasing awareness, a smoldering flame, and a heated entrancement from which there was no escape.

Sara studied the lean dark-skinned face, waiting for an answer, but when it was apparent Salem was not going to respond she clenched her teeth in frustration.

Reaching out, she picked up the glass filled with the strong drink and took a swallow. The icy cold was followed by a warming that washed away her tension and apprehension. Salem Lassiter was nothing like the men in New York, who usually were not as candid when they sought a liaison. Their come-ons were more subtle—a surreptitious glance, or even something as ambiguous as a gentle brush of shoulders in a crowded room.

"You have to know that I'm attracted to you," Salem said after he had taken a sip from his own glass.

Sara feigned indifference even though her heart pumped wildly against her ribs. "How?"

His gaze went to the rapidly pumping pulse in her delicate throat. "I can't believe you asked me that. You claim the face and body of a seductress."

"I am asking, Salem. How?"

"I'm attracted to you in the way a man likes a woman."

Her lids fluttered slightly. "Explain."

Salem decided to press his attack. He became aware that Sara Sterling had a sharp tongue except when the topic concerned male and female interaction. She claimed she was involved with a man in New York, but he did not believe her. She struck him as a woman who put her career first and a man second.

"I want to see you again, to get to know you better—"

"To sleep with me?" she interrupted.

He shrugged a broad shoulder under his jacket while arching an eyebrow. "If it comes to that."

"It won't, and it can't," she countered angrily.

"Why not, Sara?" His voice was soft, coaxing.

Suddenly she felt as if she were on the witness stand, being cross-examined. Her very composure was under attack.

"Because I don't sleep with men."

He stared, complete surprise freezing his distinctive features. "How old are you?"

"Twenty-nine."

"You're twenty-nine and you're still a virgin?" His voice was barely above a whisper.

"I didn't say I was a virgin," she hissed between clenched teeth. "I just said I don't sleep with men."

Salem successfully schooled his features to hide the relief sweeping over him. Sara was not physically involved with her New York boyfriend, and that was why both were content to spend three months apart.

"What about you, Salem?" she continued, not giving him the opportunity to come back at her. "Are you sleeping with a woman?"

"No. And I haven't for a while," he answered honestly. He had been celibate for more than two months.

It was her turn to lift her eyebrows. "Is abstinence difficult for you?"

He flashed a shy smile. "Sometimes. Why do you ask?"

"Just curious."

What she could not tell him was that being celibate had not bothered her before meeting him. That she had changed, because now she looked forward to seeing him, having him touch and kiss her, that for the first time in six years she wanted to take off her clothes and lie down with a man. She wanted to trace his body with her fingertips, feel the protective warmth of his arms around her and eventually take him into her body.

How could she tell Salem Lassiter—her parents' neighbor, a stranger—that he made her aware that she had denied her femininity for too long?

"I'm certain you know the adage about curiosity, kitten."

She affected an attractive moue. "Oh, I do. But remember, satisfaction brought it back."

"That it did," he agreed with a wide grin.

All conversation ended once the waitress returned with a tray filled with hot and cold appetizers. Sara stared at the dishes, recalling the names of spicy concoctions she had not seen or eaten in years.

Now that she was going to eat authentic Mexican food she knew she had truly come home.

It was close to the midnight hour when Sara and Salem stood on the loggia to her cabin. He curved his arms around her waist, pulling her to his chest.

"Ahéhee," he whispered in her ear. "I said thank you."

"Ahéhee," she repeated, pressing her face against his hard shoulder. "I really enjoyed myself."

Easing back, he stared down at her face in the soft light

coming from two mission lanterns that flanked the front door. "Will you go out with me again?"

"Yes."

"When?"

"Next week. I'm going up to Santa Fe tomorrow to visit a friend, and I probably won't be back until the beginning of next week. I want to be here when my family arrives."

Salem felt a sense of loss. He did not know what it was, or why he felt the need to see her—every day, if possible.

"I still owe you dinner at my place."

Sara placed a hand on his left cheek. "I won't let you forget, but the next one is on me." Leaning forward, she pressed her lips to his. "Good night."

He released her and watched as she put her key in the lock and turned it. Pushing his hands in the pockets of his slacks, he saw her open the door, then close it softly. He waited for the sound of the tumblers falling into place when she locked the door behind her.

He stood motionless, staring at the space where she had been for a full two minutes, then walked back to his car. An inner voice told him to retrace his steps and knock on the door, but he ignored it. Sara Sterling planned to stay in Las Cruces for three months, and that was enough time to decide whether he wanted to become a part of her existence.

Chapter 10

Sara smiled at the man sitting in the gatehouse at the housing development where Emily Kirkland owned a two-story, modern, three-bedroom house. He waved her through after he had verified that her name was listed on a visitors sheet.

She remembered her best friend calling her after she had moved into the newly constructed development, inviting her to a housewarming celebration. She had declined because she was in the middle of a major case with a prominent drug trafficker, but had made arrangements for the delivery of an authentic Tiffany light fixture for the ultramodern kitchen.

It had been exactly one year since she last saw her best friend. Emily had flown into New York on business, and they had met at a Manhattan hotel for dinner before the journalist flew back to Santa Fe the following morning. Sara looked forward to seeing Emily again and catching up on what was going on in the political journalist's exciting career.

Driving slowly, she looked for Emily's house number along the curbs. Then she saw her friend standing in a driveway beside a gleaming white Corvette, waving to her. Seeing the car elicited a warm smile from Sara. She recalled her friend's penchant for speed. There had been a time when Emily owned a motorcycle, but she sold it after her parents refused to talk to her. The stalemate ended after two weeks. Emily loved her mother and father too much to risk their alienation.

Maneuvering her Volkswagen Beetle into the driveway behind the Corvette, Sara turned off the engine and stepped out of the car. Her luminous eyes crinkled in a warm smile as she extended her arms.

Twenty-eight-year-old Emily Kirkland's green eyes tilted upward as she wound her arms around Sara's waist. "Welcome home, stranger."

Pulling back, Sara wrinkled her pert nose. "Before you start calling me names I want you to stop and count how many days a month *you* spend in Santa Fe."

Emily lifted her beautifully arched black eyebrows. "I'm only away from home when on assignment. I'm like a homing pigeon, because the first opportunity I get I'm back here."

Sara stared at Emily, admiring the mass of curly black hair framing her oval face and falling to her shoulders, the clear, leaf-green color of her large eyes, and the perfection of her delicate features in a face the color of polished oak. Whenever her image appeared on the television screen the network's ratings escalated appreciably. Emily had surreptitiously confessed that she received at least two marriage proposals every week via the station's website address. However, what most men could not know was that the political analyst was only interested in one man—Christopher Delgado.

Gesturing to the low-slung sports car, Sara said, "I like your ride."

"Thanks. I took it out yesterday and pushed it to ninety. Talk about a rush!" There was no mistaking the awe in her voice. Emily tunneled her fingers through her hair, pushing the thick, shiny curls off her forehead and behind her ears.

Sara laughed softly. "Whenever I want a rush I take a roller coaster ride."

Peering into the backseat of the Volkswagen, Emily spied a tapestry-covered bag. "How long do you plan to hang out with me?"

"I'm good until Tuesday. My family's due back Wednesday night.

Affecting a frown and crossing her arms under her breasts, Emily chewed her lower lip. "That doesn't give us much time together. My brother's in town for one of his rare visits, so we're expected to eat dinner at my parents' house tonight. And I've also made appointments for us to have the works at our favorite spa early Monday morning—"

"When did you plan all of this?" Sara interrupted. She opened the door to the Beetle and withdrew her weekender.

"Now, you know you can't come to Santa Fe without seeing my folks. And your looking as if you just stepped off the cover of *Vogue* doesn't excuse me—my hair hasn't been this long since high school."

"I like it."

And she did. Emily Kirkland had inherited her mother's raven-black hair and tall slender body and her father's coloring, eyes and features. The overall result had made her a shockingly beautiful woman. There were times when people saw her and Emily together and asked whether they were sisters because they shared equal height, hair color and green eyes—even though Emily's were a clearer, lighter green.

They were lifelong friends, as were their parents. Joshua Kirkland and Matthew Sterling had met in their twenties when both worked for the U.S. Army, and retired within a year of each other. Her father had moved from West Texas to New Mexico and established the horse farm, while Joshua Kirkland relocated from Palm Beach, Florida, to Santa Fe after he married Vanessa Blanchard. The elder Sterlings and Kirklands had alternated visiting each other over the past twenty-five years, becoming more of an extended family than friends.

Emily pulled the bag from Sara's loose grip. "Come in and relax. I prepared a light cold lunch because we're expected at Mom and Dad's at eight."

She led the way up three steps and pushed open the door to reveal a yawning space claiming a two-story foyer and a circular wrought-iron stairway leading to a dramatic loft. Gleaming wood floors, Palladian windows, skylights and a massive stone fireplace all drew her attention immediately.

Sara stood in the middle of the living room, staring up at recessed lights and slowly revolving fans. "Girlfriend, this is fabulous!"

"It's quite a stretch from my first apartment."

"Don't remind me," Sara said, grimacing. Emily had moved away from home during her senior year in college, and had rented a studio apartment in a less than desirable Santa Fe neighborhood. Her parents did not mind her moving out, but were appalled when they discovered she had to share a bathroom with two other tenants on her floor.

"Come on. Let me show you your bedroom before we eat. Then I'll give you a quick tour."

Following her friend up the winding staircase, Sara managed only a fleeting glimpse of the carefully chosen furnishings. The bedroom Emily selected for her was perfect—floor-to-ceiling windows offering a view of the Sangre de Cristo Mountains. The large bedroom also claimed a sitting room and a private bath with a sunken tub.

She stared at a clock on a bedside table. It was twelve-twenty. "Do I have time for a quick shower before we eat lunch?"

Emily flashed a quick smile. "Sure."

Kicking off her running shoes, Sara pulled her blouse from the waistband of her jeans. "Give me about twenty minutes."

"Take your time. It's not too hot, which means we can eat on the patio."

Half an hour later, dressed in a pair of shorts and a skimpy tank top, Sara sat under the shade of a large, dark green umbrella, accepting a chilled glass filled with a tart citrus drink from her hostess. A cooling mountain breeze feathered over her exposed flesh.

Her gaze narrowed as she stared out at the landscape stretching from the rear of the house. A soothing calming peace invaded her mind and body as she closed her eyes.

"This is truly living."

"Are you saying you don't miss the Big Apple?"

Opening her eyes, she stared across the table at her friend. "No."

Emily gave her a skeptical glance. "Do you think you'll ever come back here to live?"

"I don't know."

Emily removed a plastic cover from a large platter filled with boiled jumbo shrimp, an expertly prepared crab salad, deviled eggs and an assortment of crudités surrounding a scallion-topped mixture for dipping.

"What's keeping you in New York? Career or a man?"

"It's certainly not a man."

Picking up a plate, Emily's penetrating gaze caught and held Sara's. "Nothing has changed, has it?"

Sara shook her head and glanced away. Only Emily and her parents knew why she had ended her engagement to Eric Thompson.

"When are you going to get some help, Sara? I can't believe you're going to spend the rest of your life thinking there is something wrong with you because a man decided he preferred a same-sex partner."

"It's not as bad as it was."

"Why? What has changed?"

Slowly, methodically, she related her encounters with Salem Lassiter, seeing an expression of disbelief freeze Emily's features.

"You're involved with *him?*" She had caught a glimpse of the veterinarian when she visited the Sterlings over a Thanksgiving weekend. Dr. Salem Lassiter had stopped by to check the leg of a stallion that had come up lame during a pacing exercise.

"There's no need to make it sound as if he were a leper."

Leaning back in her chair, Emily threw back her head and laughed. "There's nothing wrong with him—at least not visually. In fact, he's the most gorgeous piece of male flesh I've seen in a long time."

"Even better than Chris Delgado?"

An attractive flush swept over Emily's face. "I don't think so."

Sara speared a shrimp and placed it on her plate. "Speaking of my brother, I think you ought to know that he broke his leg."

"Where? How?" There was no mistaking the panic in Emily's voice.

She outlined the events leading up to her brother's accident, ending with her parents traveling to Europe to bring him back. "There's no doubt he's going to be laid up for at least a month before he begins physical therapy."

Emily took a sip of her drink. "I'm not expected back at the station for another week, so I'll drive down and look in on him." A distressed look marred her beautiful face. "Do you think your brother will ever see me as a woman rather than just his younger sister's friend?"

"Chris may seem indifferent because right now politics is his passion, but I know he likes you."

Emily emitted a groan. "I don't want him to like me, Sara. I want him to love me."

"I don't know if he can do that right now. He's only thirty-three, and I happen to know that he's not ready to marry. Give him time, Emmie."

"I've given him more than half my life." And she had. She realized she had fallen in love with Christopher Delgado the year she turned twelve, and she had spent the past sixteen years waiting for him.

"Why don't you start seeing other men? You talk about me not becoming involved with a man, but I can say that I at least slept with a guy, even if I wasn't what he wanted."

"You didn't have to go there, girlfriend," Emily retorted.

"It's only a gentle reminder."

Whatever Emily was going to say was preempted by the ringing of a telephone. "Excuse me." Pushing back her chair, she went into the house to answer it.

Sara and Emily spent the remainder of the afternoon talking and bringing each other up-to-date on what was going on in their lives after a year's separation. The sun was beginning to descend behind the peaks of the mountains when they finally retreated to the house to dress for dinner at the Kirklands'.

Sara walked into the sprawling one-story house Joshua Kirkland had built the year before his wife delivered their second child. A gentle tenderness filled her gaze when she saw Michael Kirkland rise to greet her.

Twenty-four-year-old Michael was an exact replica of his father with the exception of his hair color. Joshua's pale hair was now a gleaming silver, while his son's close-cropped dark hair lay against his scalp in layered precision. And like his father he had also attended and graduated from the U.S. Military Academy at West Point.

Cradling Sara to his chest, he leaned down and kissed her forehead. "Welcome home, gypsy," he crooned against her ear.

Pulling back, she smiled up at him. "You're a fine one to talk. How long are you staying this time?"

"Two weeks."

"Where are you off to next?"

His expression changed, becoming somber, closed. "It's classified."

Vanessa Kirkland walked into the living room, her face glowing with a broad smile. "Welcome back, Sara."

Sara embraced her, kissing her cheek. "It's good to be back, Aunt Vanessa. You look wonderful."

Vanessa had recently celebrated her sixty-third birthday, and still claimed a slim, supple body. Her fashionably short black hair was liberally streaked with silver, while her face had remained virtually wrinkle-free.

Sara peered around Vanessa's shoulder. "Where's Uncle Josh?"

"Dad's in the kitchen putting the finishing touches on dinner," Emily announced, coming from that direction and licking the tips of her fingers.

"Emily Teresa Kirkland!" Vanessa wailed when she saw her daughter.

"Lighten up, Mom. You know I can't resist Daddy's cooking."

"When are you ever going to stop licking your fingers?" her mother countered.

Emily smothered a giggle. "Never." She knew nothing upset her mother more than her licking her fingers.

Joshua Kirkland entered the living room, flashing a rare smile. Time had also been kind to him. He would soon celebrate his sixty-eighth birthday, and only the tiny lines around his penetrating pale green eyes verified that he had joined the ranks of the senior citizens.

"The prodigal daughter returns," he announced, his deep, powerful voice carrying easily in the enormous room.

Sara moved forward and found herself cradled gently against his chest. Tilting her chin, she kissed his cheek. "I plan to stay three months this time."

Joshua brushed a light kiss over her lips. "Good. Tonight's going to be special because it's not often that Vanessa and I can get all of our *children* together at the same time."

Michael extended an arm to his mother. "Madam, may I escort you to the dining room?"

She took the proffered arm, smiling affectionately up at her son. "Why, thank you, sir."

Michael ducked his head. "Mom, don't."

"Well, aren't you an officer?"

"Yeah, but this is not the army."

Joshua patted his son's back. "Get used to it, son. Your mother threatened to divorce me if I didn't quit the military, but applauds you for making it your career choice. Go figure."

The good-natured bantering continued over dinner, and Sara felt as if she had truly returned home for the first time. Joshua and Vanessa had always treated her like a daughter, and for that she was grateful now. It made the wait for her parents' and brother's return tolerable.

Chapter 11

Sara and Emily shared a booth at a popular Santa Fe restaurant, laughing softly. They had spent more than five hours at a day spa under the professional ministrations of a hairstylist, esthetician, nail technician and a masseur. Their hydrated faces were shimmering under a light cover of makeup, their short coiffed hair cut in layered precision and their hands and feet smooth and dewy from rich penetrating oils that highlighted the fresh vibrant colors on their toes and nails. The two women had become so relaxed during their massages that the masseur had to wake them up.

Admiring male glances were directed at them as they flirted shamelessly with every man who passed their table. Emily affected fluttering her lashes, while Sara perfected a pout that caused some of them to stop in their tracks. Both women dissolved into hysterics and a woman forcibly turned her boyfriend's head when he stumbled while glancing over his shoulder at them.

"You're bad, Sara Sterling," Emily whispered.

Sara managed to look thoroughly insulted. "Me?"

"Sí tú."

"You're a fine one to talk. At least I'm not fluttering my lashes at every man who—" Her words trailed off when she saw Emily staring at something over her shoulder.

Shifting slightly, Sara saw Salem Lassiter coming toward their booth. She wondered what had brought him to Santa Fe. She hadn't realized how fast her heart was pumping until he stood beside her.

She wiggled her manicured fingers at him. "Hi."

Lowering his chin, he stared at her, his penetrating gaze caressing her sensual mouth. "Hello, Sara."

"Please, sit down."

Moving to her left, she patted the space beside her. He sat down next to her and everything about him enveloped her like a comforting cocoon. He was casually dressed in a pair of laundered jeans, a white snap-button shirt and a pair of boots. He had secured his hair at the nape of his neck, displaying the silver hoops in his pierced lobes.

Emily extended her right hand. "I don't know if you remember me, but I met you once at—"

"The Sterlings, over a Thanksgiving weekend," Salem said, completing her statement and taking her proffered hand. "It's a pleasure to meet you again, Miss Kirkland."

"Emily," she admonished softly. "Same here, Salem."

"What are you doing in Santa Fe?" Sara asked, her gaze fixed on his profile. Not seeing him for four days made him more attractive than she had remembered.

He turned to stare at her, his dark gaze burning her face with its intensity. "I'm waiting to pick up Ginger's foal."

"Did you fly up?"

"No, I drove up."

"Maybe Sara can go back with you instead of driving back by herself," Emily volunteered quickly.

A slight frown furrowed Sara's smooth forehead. "And who's going to drive my car?"

"I will," Emily offered. "I plan to come down to see Chris, so I'll bring it back for you."

"I wouldn't mind the company on the return trip," Salem remarked smoothly.

He had not said that he had not realized how much he had missed seeing Sara until he walked into the restaurant. He had recognized Emily Kirkland's face first because she was facing him, but had been totally unprepared to see Sara.

"Well?" Emily questioned, staring at her friend.

Sara stared back at Emily, then Salem. He shifted his eyebrows in a questioning expression.

"Okay," she agreed. She knew she had fallen into a trap when she heard Emily's and Salem's collective sighs.

Salem smiled at Emily, giving her an imperceptible nod. He noted two menus and two glasses of water on the table. "Have you ladies ordered yet?"

"No," they chorused in unison.

He reached for Sara's menu, studying it while she glowered at Emily. So, her friend was into matchmaking. Well, two could play the same game. Emily wanted Christopher Delgado. Well, she would offer her brother up to her— broken leg *and* dislocated shoulder.

The return drive to Las Cruces, which normally would have taken four hours, stretched into six. Salem had elected to take the local roads instead of the interstate because he was pulling a trailer with the foal. She noticed that he steered with his right hand, while resting his left on his thigh.

"You look very nice today," he mentioned after a lengthy silence.

Opening her eyes, Sara smiled at him. "Thank you."

"How often do you and your friend get together and flirt with men?"

Her mouth opened and closed several times before she was able to speak. "Flirt?"

He gave her a quick glance. "Yes, Sara. Flirt."

Heat suffused her face. "Well, we actually weren't flirting."

"Oh, really? Before Emily Kirkland saw me I saw her fluttering her lashes at a man who I though was going to need CPR."

"I suppose we did act up a little."

He chuckled softly. "It's encouraging to know that the very stiff and proper district attorney can relax enough to *act up*."

"I'm not stiff."

"Yes, you are," he insisted. "Do you ever permit yourself to be spontaneous? Have you ever given in to a reckless impulse?"

"And do what?"

"Just let yourself go?"

"No."

"Why not, Sara?"

"Because that's not who I am." Her voice had risen slightly, indicating her annoyance.

There was only the sound of the tires hitting the smooth surface of the road as Salem concentrated on his driving. It was another ten minutes before he spoke again.

"You're annoyed with me." His question came out as a statement.

Sara stared through the windshield. "It's not you, Salem."

"If not me, then who?"

Sighing, she tried composing her thoughts. She could not believe she had to grope for an explanation. She, who earned her living by talking, debating, was at a loss for what to say.

Her gaze clouded with painful visions of her past. How could she tell him, a disturbing stranger, of the insecurities she had hidden from everyone but her parents and Emily Kirkland? Would he understand? She took a deep breath and decided to try.

"It's me," she began quietly. "I think, I believe..." She began again. "I believe I'm frigid."

Salem's head spun around and he stared at her. The truck veered to the right, and he quickly returned his attention to the road.

"Who told you that?" There was an ominous tone in his voice.

"No one told me."

"Then how did you come to that conclusion?" It was his turn to sound annoyed.

"I don't feel anything—no desire when a man touches me."

"How about when he kisses you?"

"Nothing."

Salem chanced another glance at her pained expression. "What did you feel when I kissed you, Sara?"

"It was different with you."

"How?"

A secret smile touched her soft mouth. "It felt good. Very good."

He successfully concealed a smile. "Why is that?"

She shrugged a slender shoulder. "I don't know."

"And neither do I," he countered. "However, we do have three months to uncover why."

He had thrown down the gauntlet, leaving her to accept his challenge. Did she want to? Could she afford to?

Yes, a silent voice whispered. Yes, she could.

Turning her head, she stared at him. "You're right about that, Salem. We do have three months. But I doubt whether it will prove anything."

His mouth curved into an unconscious smile. "Only time will tell. Right or wrong, kitten?"

"You're right," she conceded.

Salem wanted to tell Sara that he did not want her only for sex, but for companionship, too. When he had taken her to Mexico he had almost forgotten how much he liked the close intimate contact and all of the things about a woman that appealed to his maleness. After leaving her at her cabin, he had returned home recalling her feminine warmth and fragrance. He had enjoyed dancing with her, hearing her tinkling laugh, her intelligence, and there was never a moment when he hadn't wanted to be with her.

The sun was setting as they crossed the boundary markers indicating Sterling Farms. Sara deactivated the security system and opened the barn while Salem unloaded the foal from the trailer. He carried the tiny horse to the stall where it had lain laboring for each breath a week ago. Ginger whinnied when she detected the scent of her baby.

Salem motioned with his head. "Please move back, Sara."

She stepped away from the stall, watching him as he used his booted foot to open the kick bolt. Shifting the foal, he pulled back the door and placed him on a layer of clean shavings. He closed the door to the stall, but not before Sara saw Ginger nuzzle her baby.

Salem offered his hand, and he wasn't disappointed when she placed her smaller hand in his, permitting him to lead her out of the barn. She reset the security code and turned to face him. The sky was a clear royal-blue with an abundance of stars resembling a spray of blue-white diamonds.

Staring down at her, he wound his arms around her waist. "Are you going back to your cabin, or are you going to stay at the main house?"

Sara tried making out his expression in the waning light. "I'm going back to the cabin."

He tightened his hold on her waist, pulling her closer to his body. "Do you need a ride?"

"No. I'll take my mother's car."

"I can drive you."

"And how will I get back?"

"I can pick you up in the morning. Either that, or you can spend the night with me."

Her eyes widened. "I told you before that I don't sleep with men."

"Did I ask you to share my bed?"

She could not stop the heat stealing into her face when she registered the condescension in his query. "No, you didn't. But whenever a man asks me to spend the night with him it usually translates into that."

"Don't ever lump me in the same category with your double-talking slick New York brothers. If I want you to share my bed I'll come out and say it."

Her hands came up and she pushed against his chest, freeing herself. Turning on her heel, she headed for the house.

When she had almost reached the house a few moments

later, he caught up with her, his fingers curling around her upper arm.

"Sara!"

"Let me go!"

He tightened his grip, spinning her around until they were facing each other. "Sara." This time her name came out in a raspy whisper. "Please, let's not fight."

"I'm not fighting, Salem. I'm going into the house. Now, please let me go."

He released her, watching as she made her way to the front door. He waited, wondering why she had not opened the door. He did not have long to wait for an answer when she retraced her steps.

"I left my purse in your truck. I need my keys."

He stared at her, unable to summon a modicum of anger. He was still trying to comprehend her believing she was frigid. Who could have possibly led her to believe she was a cold, unresponsive woman?

"I'll get it."

He returned to his vehicle and found her purse on the seat. She was still standing in the same spot when he handed it to her.

"Thank you." Her voice was barely audible.

"I'll wait here until you're in."

"Thank you," she repeated.

She felt the heat of his gaze on her back as she walked to the door, put the key in the lock and turned it. The last time she saw Salem he had waited for her to unlock her door, and then she had kissed him good-night. That would not happen tonight. She felt naked, totally vulnerable because of her revelation that she was frigid. He must have been laughing when she told him what only three other people knew.

She opened the door, stepped in and closed the door.

She waited until she heard Salem drive away, then made her way to the kitchen. The house was silent, empty, and she knew Marisa had gone home. Lamps on timers set at different intervals provided enough light.

It wasn't until she had locked the door to her cabin behind her that she broke down and cried until spent. A pile of damp tissues dotted her bed after she'd blotted the moisture from her face. Her gaze fell on the letter from John. Reaching for the telephone, she dialed his number. He answered after the second ring.

"Bohannon."

"Hi, John." Her voice was low and husky after her crying episode.

"Sara! How are you, darling?"

"Well," she lied smoothly. "I got your letter. You must have mailed it the day I left New York."

"I must admit that I wrote it before you left and mailed it a couple of days later."

"How are things in New York?"

"SOS. Same old stuff. What's happening with you?"

"Nothing much."

"I miss you, Sara."

"And I miss you, John." There was a pregnant silence before she said, "Look, I just called to acknowledge the receipt of your letter."

"Give me your number. It's not showing up on my caller ID."

Sara gave him the area code and the number at the main house. She did not want him calling her at the cabin and monitoring her whereabouts. There were times when she found John Bohannon a little too intense. The first time he called her at her apartment he had questioned where she had been at ten-thirty on a Thursday night. She did not tell him that she had been home, reviewing evidence for an upcoming trial. She had made it a practice to leave her answering machine on at all times.

"Do you mind if I call you every once in a while?"

"No, I don't. I know it's late in New York, so I'm going to hang up."

"I love you, Sara."

She had called him to hear his voice, not a confession. "Good night, John."

She hung up, and lay across the bed fully clothed. She had called him because she needed to connect with something she was familiar with. She was New Mexican born and raised, and she could not understand why she felt so detached from her roots. She had enjoyed the time she had spent with Emily and the Kirklands, but something was missing. Something she could not quite identify.

Closing her eyes, she listened to the sound of her own breathing. What she did not want to admit was that the presence of Salem Lassiter disturbed her—disturbed her so much that she had begun to doubt herself and her future.

Sara sat in the terminal for international arrivals, watching the computerized board for verification that the flight from Zurich had touched down. She breathed out an audible sigh of relief when the flight number appeared on the screen. It would take some time before her family cleared customs, but at least she knew they had arrived safely.

She saw her father and brother first, then her mother. Christopher Delgado sat in a wheelchair pushed by his stepfather, his outstretched left leg encased in plaster and left arm cradled by a sling, while his mother followed a redcap pushing a cart with their luggage.

She waved, and Chris returned her wave with his uninjured arm. Despite his injuries he looked wonderful. His face was deeply tanned and his wavy hair was longer than she had seen it in years. Observing him made her aware that he was the perfect mate for Emily Kirkland. He was an even six feet, and his one hundred and seventy pounds was evenly distributed over his athletic physique. He looked nothing like their mother—except for his eyes. They were a compelling magnetic jet-black. When he was angry, they glowed with a lethal calmness that sent a shiver up her spine, and she had learned never to cross the line to test his temper.

Eve Blackwell-Sterling rushed forward to meet her daughter. "I'm sorry we weren't here when you arrived," she apologized, hugging her tightly around her neck.

Sara kissed her mother. "It's all right, Mama."

Eve's eyes filled with a rush of hot tears. It had been years since her daughter had called her *Mama*—not since she was a little girl. Pulling back, she stared at her.

"Are you okay?"

Sara forced a bright smile. "Of course I am."

Easing out of her mother's embrace, she moved over to her father. Matthew Sterling picked up his daughter, holding her to his heart. Eyes so much like his own crinkled as she smiled.

"Hi, Daddy."

"Hi back to you, baby." He kissed her soundly on her mouth.

"Don't I get a kiss?" Chris complained, flashing a wide grin.

Matt released her and she hunkered down beside the wheelchair. "I should go upside your head instead of welcoming you home," she teased.

Chris reached for her hand, pulling her closer. "Have mercy on your poor busted-up brother." Tilting his head, he offered her his lips, and he was not disappointed when she kissed him. He winked at her. "You're looking good, baby sister. Have you fallen in love?"

"Hardly." She smiled at her father. "Why don't you all wait here while I bring the truck around?"

Holding out a callused hand, Matt shook his head. "Give me the keys and I'll get it."

Reaching into her handbag, she retrieved the keys and gave them to him. She moved over to her mother and wound an arm around her waist, watching her father as he walked through the automatic doors to the parking lot.

Both her parents were completely gray. There had been a time when Matt Sterling could still count the number of ebony strands in his thick wavy hair, but even that was now a part of his past. Even though her father and mother were sixty-eight and sixty-four respectively, both appeared years younger. They exercised regularly and were mindful of their diets. She knew they wanted to see their children married, and possibly claim a few grandchildren, but she and her brother were reluctant to form relationships that could lead to marriage.

Matt returned with the truck bearing the logo of Sterling Farms on the driver and passenger doors. He rolled the wheelchair out to the curb, then picked up Chris with a minimum of effort and placed him on a seat in the rear of the oversize four-wheel-drive vehicle.

The luggage was loaded in the cargo area, and within a quarter of an hour Sara maneuvered out of the airport traffic and headed for Sterling Farms. She accomplished the trip in complete silence. Her family had fallen asleep. She knew they were experiencing the effects of jet lag, and it would be at least two days before their bodies' circadian rhythms would adjust to their crossing the international date line and several U.S. time zones.

Chapter 12

"Why is she still alive?"

"Because I haven't killed her, that's why!"

"Don't mouth off at me! In case you've forgotten, I'm the one holding the Benjamins."

"And you'll get your money's worth. Just let me do my job my way."

"Is her father back?"

"Yeah. He's been back for a couple of days."

"I hope you know this will change everything."

"It changes nothing. If I have to I'll eliminate him, too."

"What the hell is wrong with you? I want you to pop Sara Sterling, not take out her family. I don't need this to blow up into something that will—"

"Don't ever tell me what I can and cannot do. I will take care of her—my way."

Kareem Daniels pressed a button on his cellular phone, ending the call. He hated impatient clients. Most times they were more danger to him than the people who surrounded his target.

Shifting positions, he tried finding a comfortable spot on the too-soft mattress. He had rented a furnished room in a charming boardinghouse that boasted a sign proclaiming that Billy the Kid had slept there a week before he was gunned down by Sheriff Pat Garrett on July 14, 1881. Kareem had filed the date away in his mind, because he planned to use it as his unofficial final deadline to complete this assignment. It had only taken two days of inhaling strong urine and shoveling horse manure to conclude that he hated horses. And he sensed they didn't like him, either, because they tended to rear and buck whenever he approached them.

He glanced at the date on his watch. It was June 15. Maybe, if he were truly blessed, he would be able to leave New Mexico soon. He wanted to return home and reunite with his wife and sickly child.

Sara woke, startled, and sat up. She was back in her cabin after spending three nights in her old bedroom in the main house. She had seen little of her brother and parents their first day back, and had amused herself riding Blaze and helping Marisa cook. She had surprised the cook with her newly found culinary skills, finally admitting that she had enrolled in several cooking classes.

She stared at the glowing red numbers of the clock on the bedside table. It was only 3:17. Combing her fingers through her short hair, she eased back against the pillows, cradling her shoulders, wondering what it was that had jolted her out of a deep slumber. Going completely still, she listened intently for something out of the ordinary, but encountered silence. She relaxed enough to close her eyes in an attempt to go back to sleep.

Then she heard it. Something or someone was moving around outside her bedroom window.

Pushing back a sheet and lightweight blanket, she slipped off the bed and crept over to the window. She thought about turning on a lamp, but dismissed the notion because she did not want to alert or startle her early-morning visitor. Cool, dry, desert air flowed through the screened open windows. Pulling back a panel of white-on-white striped voile, she peered through the screen.

Standing outside her window was the shadowy figure of a large dog. The dog moved closer, his glowing eyes shimmering eerily in the diffuse light coming from the lanterns placed strategically around the cabin.

"Shadow," she whispered softly. It was apparent the dog heard her, because he whined in response. Her initial fright in believing he was a wolf had fled with Salem's reassurance that Shadow would not attack her unless he directed him to.

"What's the matter, boy?" she asked softly.

Reaching for a satin dressing gown on a nearby chair, she pulled it over her revealing matching nightgown and walked on bare feet to the door at the rear of the house and stepped out into the night.

She couldn't stop the small gasp escaping her constricted throat when she saw Salem leaning against the post supporting the oversize hammock. His face was in the shadows, making it impossible for her to see his expression.

"What are you doing here?" There was no mistaking the husky timbre in her voice as she tried to slow her accelerated pulse.

"Waiting for you to wake up." His voice seemed detached from his body.

"But…but it's three o'clock in the morning."

"And you're awake."

"Because you woke me up."

"I didn't wake you up. You woke up on your own."

She pulled her dressing gown around her body in a protective gesture when he straightened from his leaning position and closed the distance between them.

"You're trespassing," she said accusingly.

Salem stared down at the slim, ethereal figure she presented in the muted light. She was so sensually alluring that he pushed his hands into the pockets of his jeans to keep them from reaching for her.

"Your father pays me quite well to trespass."

Her eyes widened. "Is there something wrong with one of the horses?"

He arched an eyebrow. "If there is, I haven't been called." A mysterious smile curved his mouth. "I'm here because Shadow and I decided to take a walk in the moonlight and we happened to wind up here."

She glanced up at the quarter moon in a navy blue sky. "There's not much of a moon tonight."

"It's still a moonlit sky," he countered in a soft voice.

Sara did not believe she was standing on her back porch in her nightgown and robe in the middle of the night, talking to Salem Lassiter. He stood close enough to her for her to inhale the citrus scent of his cologne and feel the heat from his large body.

Tilting her chin, she visually admired his unbound hair. It was only the third time she had seen him with his hair loose—and she much preferred seeing it that way. When he pulled it back it made him appear stoic—too severe. The hair floating around his face and over his shoulders softened his expression and made him look much younger than thirty-six.

"I know you were taught not to visit a woman unannounced," she chided softly.

He smiled, revealing his straight white teeth. "I was, but if that woman in question won't give me her telephone number, then what am I to do? I can't continue to slip notes under her door."

"Why haven't you asked that woman for her number?"

Sara could not believe she had said that. She was actually flirting with him, and it had been a very long time since she had seriously flirted with any man. The antics she and Emily Kirkland had executed in the restaurant in Santa Fe were a throwback to their adolescence. Whenever they got together they usually shed what they had come to think of as their newfound sophistication and did what fifteen- and sixteen-year-old girls were expected to do—flirt with the opposite sex.

Leaning closer and lowering his head, Salem pressed his lips to her ear. "I'd like your number, Miss Sterling."

She shivered noticeably, and her nipples sprang into prominence under her satin garments. Rising on tiptoe, she whispered her number. "It's private, so please don't give it out."

"I'll guard it with my life."

She laughed, the sound floating and lingering in the night air. "How often do you take your moonlight walks?"

"Often. Now that you're up, would you like to join me?"

He did not say that after he buried Grace and Jacob he had found himself walking every night. He walked in the heat and he walked in the rain. Walking had become a balm—a time when he could think and reflect. A time given him to rid himself of the guilt and a time to heal.

She shook her head. "No, thank you."

"Are you going back to bed?"

Her gaze locked with his, and she tried ignoring the

silent sensual magnetism pulling them closer. Numbly, as if in a trance, she shook her head.

"I can't now," she admitted. "I'm too wide-awake."

Biting down on her lower lip, she lowered her gaze, staring at the middle of his broad chest. The words she had not been able to say to any man in more than six years were poised on the tip of her tongue. All she had to do was open her mouth.

Her gaze shifted upward as she stared at Salem staring intently at her. "Would you like to come in, perhaps share a cup of coffee or tea?"

His expression did not change with her offer, and as soon as the words were out she berated herself for her brazenness. Why did she find herself so insecure with men, though she exuded an abundance of confidence in the courtroom?

After what seemed to be an interminable silence, Salem nodded. "Thank you, Sara. I'd like that very much."

He motioned to Shadow not to move, then turned and followed Sara into the cabin.

She flipped a switch on the wall near the back door, and the living room and dining area were bathed in soft golden light from table lamps and an exquisite, delicate crystal chandelier over a table with six accompanying chairs. Her bare, slender feet were silent on the thick pile of a cream rug with a blue-gray border.

She smiled when noting the stunned expression on Salem's face. Anyone who had visited her cabin always reacted in a similar manner when they saw the white and near-white furniture and accessories.

"Please make yourself at home. I'll be back as soon as I change my clothes."

Salem nodded as he walked across the living room and stared at the silver-framed photographs lining the decorative molded plane of a Victorian mantelpiece. The pictures showed various stages of Sara—from infancy to a picture taken when she had received her law degree. There was a family pose showing her smiling and sitting on Matthew Sterling's lap, while Christopher Delgado leaned against his mother's shoulder. He estimated she had to be five or six, because she was missing her two front teeth.

Peering closer at an adolescent Sara, he recognized the emerging seductiveness that she seemed totally oblivious to. And he wondered, not for the first time, how she could believe she was frigid. She exuded a sensuality many women would be tempted to sell their souls for.

He shifted over to a wall of built-in bookcases. One entire shelf was stacked with volumes of Nancy Drew books. He removed one, opening it to the title page. A slight smile curved his mouth. The first-printing hardcover books had belonged to Eve Blackwell when she was a girl. He replaced the book, then examined a shelf filled with CDs. Sara had stacked them alphabetically. He noted the names of various artists: George Benson, Michael Bolton, Randy Crawford, Luther Vandross, Peter White and the Yellow Jackets. He also noted Tupac's greatest hits, along with several CDs of Maxwell's. Sara Sterling's musical tastes were obviously eclectic.

A white wicker étagère cradling the components of a sophisticated stereo system stood in an alcove that had once been a walk-in closet. Everything in the room appeared pristine, virginal—as untouched as Sara Sterling's celibate body.

A large round table covered with a lace tablecloth cradled several Native American and African artifacts. He picked up a small clay bowl with a chip along the outer edge. The bright red and yellow colors were faded, but he recognized the markings on the underside as Apache, and remembered Sara mentioning that her undergraduate minor had been ethnology. He leaned closer and examined the figures in a carved tribal mask. The entwined images of a man and woman were locked in a pose depicting an act of copulation. There was no doubt it was a fertility totem—a totem she certainly had no use for at the present time.

She had asked him to teach her the Navajo language when all he wanted to teach her was passion. Closing his eyes, he whispered an ancient prayer. He would use every day given him to try to convince Sara Sterling not to return to New York. And if he failed it would be because the breath loaned to him for this lifetime had been reclaimed by a spirit greater than his.

Sara returned to the living room, her damp hair brushed off her face, dressed in a shirt that had belonged to her brother. Instead of her usual jeans she had pulled on a pair of walking shorts, and running shoes had replaced her boots. She flashed a warm smile when Salem turned to stare across the space at her.

"At four o'clock it's a little early for breakfast, but if you want something to eat I'll fix us something."

He returned her smile. "What's on the menu?"

Folding her hands on her slim hips, she pursed her lips. "Pancakes, waffles, omelettes. I have fresh blueberries, so if you want blueberry muffins—"

"No. You didn't say blueberry muffins."

"Yes, I did. Why?"

He headed toward her and she noticed the silent stalking that made it impossible for her to detect his approach. He picked up and put down his feet in a seemingly floating fashion, while his arms barely moved. She hadn't realized that she hadn't exhaled until he was only a breath away.

Lowering his chin, his eyes widened as he stared down at her stunned gaze. "I have a serious weakness for blueberry muffins."

"I'm rather partial to them myself," she admitted.

Reaching up, he cradled her face between his large hands, his fingers splaying over the gold studs in her pierced ears. "I also find that I have a serious weakness for a certain district attorney," he whispered seconds before his mouth closed over hers.

Sara's trembling hands covered his, and she made no attempt to pull them away. Instead, she took a step closer, winding her arms around his waist.

His lips were warm and sweet, and she sank into his comforting embrace. There was no dizzying panic or fright, just a heated throbbing that made the blood sing in her veins.

Salem's hands moved from her face to her waist and he wrapped his arms around her midriff, making her his willing prisoner. He marveled that she fit so perfectly within his embrace. It was as if she had been created expressly for him.

His kisses were gentle, controlled. He did not want to frighten her, but wanted her to feel what he was beginning to feel for her—a slow, heated ache that would have to be assuaged at another time.

His mouth throbbed with a passionate message—one that called silently to her that she had nothing to fear, that she was the day to his night, the healing balm to his lingering pain, and the woman he had been waiting for who could teach him to trust again.

Sara found her senses spinning as she lost herself in the scent of his warm, hard body and the soft nibbling kisses that teased and tantalized. She could feel the heat of Salem's body course down the entire length of hers, and she could not disguise the changes in her body as her breasts grew heavy against his chest, while the shock of moisture bathing the secret place between her thighs left her shaking and gasping with an awakening sexuality she had forgotten existed for her.

Shivers of rekindled desire sang through her veins, and she held on to Salem, her fingernails biting into the muscles of his solid shoulders under his navy blue T-shirt. Moaning, she tore her mouth away and buried her face against his shoulder. Her heart was beating as rapidly as a frightened bird's, and she prayed he would not release her—not yet, not until she regained some of her composure.

Salem held her gently, one hand stroking her back until her trembling subsided. Closing his eyes, he waited for his own passions to wane. Then his breathing slowed, and he was once again in control of himself and his emotions.

"Are those muffins still on the menu?" he whispered in her ear.

"Yes. Why?"

Easing back, he smiled down at her. "I've just discovered something that I'd much rather eat than blueberry muffins."

She cocked a questioning eyebrow. "What?"

"You."

Heat flooded her face, her mouth gaped in shock, and Salem threw back his head, laughing. Thoroughly humiliated, she pounded his hard shoulder with a fist. He caught her hand and swung her up in his arms.

"You're a pig," she spat out.

His smile vanished, replaced by a warning frown. "Didn't I tell you about calling me out of my name?"

Embarrassment made her reckless. "Yes, you did. And what are you going to do about it?" she challenged.

Lowering his head, he captured her mouth with the speed of a falcon swooping down on its prey. This kiss was nothing like the one they had just shared. His tongue eased into her open mouth, searching, plundering and claiming the passion she had never offered any man.

Her arms tightened around his neck, increasing the pressure of his mouth on hers, and when he raised his head he knew they were not the same people they had been before the kiss.

Bending slightly, Salem lowered her to the rug. They stared at each other for a full minute, their chests rising and falling heavily. The spell was broken when Sara turned and made her way to the kitchen, and it was another full minute before Salem made the attempt to follow her.

Chapter 13

Sara did not make eye contact with Salem while they worked side by side in the narrow kitchen. She prepared the mixture for the blueberry muffins while he diced the ingredients for omelettes. While the muffins were baking, she ground fresh beans for a pot of coffee, then set the table with plates and silver.

Salem stood at a window in the kitchen, staring out at the brightening sky and the sun rising behind the mountains. He hadn't noticed that Sara had turned on a powerful ministereo player until he recognized the familiar strains of the soundtrack from *The Piano*.

Shifting, he turned to look at her. She was so absorbed in cooking that she failed to notice him watching her until he had gotten his fill.

She flashed a strained smile. "Do you want to cook the omelettes?" She wanted him to do anything except stand there and stare at her.

KIMANI ROMANCE™

An Important Message from the Publisher

Dear Reader,

Because you've chosen to read one of our fine novels, I'd like to say "thank you"! And, as a special way to say thank you, I'm offering to send you two more Kimani™ Romance novels and two surprise gifts—absolutely FREE! These books will keep it real with true-to-life African American characters that turn up the heat and sizzle with passion.

Please enjoy the free books and gifts with our compliments...

Glenda Howard
For Kimani Press™

Peel off Seal and Place Inside...

We'd like to send you two free books to introduce you to Kimani™ Romance books. These novels feature strong, sexy women, and African-American heroes that are charming, loving and true. Our authors fill each page with exceptional dialogue, exciting plot twists, and enough sizzling romance to keep you riveted until the very end!

KIMANI ROMANCE...LOVE'S ULTIMATE DESTINATION

Your two books have combined cover price of $12.50 in the U.S. $14.50 in Canada, but are yours **FREE!**

We'll even send you two wonderful surprise gifts. You can't lose!

THE EDITOR'S "THANK YOU" FREE GIFTS INCLUDE:

➤ Two Kimani™ Romance Novels
➤ Two exciting surprise gifts

YES! I have placed my Editor's "thank you" Free Gifts seal in the space provided at right. Please send me 2 FREE Books, and my 2 FREE Mystery Gifts. I understand that I am under no obligation to purchase anything further, as explained on the back of this card.

PLACE FREE GIFTS SEAL HERE

168/368 XDL FJKD

Please Print

FIRST NAME

LAST NAME

ADDRESS

APT.#   CITY

STATE/PROV.   ZIP/POSTAL CODE

Thank You!

The Reader Service - Here's How It Works:

Accepting your 2 free books and 2 free gifts (gifts valued at approximately $10.00) places you under no obligation to buy anything. You may keep the books and gifts and return the shipping statement marked "cancel." If you do not cancel, about a month later we'll send you 4 additional books and bill you just $4.94 each in the U.S. or $5.49 each in Canada. That is a savings of at least 21% off the cover price. Shipping and handling is just 50¢ per book in the U.S. and 75¢ per book in Canada.* You may cancel at any time, but if you choose to continue, every month we'll send you 4 more books, which you may either purchase at the discount price or return to us and cancel your subscription.

*Terms and prices subject to change without notice. Prices do not include applicable taxes. Sales tax applicable in N.Y. Canadian residents will be charged applicable taxes. Offer not valid in Quebec. All orders subject to credit approval. Credit or debit balances in a customer's account(s) may be offset by any other outstanding balance owed by or to the customer. Offer available while quantities last. Books received may not be as shown. Please allow 4 to 6 weeks for delivery.

If offer card is missing write to: The Reader Service, P.O. Box 1867, Buffalo, NY 14240-1867 or visit www.ReaderService.com

BUSINESS REPLY MAIL

FIRST-CLASS MAIL   PERMIT NO. 717   BUFFALO, NY

POSTAGE WILL BE PAID BY ADDRESSEE

THE READER SERVICE
PO BOX 1867
BUFFALO NY 14240-9952

NO POSTAGE
NECESSARY
IF MAILED
IN THE
UNITED STATES

He nodded and returned to the stove. Quickly, expertly, he turned the egg mixture into a prepared pan, while she transferred the warm, freshly baked muffins to a serving platter and took them to the dining area. Within minutes the table held a carafe of steaming coffee, a pitcher of freshly squeezed orange juice and a platter filled with omelettes.

Salem seated Sara, then rounded the table to take a chair opposite her. He stared at her when she lowered her head and silently said grace. Sheepishly, he lowered his own head and followed suit. When, he thought, had he forgotten all that he had been taught as a child? It had not mattered to Grace whether she blessed her food or her table. Nothing had been important to her—not her husband or her child. She had existed only for one man who claimed he'd loved her yet had systematically rejected her, and in the end she lost everything—husband, child and lover—when she took her own life.

Raising her head, Sara surveyed the table. Her mother had not taught her to cook, but had insisted she learn to set a proper table. And by proper Eve Sterling meant china, crystal, sterling and lace tablecloths.

Handing Salem her plate, she waited for him to serve her. He spooned a fluffy omelette onto her plate and handed it back to her. He also filled her cup with coffee and her goblet with juice. She waited until he served himself, then picked up her fork.

They ate in silence, listening to the music coming from the kitchen. Each time Salem turned his head, his heavy black hair rippled over his T-shirt-clad shoulders like a curtain of silk.

The last note on the CD faded, and there was complete silence. The sun was up, and streams of light poured in through the sheer panels gracing the windows.

A distinctive sound shattered the early-morning hush. Sara had recognized the sharp crack seconds after Salem registered it. He stood up, and the sound reverberated through the air again. By the time he reached the front door, Shadow was barking uncontrollably.

Seconds after Sara rose to her feet, she heard the screams—blood-chilling screams. Sara stopped. Instead of going outside, she retreated to her bedroom and raced over to a massive armoire. Flinging open the doors, she pulled open a drawer and searched under a pile of cotton socks for her automatic handgun.

She located a full clip of bullets, slipped it in place in one continuous motion and raced out of the house. The sunlight nearly blinded her, and she blinked furiously to clear her vision. She saw the shattered windshield of the blue Volkswagen she had left in Santa Fe with Emily Kirkland first. Then she saw her friend lying motionless on the ground.

Salem knelt over Emily, feeling for a pulse along the column of her neck. A stream of blood oozed from a wound along her hairline, disappearing into her shortened black hair.

Taking slow, measured steps, Sara stood over them, the gun pressed to her thigh. The blood roared in her ears like the rushing thunder of a waterfall.

"How is she?" She did not recognize her own voice. A cold knot had formed in her stomach, making it impossible for her to move.

Salem curved an arm under Emily's head and the other under her knees. "She's all right. It appears a piece of glass is embedded in her forehead." He shouted something in Navajo to Shadow, and the frantic barking stopped.

"Why is she so still?"

"She's probably in shock." His gaze met Sara's for the

first time since hearing the gunshot, and he recognized fear—stark and naked—in her wild gaze. "Let's get her inside."

Sara turned, and he saw the gun in her right hand. A violent shiver raced down his body, chilling his blood. Why did she have a gun? Who or what did she have to fear?

He wanted and needed answers, but that would have to wait. Right now his first priority was Emily Kirkland.

Sara led the way to her bedroom, directing Salem to put Emily on her bed. She did not put the automatic pistol back in the armoire, but placed it on her dresser.

Salem leaned over Emily and checked her pupils. "Get me a tweezer, a bottle of alcohol and a cold compress. And see if you have any gauze bandages." He had barked out his demands like a drill sergeant.

Sara left to do his bidding and he undid several buttons on Emily's blouse. As he removed her boots, her lids fluttered and she opened her mouth to scream, but he cut her off when he placed a hand over her trembling lips.

"It's all right, Emily. No one is going to hurt you. You're safe now." Her clear green eyes widened in recognition, then filled with tears.

Sara returned from the bathroom with the items he had requested, and found Salem holding Emily while she sobbed against his chest. She closed her eyes and prayed a silent prayer of thanks that her friend was okay.

Salem eased Emily down to the pillows, then took the cool cloth Sara handed him. He managed to wipe away most of the blood. He had to remove the shard of glass and stanch the flow of blood. He motioned for Sara to hold Emily's hands.

She sat on the opposite side of the bed and held her friend's hands. "Emmie, it's me. Sara. Try to relax."

Emily sniffled, squeezed her eyes shut and bit down on her trembling lower lip. "Sara?"

"I'm here, Emmie."

Salem poured a trickle of alcohol over the sharp, slanting tip of a tweezer. "Don't move, Emily."

Emily moaned, trying to free her hands, and Sara tightened her grip. "Do as Salem says and try to relax."

"I never heard the first shot," she whispered. "The windshield shattered right before my eyes, and when I turned my head I heard the next one."

"Did you see anyone?" Sara asked, hoping to distract Emily enough so that Salem could extract the sliver of glass.

Emily closed her eyes. "No." She inhaled, then let out her breath in a ragged sigh. "Ouch!" she gasped.

"It's out," Salem stated, pressing the cool cloth against the wound. He held it against her forehead, checking to see if the bleeding had begun to subside. "Sara, I need you over here. Hold the cloth against her head until I tell you to let it go."

She circled the bed and held the cloth while Salem opened a prepackaged gauze bandage. Two minutes later, Emily Kirkland lay on the bed, her forehead swathed in gauze. The natural color had left her face, resulting in a sallowness under her normally golden-brown skin.

Opening her eyes, she groaned through clenched teeth. "I think I'm going to be sick."

Salem swooped her up from the bed and carried her into the adjoining bathroom. Sara sat on the side of the bed, listening to the sounds of violent retching.

Ten minutes after Sara placed a call to the main house Matthew Sterling walked into his daughter's bedroom. His green-gold gaze swept around the space, missing nothing.

When he'd entered the cabin he had noticed the remains of a meal shared by two people, and when he came into the bedroom he saw the tall figure of Salem Lassiter standing behind his daughter. They weren't touching, but they did not have to. There was something possessive in the veterinarian's stance that he recognized immediately. He dismissed the notion of his daughter becoming involved with his neighbor to stare at the handgun on the dresser. Then he turned his attention to Emily Kirkland.

She lay on the bed, her chest rising and falling in a gentle rhythm. It was apparent she had fallen asleep.

Folding his arms over his massive chest, he turned his fiery gaze on the couple. "The doctor, sheriff and a tow-truck driver are on their way. But before they get here we need to talk."

Sara nodded. "Let's talk in the living room." She led the way out of the bedroom, followed by her father, then Salem. She sat down on the sofa and patted the cushion beside her for Matt, while Salem took an armchair.

Placing his booted feet firmly on the rug, Matt leaned forward and stared at his daughter's profile. "What the hell happened here?"

"We're not certain, Dad. Salem and I were eating breakfast, then we heard a gunshot. Shadow started barking right after the second shot. Salem got to Emily before I did."

"What did you see?" This question was directed at Salem.

"Nothing," he replied. "By the time I got to her she was in shock. If she hadn't been bleeding I probably would have taken off to see if I could find someone."

Matt looked at Sara. "Did you know Emily was bringing your car back today?"

A frown creased Sara's smooth forehead. "Yes. She

called me last night and said she was driving down this morning. I just didn't expect she would be here this early."

Running a hand over his cropped gray hair, Matt massaged the back of his neck. "This doesn't make sense. If someone had shot out the windshield down on the interstate or along a local road I'd be apt to believe it was some drunk or drug-crazed idiot deciding to use passing vehicles for target practice."

"What are you saying, Matt?" Salem questioned.

"Someone was shooting at Emily on Sterling Farms property. And that means it had to be a trespasser."

"But why shoot at Emily Kirkland?"

Closing her eyes, Sara repeated Salem's query to herself. An inner voice whispered, *Maybe they weren't shooting at Emily Kirkland. Maybe they were shooting at the car because someone thought I was driving.*

Matt noticed his daughter's strained expression. "What's the matter, baby?"

Opening her eyes, she stared at her father, forcing a smile she did not feel. "Nothing."

She hoped she was mouthing the truth. She did not want to think the mobster's death threat had followed her from New York to New Mexico.

"I'm going to have to call Joshua," Matt announced.

"Oh, Daddy, no," Sara whispered.

Matt stood up. "He has to be told. How do you think I'd feel if you went up to Santa Fe and something happened to you and he didn't tell me?" One thick black eyebrow curved dramatically over his luminous eyes, then lowered as he stared at Salem.

Salem stood up and extended his hand to Matt, his solemn expression never changing.

Matt took the proffered hand, nodding. "I'm going to see if I can find an empty shell casing. The sheriff's going to need something to go on other than a shattered windshield." He walked across the living room and out of the cabin, leaving Sara and Salem staring at his broad shoulders.

The door closed behind Matt, and Salem moved over and sat down beside Sara. "What didn't you tell your father, Sara?"

Her head snapped around. "What are you talking about?"

"You're hiding something," he insisted.

"You're imagining things."

"If I am, then why did you come out of the house with a loaded gun?"

"Because it was apparent you didn't have one. And whoever shot at Emily could have just as easily shot you."

"You can come up with a better defense argument than that."

She went completely still, her eyes narrowing in anger. "Are you calling me a liar?"

"No, I'm not. I'm just saying that I don't believe you."

"That's the same as calling me a liar!"

"That is your opinion, and I don't intend to sit here and debate semantics. The fact remains that Emily Kirkland could have been killed because she happened to be driving your car."

Tunneling her fingers through her hair, Sara slumped back into the cushioned sofa, shaking her head. "I don't want to believe someone thought Emily was me."

"Why not? It's easy enough for someone to mistake her for you. Especially now that she's cut her hair."

Staring at a crystal vase on a low table filled with a profusion of newly opened, creamy white roses and peonies, she prayed he was wrong. How far would a person go to exact revenge because he was forced to relinquish his freedom for the next eight years? He had chosen to embark on a life of criminal activities. Had he thought he was right, and she was wrong for prosecuting him?

Salem curved an arm around her waist, pulling her closer to his side. He dropped a kiss on her hair when she rested her head against his shoulder.

"Death is following you, kitten."

The warning voice in her head whispered he was right. As much as she did not want to accept the truth, she knew he was right.

"How do you know, Salem?"

"I can feel it."

Raising her head, she stared at him. His black eyes impaled her. "How?"

He shook his head. "I don't know, but I can. I know when you're frightened, angry, sad."

"Sad?" There was no mistaking the incredulous quality in the single word.

"You cried the night we came back from Santa Fe with the foal."

"What were you doing? Standing outside my window like a Peeping Tom?" She pulled out of his embrace and stood up.

He rose to his feet, a slight frown furrowing his smooth, intelligent forehead. "No, Sara. I didn't have to spy on you."

She threw up her hands in a gesture of dismissal. "I don't want to hear anymore. Just what exactly do you call yourself other than veterinarian? Soothsayer? Seer? Shaman? Warlock?"

"Salem Lassiter, ma'am." His voice was cold, the words exacting.

She shifted, showing him her back as she wrapped her arms around her body in a protective gesture. She knew she should have told her father about the death threat, but she had not wanted to alarm him.

Matthew Sterling had once lived a double life as an independent operative for an intelligence agency, and after he retired thirty years ago he vowed he would never go back. But if she told her father that a member of an organized-crime family had placed a price on her head, that vow was certain to be broken.

And if her would-be assassin had shot Emily Kirkland in error, then Joshua Kirkland also would be drawn into the drama. He had retired from military service as Colonel Kirkland, former Associate Coordinating Chief of the Defense Intelligence Agency. And, like her father, he had taken a vow not to return to the shadowy world of military intelligence.

Both fathers were approaching seventy years of age, yet would embark on a mission to protect their children with a ferocity that would take the nerve of men half their age.

Lowering her arms, she turned to face Salem. Tilting her chin in a gesture of defiance, she nodded. "You're right about one thing. I have been threatened with death." One moment she and Salem were standing two feet apart, and before she could blink she found herself in his arms.

His warm breath swept over her face. "Tell me about it."

"I will, but you must promise me you won't tell my father."

He gave her a questioning look. "Why not?"

"Promise me you won't tell him."

Salem saw the silent pleading in her eyes, and he realized he could not deny her anything—not when he knew he was falling in love with her.

"I promise."

Pulling him back down to the sofa, Sara held his hand

tightly and told him everything about the trial, the jury verdict and the sentencing. She left nothing out. Her eyes were brimming with unshed tears when she finished, the last word lingering in the quiet room like a fading sigh.

Lowering his head, Salem brushed his mouth over hers, increasing the pressure until she returned his kiss with a passion she summoned from her very soul.

"I will take care of you, kitten," he crooned, placing comforting kisses over her cheekbones and down the silken column of her elegant neck. "I would give up my life to keep you safe."

He hadn't lied to her, but on the other hand he hadn't been completely truthful, either. He had not told her that he loved her.

Chapter 14

The next six hours passed with accelerated expediency for Sara. Her father, the sheriff, and his deputy found both spent shell casings, the lawmen verifying that they had come from a high-powered rifle. The sheriff concluded from the trajectory of the bullets that had shattered the windshield that someone had lain in wait for the car. A further search of the area supported his claim when his deputy found a section of grass trampled down at the precise angle from where the shots were apparently fired.

Salem informed Sara that he had to return home to check his beeper and answering services for calls, promising to return as soon as he could. Matt told him firmly that Sara and Emily would not be staying at the cabin. He planned to take them back to the main house.

Nothing in Salem's implacable expression had indicated his annoyance with Matthew Sterling's decision. He simply nodded, signaled for Shadow, then headed in the direction of his house.

* * *

Joshua and Vanessa Kirkland had arrived in Las Cruces, anxiety clearly etched on their faces. Both were visibly relieved when they saw the Steri-Strip the doctor applied to the minute cut, replacing Salem's gauze dressing. Both had feared the worst when Matt called them with the news that their daughter had been injured in an auto accident.

It was early afternoon when Sara, Emily, Vanessa and Eve gathered on cushioned lounge chairs in a screened patio. The four women sipped from tall glasses of iced tea while Matt, Joshua and Chris retreated behind a locked door in a room that doubled as Matt Sterling's office.

Vanessa sat down on a chaise next to her daughter. "Are you in any pain?"

Emily gave her a reassuring smile. "No, Mom." And she wasn't. Closing her eyes, she mentally dismissed the episode where she actually saw the car's windshield shatter outward in a spiderweb pattern seconds before the second shot blew out the driver's-side window. She would readily admit that she had been frightened, more frightened than she had ever been in her life, but told herself that she could not let the fear paralyze her. She was a television journalist with a recognizable face, and she was aware that she had to conquer her fear or it would destroy her as well as her career.

Sara's gaze was fixed on Eve Sterling's solemn expression. "Why the long face, Mama?"

Eve turned to stare at her daughter, her ebony gaze filled with trepidation. "I don't like this, Sara. Your father and Joshua are carrying guns, and if Chris wasn't laid up with a broken leg, and Michael hadn't left for his assignment, I'm certain they would also be packing guns."

"They're just being a little macho," Sara replied flippantly.

She did not tell her mother that she was carrying a gun

in her purse. She knew how much her mother detested fire-arms, because her parents had argued incessantly when Matt Sterling stated he wanted his children to learn to operate handguns. It was the only time she remembered her parents not sharing a bed. Eve had moved out of her bedroom, sleeping in one of the guest rooms until her son and daughter completed their firearms training.

"It has nothing to do with machismo," Eve countered. Her words were layered with repressed anger. "Your father and Joshua lived lives both would like to forget, and seeing them like this is like a flashback. I met and married your father in Mexico, and when I left there three months later I did not know whether he was dead or alive. I came back to the States to a son I hadn't seen in nine months, while I'd carried another child beneath my heart who would never know its father if he never returned."

"Vanessa and I have had to go through hellish periods of waiting to see whether we would get our husbands and the fathers of our children back whenever they decided to undertake a *mission.* And I see this as another mission, Sara."

She heard the pain in Eve's voice and saw fear in her dark gaze. Could she tell her mother that she had been tar-geted for death? That someone wanted to exact revenge because they felt she was responsible for putting them in prison? *No, you can't,* a silent voice whispered to her. She would hide the danger surrounding her from her parents for as long as she could.

At twenty-nine she was an independent adult who had learned to protect and take care of herself. Her father had taught her all there was to know about firearms, and if she had to use one to protect herself or her family she would.

"You, Dad, Uncle Josh and Chris may be overreacting."

Eve shook her head in disagreement. "I don't think so, Sara. I've lived with your father long enough to know when something is not right. I feel his apprehension, and something else he's never exhibited in the thirty years we've been married."

A foreign emotion swept over Sara, gnawing away at her confidence, and she knew what her mother was going to say before the single word was uttered.

"Fear," Eve stated, confirming her thoughts. "Even though he's always treated Chris like a son, I've always known that you're his world, Sara. From the moment you were born he has existed solely for you."

"But he loves Chris."

"That he does, but he loves you more. And if anything were to happen to you it would literally kill him."

"What are you trying to say, Mama?"

Again, Eve registered the form of address from Sara's childhood. She knew something was not right with her daughter, and she wanted to shake her and force her to reveal what she was hiding from those who loved her most.

"You're a very bright woman, Sara Ellen Sterling. Figure it out." Swinging her legs over the chaise, she stood up and walked out of the patio, leaving her daughter staring at her retreating figure.

Falling back on the cushioned chair, Sara closed her eyes. She hadn't missed seeing the tears welling up in her mother's eyes. She had witnessed Eve Sterling's unbridled temper on occasion, but could not remember the last time she saw her cry.

She wanted to blame herself for Emily's brush with death, yet she wasn't absolutely certain that the sniper was trying to kill her or her friend.

A restlessness assailed her and she knew she had to get up, move around and do something—anything except lie around and think about the danger threatening her very existence.

Salem's warning came back, bringing with it an icy chill that left her trembling despite the summer heat. *Death is following you, kitten.*

Moving off the chaise, she left the patio and walked into the kitchen. Marisa stood at the sink, mumbling under her breath.

"Do you need help, Miss Marisa?"

The petite cook turned and glared at her. "Not if you're going to grunt at me, too."

"Who grunted at you?"

"Your mother. All I asked her was if the Kirklands were staying the night."

"Mom's kind of stressed right now," she stated, coming to Eve Sterling's defense.

"Who isn't?" Marisa countered. "First Christopher nearly breaks his neck, then you come home and fall off a horse and now someone wants to use Emily Kirkland for target practice. This generation will have their parents in the grave before it's their time." Handing Sara a sharp chopping knife, she pointed to half a dozen whole chickens on a cutting board. "You can finish cutting those into quarters while I baste the ribs."

Now who's testy? Sara thought, taking the knife. She had cut up one chicken and had reached for the second one when the doorbell rang.

"I'll get it," Marisa volunteered, running her hands under water before she dried them on a terry cloth towel.

Sara went completely still when she felt the wave of heat sweep over the back of her neck. She did not have to turn around to know that Salem Lassiter had entered the kitchen, feeling his heat and energy as surely as if he had touched her.

Closing her eyes, she swayed slightly. "Salem?"

"Yes, Sara."

Turning slowly, she saw him leaning against the entrance to the kitchen, her gaze widening as he seemed to pull her into his force field. He wore a pale blue cotton shirt and matching jeans. He had brushed his hair off his face, securing it at the nape of his strong neck. The light blue color was a startling contrast to his deep copper-brown coloring. She also noticed that he had attached a beeper and small cellular telephone to the belt encircling his slim waist.

Marisa brushed past him, well aware of what had silently passed between her employer's daughter and his veterinarian.

"The boss is waiting for *you*," she threw over her shoulder.

Salem smiled. "Thank you, Miss Marisa." Nodding to Sara, he turned and walked away.

Sara forced back a smile as she resumed cutting up the chickens. "What are we having for dessert?"

"I'm thinking about strawberry shortcake. I need to use up the strawberries before they start growing whiskers."

"I was hoping you'd say German chocolate cake."

Marisa glanced up at the clock on the built-in microwave oven. "If we're not going to eat until seven, I think we'll have time to make both."

The setting sun fired the pipelike spires and pinnacles of the Organ Mountains, turning everything along the western slopes a dazzling, spectacular, flaming red. The five couples sitting at the long table carved from the trunk of an oak tree paused and stared at the awesome sight. Matt and Joshua had moved the table from the patio to the rear of the house in order for the diners to take advantage of the cooler evening temperatures.

Sara felt the heat of Salem's gaze on her face, refusing to meet his knowing dark eyes. Each time he pressed his thigh against hers, she felt a rush of desire sweep over her body. He had remained behind the closed door with her father, brother and Joshua Kirkland for more than an hour, and when the men emerged it was with a merriment that had been missing earlier that morning. It wasn't until she had curved an arm around Chris's waist as he leaned heavily on a cane that she detected the odor of brandy on his breath. The men had been talking *and* drinking.

"This sure is a pretty sight," Joe mumbled, shaking his head in amazement. Reaching under the table, he grasped Marisa's hand.

Rising to her feet, Sara placed her napkin beside her plate. "I need to walk off some of this food before I even think about dessert."

She had sampled portions of grilled chicken, steak and Marisa's tender barbecued spareribs, along with their mother's delicious potato salad, Vanessa's tossed salad and homemade bread. Matt and Joshua were responsible for the alcoholic and nonalcoholic concoctions.

All gazes were fixed on her as she turned and walked in the direction of the stables. Salem looked across the table at Matt, who lowered his lids in a gesture of approval.

Placing his napkin beside his place, he rose to his feet. "Excuse me, but I'm going to join Sara in that walk."

The couples pushed away from the table in pairs: Joshua and Vanessa, Matt and Eve and finally Joe and Marisa. The only remaining two were Christopher Delgado and Emily Kirkland, who sat regarding each other with curious stares.

"Why are you following me?" Sara asked without turning around.

Salem stared at her strong, shapely, long legs, not responding. She had elected to wear a white, fitted tank dress that ended several inches above her knees. He had found it difficult to control a rush of desire when she came out of the house wearing the dress, because it was the first time he had seen her reveal so much flesh.

His gaze was fixed on the firm muscles in her calves as she placed one foot in front of the other. "Are you aware that you have very sexy legs?"

She stopped abruptly, turning and facing him. The setting sun turned her into a statue of fiery bronze. It fired the gold in her eyes and the gold undertones of her brown skin.

Folding her hands behind her back, she smiled up at him. "No." The gesture caused a soft swell of breasts to rise above the revealing neckline.

He moved closer. "No man has ever told you—"

She placed her fingers over his lips, stopping his words. "Don't, Salem," she whispered. "I don't want to talk about other men."

Curling his fingers around her delicate wrist, he pulled her hand away from his mouth. "What do you want to talk about?"

"Anything, except other men."

Lacing his fingers through hers, he nodded. "Can we talk about you?"

She shrugged her bare shoulders. "That all depends on what you ask."

He began walking, and she fell in step with him. "What do you want for your future?" he asked, startling her with the question.

There was a comfortable silence before she said, "I honestly don't know. I thought I knew exactly what I wanted before I came back here."

"And what was that?"

"To work in the D.A.'s office for another three or four years, then trying the other side of the table."

"You mean you'd want to become a defense attorney?"

"Yes. I've thought about taking on cases where the defendants are young African Americans who are first offenders. I'd like to be responsible for offering them a second chance before they go to prison."

"Would you do that in New York?"

"It could be New York, New Jersey, New Mexico or Florida."

"Why so many states?"

"I'm licensed to practice law in those states."

Salem schooled his features not to reveal his relief. So, it was possible she might return to New Mexico in the future. "What about your personal life?"

Sara stared at the toes of her white, ballet-slipper–style shoes. "Are you talking about marriage and children?"

He nodded. "Yes."

Raising her head, she stared up at him, meeting his direct gaze. "I don't think I'm ready to become a wife, and certainly not a mother."

"I take that to mean that you don't like children."

"I like children, but I've never thought of myself becoming a mother. There are certain women who are born to have children, and I don't think I'm one of them."

"Maybe you will change your mind when you meet Mr. Right."

"You could be right about that."

She did not say that she knew she had met Mr. Right, but it would remain her secret. Salem Lassiter was her Mr. Right.

They walked in silence past the stables and the fields where the horses were turned out to graze, then turned in the direction of the stream separating the two properties.

The sky had darkened from a fiery red to a clear royal blue with a liberal sprinkling of stars. Sara stopped and looked upward, marveling at the beauty of her surroundings.

Salem released her hand, pulling her into a close embrace. She laid her head on his chest, counting the strong, steady beats of his heart. Everything about him was so virile, so male, that it literally took her breath away.

Winding her arms around his waist, she felt a warming, healing peace she had not felt in years. With Salem she was safe and complete.

Raising her head, she smiled up at him. "Why did my father call you to come over?"

He arched an eyebrow. "He invited me to come for dinner."

"Is that all?"

"What else would there be, Sara?"

She shrugged a shoulder. "I don't know. I thought he wanted to talk about what had happened this morning."

"Did you think he was going to take me to task for being at your place so early in the morning?"

"I doubt if Daddy would mention that."

"If you think that, then you don't know your father as well as you should. If he felt I was taking advantage of you he would confront me."

"But you're not."

"That's because I never would, despite what you may have heard about me."

"I haven't heard much about you, except that I should stay away from you because you may have been responsible for your wife taking her life."

His expression changed, making him look as if she had struck him in the face. "What do you believe, Sara? Do you think I'm such a monster that I'd drive a woman I loved to take her life and our son's?"

She did not know how, but at that very moment she felt his pain, his anguish and his loss. "I've seen you with animals—"

"Answer me," he snarled, his hands moving from her waist to her shoulders. He gave her a slight shake.

"No, Salem!" she screamed. "No, I don't think you're a monster. And no, I don't believe you'd make someone take her own life just to be rid of you."

He cradled her to his chest in a savage grip that made it difficult for her to breathe. Lowering his head, he kissed her hair, forehead, ear and jaw as his lips trailed down to the side of her neck.

Sara groaned softly, turning her head and searching for his mouth. She felt the moist heat of his breath seconds before their mouths were joined in a tentative, cautious meeting. Rising on tiptoe, she wound her arms around his neck.

Salem picked her up until her head was level with his, savoring the healing passion she offered him. He had tasted her mouth, but that was not enough. He wanted more—all of her.

Lowering her to the grass, he slipped his hands under the straps of her dress and pushed it off her shoulders. She froze, her eyes widening in fright as he exposed her breasts to his hungry gaze.

Sara's impulse was to cover her breasts with her hands. She was thwarted when Salem captured her wrists, not permitting her to move. She tried to quell her panic as her chest rose and fell with the lingering fear that she would not be able to please a man.

Moving closer, he reveled in the fullness of her high, firm breasts pressed to his chest. "You're perfect, Sara

Sterling. Perfect and so beautiful." He could not disguise the awe in his voice.

"Salem." His name came out in a sob.

"It's all right, kitten," he crooned close to her ear. "I'm not going to touch you."

"I…I can't," she gasped.

"You don't have to. There will come a time when you'll want to lie with me, and I'm willing to wait for that time." Releasing her wrists, he pulled up the straps and settled them over her shoulders. He pressed a kiss over each eyelid. "Let's go back before your father comes gunning for me."

Chapter 15

"*Daniels here. What the hell is going on?*"

"*What are you talking about?*"

"*Someone else tried taking out Sara Sterling.*"

"*Who?*"

"*That's what I want to know.*"

"*What happened?*"

"*They shot at her car.*"

"*Is she dead?*"

"*What the hell kind of question is that? If she was dead do you think I'd be calling you? Look, don't play shady with me, or—*"

"*Don't threaten me, Daniels. If you think I sent someone to shoot that Sterling bitch, then think again. The reason you were referred to me is because you don't use a gun. But if you're having a problem getting rid of the lady, just let me know.*"

"*There's no problem. I'm just careful.*"

"Don't be too careful, because if someone gets to her first, then consider what I gave you as payment in full."

"I need that money."

"And I need a dead district attorney. Look, I have to go because I'm late for a breakfast meeting. Don't call me again until you have good news for me."

Kareem pressed a button, ending the call, then flung the phone across the room. It bounced off the wall and landed on the worn carpet. Running a hand over his head, he squeezed his eyes tightly. He *had* to kill Sara Sterling because he needed money—money for his son's operation.

Burying his face in his callused hands, he moaned in frustration. Since he had come to work at Sterling Farms he hadn't been given the opportunity to be alone with Sara. The one time had been when he went to her cabin with the letter. He had not expected the vet to show up. What had unnerved him was that he hadn't heard him come up behind him, and he knew his chances were getting slimmer with each sunrise.

Her father was back, and he rarely left the ranch, while her injured brother never left the ranch. He also noticed that Matt Sterling had taken to wearing a gun, and Joe Russell now kept a loaded rifle on a rack in the barn.

Kareem would sooner face down a bear than pick up a gun. Two days before his twelfth birthday he awoke to the sound of a gunshot and discovered his father had spattered his brains on the bathroom wall. His mother had returned home four hours later to find him standing in the same position—in shock. He glanced down at his watch. It was almost seven; time he left for work.

Sara met Joe as he led a high-spirited, prancing stallion out of the stable. "Good morning." Her voice was as light as her step.

"Mornin', missy. I'm surprised you're up this early. You planning to ride Blaze?"

"Yes."

"Wait a few minutes for me to take Temptation out to the field, then I'll saddle her up for you."

"Don't bother. I'll saddle her myself."

Joe raised his bushy reddish eyebrows. "You sure?"

"Of course I'm sure."

"Don't go too far," Joe warned.

"I won't."

She did not tell Joe that she had tucked the small automatic pistol into a boot under her jeans. And she was up early because she hadn't slept more than three hours all night.

After she and Salem returned to the house she had spent the next hour watching him warily while he interacted with her family and the Kirklands.

Each time he glanced her way she felt naked and as vulnerable as she had been when he had exposed her breasts. It wasn't until she lay in bed, though, that she recalled everything she had felt when he pressed his chest to hers.

A rush of heat had swept over her body, leaving her shaking with desire. She realized she wanted to share her body with Salem, but whenever he touched her she froze like a frightened rabbit. She hadn't been that frightened her first time with Eric.

She selected a bridle and noseband from several hanging on a hook, whistling softly as she walked down the path; she stopped in front of Blaze's stall.

"Good morning, girl. I'm sorry I didn't get to see you yesterday. We had a little commotion," she crooned softly as she opened the door to the stall.

The horse reared up, but settled down when she patted her neck. She slipped the noseband up the mare's muzzle and fastened it around her head, then attached the bridle.

"How fast do you want to go this morning?" she asked, leading the horse over where she could saddle her.

A door opened and closed and Kareem Daniels stepped into the stable. Blaze reared again, her front hooves coming dangerously close to Sara's shoulders. He saw the rearing horse and backed up, waiting for Sara to settle the excited mare.

Glancing up, Sara noticed Kareem for the first time. "Good morning."

He nodded his head. "Good morning, Miss Sterling. Your horse giving you trouble?"

"A little. She seems out of sorts today."

"Do you want me to get Mr. Russell to help you?"

"No. I'll handle her."

Kareem watched as Sara placed a saddlepad on the horse before she picked up a saddle and swung it easily over the mare's back. He hadn't thought she was that strong, given her slender figure. He curled his fingers into fists to keep from putting them around her neck. It would have been so easy to snap her neck, but he knew he would never make it out of Las Cruces if someone discovered her body. A knowing smile softened his boyish face. He still had time, and now he knew which horse she rode.

"Do you need a hand up, Miss Sterling?"

"No, thank you." She placed her booted foot in the left stirrup and swung her leg over the horse in one smooth graceful motion.

Stepping aside, he opened the door and watched her as she cantered across the field. Kareem was still standing and watching the horse and rider grow smaller when Joe Russell returned to the stable. It was his cue to begin mucking out the stalls of the horses that were grazing in the field.

* * *

Sara stopped under the spreading branches of a lone tree in the pasture, slipping off Blaze. She looped the reins over one of the lower branches, leaving the horse to graze on the sparsely growing sweet grass. Raising her arms above her head, she executed a series of stretching and bending exercises.

She had a feeling someone was watching her. Turning, she saw Shadow standing about ten feet away. Blaze stomped nervously, backing up. Moving over to the horse, she curved an arm around her neck, hoping to settle her down.

Shadow's golden eyes regarded her keenly from a thick coat of light and dark gray fur. Salem had said he was mixed with shepherd, but Shadow's bulky body and longer legs verified that his sire's wolf characteristics were dominant.

"Where's your master?" The dog looked around as if he understood what she was saying. "Where is he, boy?" As if in answer to her question, Salem appeared over a rise. He slapped his left thigh, and Shadow trotted back to his side.

"Good morning, Miss Sterling."

"Good morning, Dr. Lassiter."

Crossing his arms over his chest, he smiled at her. "You're looking well this morning."

"Thank you."

"You're up early."

"I couldn't sleep."

"Why didn't you call me?"

"Whatever for, Dr. Lassiter?"

"Because I have the perfect remedy for insomnia."

She flashed a saucy smile. "And that is?"

"I can't tell you. I'd have to show you."

"Perhaps another time."

He inclined his head. "Another time, then."

"You're up early, too. Did you have trouble sleeping?"

He walked toward her, his gaze fixed on her mouth. "No. In fact, I slept quite well last night." He stopped in front of her. "You shouldn't be out here alone, especially after what happened yesterday."

"I'm not alone. I have you and Shadow to protect me."

"What if we're not around?"

"Then I have a little friend in my boot that should help me out."

Vertical lines appeared between his eyes. "I don't like the fact that you're carrying a gun."

"Neither does my mother."

"Then why do you carry it?"

"Because I feel safer with it than without it."

"What if I give you Shadow?"

"I can't take him from you."

"Then move in with me. I'd be able to protect you."

"And so can my father, if I decide to stay at the main house," she argued.

"You slept at the main house last night, and you're out here by yourself this morning."

"How would that change if I moved in with you?"

"Shadow would never let you out of his sight."

She shook her head. "Thank you for the offer, but I can't."

"You can't, or you won't?"

"I can't, Salem."

He hid his disappointment well as his gaze lingered on her face and then dropped to her shoulders and breasts. "May I call on you this evening?"

Sara felt something intense flow through her with his entrancement. It was as if he had opened her blouse and bared her breasts to his fiery gaze again. She did not know what it was about Salem Lassiter, but he had unlocked her heart and touched a chord of passion deep within a core of her very being.

He had asked her to move in with him, not sleep with him. And he had promised not to touch her until she was ready to welcome him into her body. Could she trust him enough to keep the promise? Could she trust herself enough not to come to him until she was ready?

"Yes, Salem," she whispered softly. "Yes, you may call on me tonight."

"How does dinner and a movie sound?"

"Wonderful."

The corners of his mobile mouth tipped up in a smile. "Seven?"

"I'll be ready."

"Shadow will escort you when you're ready to go back to the stables."

She glanced at the dog, who had stretched out on the ground, but stood up alertly at the mention of his name. Salem patted his thigh and he trotted obediently over to him. She did not understand what he told the dog when he spoke to him in Navajo. Shadow moved over and stood beside her left leg, waiting.

"I'm going back now."

Salem made his way to Blaze, patting her neck. He crooned to the horse as he untied the reins. The mare nudged the vet, looking for a treat.

"I'm sorry, Blaze, I don't have anything for you right now. When I come visiting I'll bring you your apple."

Sara raised her left leg to mount the horse but was thwarted when Salem curved his hands around her waist; he lifted her effortlessly, seating her and handing her the reins.

"Shadow will follow far enough behind not to frighten your horse."

Leaning down, she pressed a kiss to his eyebrow. "Thank you. I'll see you later."

Nodding, he stepped back, watching as she urged the horse up over the incline, Shadow loping behind at a comfortable distance.

He did not know what had prompted him to invite Sara to come live with him. Closing his eyes, he shook his head, trying to clear his muddled thoughts. Was he seeking an instant replay of his life? Grace had lived with him a month before she left, and if Sara agreed to live with him it would only be for two months before she left to return to New York.

He was supposed to be growing older and wiser, but since Sara Sterling had come into his life she had turned his world upside down. With her he was willing to play the fool because she was the first woman with whom his inner spirit had connected. She was the one who fulfilled his vision as a Dream Walker. The night he had stood outside her window was the beginning—the first time he was able to enter her dreams and make them his own.

The feeling was as strange and powerful as his deceased grandmother had predicted. It had taken thirty-six years for him to become *mai-coh,* or witch, a Navajo synonym for the wolf.

Sara lay on a wooden bench, squinting at her mother through a haze of steam. She inhaled deeply, filling her lungs with moist heat. The sauna was working. The tightness in her arms and legs was easing. She could not believe that not working out for two weeks had taken such a toll on her well-conditioned body.

After she returned from her morning ride, she and her family shared a farewell breakfast with Joshua, Vanessa and Emily before the Kirklands returned to Santa Fe. Then her mother suggested she accompany her to a health club where the elder Sterlings had been members for the past ten years.

She and Eve swam laps in the Olympic-size pool, but Sara had to stop after completing her third lap. Sitting on the side of the pool, she watched Eve's strong body glide through the water like a sleek fish as she swam the length of the pool, before reversing direction eight times. After catching her breath, Sara managed another two laps before stopping.

Turning her head, Eve stared at her daughter's profile as she now lay with her eyes closed. "Do you have any plans for tonight?"

Sara let out her breath slowly. "I've committed to dinner and a movie with Salem."

Eve shifted her delicate arching eyebrows. Droplets of moisture dotted her sable-brown face and shimmered on her short, silver, naturally curly hair.

"How involved are you with him?"

Opening her eyes, Sara stared at Eve. "What do you mean by *involved?*"

"Is he a neighbor, friend or something more?"

"Something more?"

"Stop answering my questions with a question, Sara!" Eve snapped angrily. "I'm not on the witness stand."

She knew what her mother was implying. She wanted to know if she and Salem were sleeping together. "I'm sorry," she replied, apologizing. "The answer is that Salem and I are friends and neighbors, nothing more."

"Is this the first time you've gone out with him?"

Sara wondered how much her mother knew about her and Salem. Had Marisa revealed what she had observed between her and the veterinarian, or had her father told his wife what he'd seen the morning she'd summoned him to her cabin?

"No." Her admission was soft, almost caressing.

"You like him, don't you?"

"What's there not to like, Mom? He's gorgeous, intelligent and quite interesting in a very mysterious way."

A slight smile curved Eve's mouth. "You know he's in love with you."

Sara sat up, holding the towel covering her nude body over her breasts. "He can't be!" Her eyes were wide and shimmering with dark green points of light.

Eve did not move from her reclining position. "And why not?"

"We…he…he doesn't even know me. We've never—" Her words trailed off when she realized what she was going to say.

This prompted Eve to sit up. "You've never what? Are you saying he can't love you because he's never slept with you?" Closing her eyes and biting down hard on her lower lip, Sara nodded. "Do you think you'll ever sleep with him?"

Returning to her reclining position, she shook her head. "I'm not certain. He makes me feel something I can't feel with other men."

"I think the *thing* you're talking about is desire."

Sara stared at her mother, seeing amusement in her dark eyes. "How would you know?"

"You're my daughter, Sara," she began gently, "and I see a lot of myself in you at your age. I kept every man who appeared the least bit interested in me at a distance until I met Chris's father. Alejandro Delgado was worldly, handsome, elegant and he was a very passionate man. He literally swept me off my feet, and I married him a month after our first date. I believed he loved me, but he did not have the capacity to be a faithful husband."

"I hope you don't think I'm going to marry Salem."

Shifting her eyebrows, Eve said, "You could do a lot worse."

"What's this all about, Mom? Are you trying to marry me off so that you can get grandchildren?"

The older woman managed to look insulted. "Of course not."

"Then why are you trying to match me up with Salem when everyone else doesn't seem to approve of me seeing him."

"Who's everyone?"

"Marisa. And Daddy didn't seem too pleased to see Salem at my place the other morning."

"Marisa's biased. She was fond of Grace Lassiter, who used to complain to her about Salem. And your father would overreact to any man who would attempt to take his princess away from him."

"Are you saying Daddy likes Salem?"

"He has the highest respect for the man."

There was a comfortable silence before Sara spoke again. "Do you know what drove his wife to take her life and that of their son?"

Suddenly Eve's expression went grim. "Yes, I do. But I promised Salem I would never tell anyone. If you want to know, I suggest you ask him."

Her gaze caught and held her mother's. "I intend to do that when I see him tonight."

Chapter 16

You know he's in love with you. Sara recalled her mother's statement when she opened the door and stared up at Salem staring back at her. There was nothing in his gaze that indicated any emotion other than awe as he visually examined her body-hugging, sleeveless, black dress in a stretch knit with a scooped neckline. The hem of the dress ended several inches above her smooth knees, and her professionally groomed feet were shod in a pair of black faille, sling-back, high-heeled sandals. A light cover of makeup accentuated her large eyes and lush mouth, and she had brushed her hair off her face in a style which would have been too severe for a woman with harder features.

An admiring smile parted her lips. Salem had elected to wear a short-sleeved silk shirt in a smoky gray-blue with a pair of tailored navy blue slacks. A pair of highly polished, low-heeled, black boots had replaced his usual dusty pair.

"You look very nice, Salem."

He gave her a dazzling smile. "Thank you."

"I'm ready," she said, reaching for her small evening purse on the drop-leaf table.

His lazy gaze moved over her face, down her body, then reversed itself. "Where have you hidden it?"

A slight frown appeared between her eyes. "What?"

Leaning closer, he whispered, "Your friend. I don't believe your purse is large enough for it, unless you're carrying a derringer."

A light laugh escaped her lips, the gesture crinkling her expressive eyes. "I decided I didn't need it tonight because I'll be with you. Besides, where would I hide it?" Spinning around, she gave him a thorough view of her slim curvy body.

Salem felt his breath catch in his chest as he surveyed the perfection of her slender body. And not for the first time he found himself admiring her long, well-shaped legs.

"Are you asking me to search you?"

Turning around, she faced him, feeling the wave of heat in her cheeks. "Not without permission."

Throwing back his head, he laughed a full-throated laugh. "Will I need a search warrant, Counselor?"

Sara affected a saucy grin. "That all depends."

He took a step closer, staring down into her compelling magnetic eyes. "On what?"

Curving her bare arm over his, she lowered her lashes demurely, charming him with the innocently seductive gesture. "How much I enjoy dinner and the movie."

He laughed again. "Then I'm in for a real treat, because I'm certain what I've planned for tonight will please you." He led her out of the house, closing the door behind them.

Salem steered Sara to his car in the driveway behind Matthew Sterling's truck bearing the Sterling Farms logo.

Opening the passenger-side door for her, he waited until she settled herself on the leather seat, then rounded the Jaguar and took his own.

As he turned the key in the ignition the powerful sports car roared to life, and within seconds it ate up the road in front of them. Instead of driving across the stream, he took a longer route, crossed a stone bridge, then came around his property from a northerly direction.

Sara stared at the expansive two-story house coming into view before she glanced at Salem. "Did you forget something?"

He shook his head. "No." Pressing a button on a remote control garage opener, he waited until the door opened to reveal a three-car garage; he maneuvered the Jaguar into a space beside his sport utility vehicle. He turned off the engine and pushed open his door.

She opened her mouth to question him further, but he had already come around to open her door. "Why are we here, Salem?"

He extended a hand. "Come, I'll show you." He wasn't disappointed when she grasped his hand, permitting him to pull her to her feet.

Curving an arm around her tiny waist, he led her along a slate path to the patio. A round table had been set for two with a snowy-white tablecloth, china, crystal and gleaming silver. Dozens of glasses, positioned in measured intervals around the perimeter of the patio, held lighted votive candles that flickered like sparkling stars in the waning daylight.

Turning, she stared up at Salem as he smiled down at her. "What a wonderful surprise."

"So are you, Sara Sterling," he whispered reverently.

Curving her arms around his waist, she pressed her lips to his. "What's on the menu?"

He pulled her flush against his body. "A little of this and a little of that."

Her eyes crinkled in a smile. "That sounds a little vague. What are you serving for dessert?"

His gaze widened as he took in the tempting curve of her full lips. "I don't know yet."

"Why not?" Her moist breath caressed his throat.

"I'll have to see how the evening progresses," he replied mysteriously.

"You're a tease, Salem Lassiter."

"No, kitten," he countered, "you're the one who's a tease. How do you expect me to keep my wits about me when I see you in that dress?"

Reaching up, Sara pulled his hair from the confines of the elastic band, the heavy, shiny strands falling from a natural center part to sweep over the silk on his shoulders.

"Now, we're even," she whispered.

Cradling her face in his hands, he lowered his head and took possession of her mouth, his tongue searching and parting her lips. The dread, fear and apprehension she had carried for the past six years were swept away—forever—with the demanding mastery of his persuasive kiss.

She forgot Eric, his heartbreaking confession and the self-sacrifice she had endured for more years than she wanted to remember as she succumbed to the healing Salem offered her.

Salem forced himself to stop, stop before he swung her up in his arms and retreated to the house and his bedroom. Once there, he knew there would be no turning back. But he also knew he had to take it slow with Sara, gain her confidence. He had proven to her that she was not frigid, and if they shared a bed it would have to be her decision and on her terms.

Easing back, he rested his chin on the top of her head,

his unbound hair grazing her cheekbones. "Come, sit down while I bring out the appetizers."

Sara nodded, not trusting herself to speak. If Salem hadn't ended the kiss, she knew she would have begged him to make love to her. Her insides were quivering like gelatin, and her runaway pulse had left her weak and light-headed. The instant his mouth touched hers all semblance of reason had fled, leaving her vulnerable to whatever he sought from her.

He escorted her to the table, pulled out a chair, and then seated her. "Don't run away," he teased.

"I don't want to," she admitted, her gaze fusing with his.

His smile broadened in approval. "Good."

She watched his tall figure as he turned and retreated into the house by a rear door, a gentle smile tilting the corners of her mouth. Tonight there were no shadows across her heart, and her newly awakened senses flowed with delight. She felt free—freer than she had ever been during any other time in her life.

Closing her eyes, she savored the cloying scent of damp earth. There was still enough natural light left for her to see droplets of water clinging to the leaves of the flowering plants surrounding the property. There had been a very brief thunderstorm earlier. She felt a whisper of a breeze caress her face like the velvet wings of a butterfly brushing bared flesh, and she listened for the nocturnal sounds that became more conspicuous with the advent of nightfall.

I love it here, she mused. *And I think I'm falling in love with Salem.* Opening her eyes, she couldn't believe the unspoken confession that swirled in her head, leaving her gasping for her next breath.

She shook her head as if to rid herself of the startling

revelation. How could she love Salem when she did not even know him? He was as much a stranger to her as she was to him—in spite of the invisible bond drawing them together. He found her attractive, as she did him, but mutual attraction was not enough on which to base love, or even a relationship. That was too shallow, much too superficial.

Despite his usual stoic expression, she had discovered he liked to laugh, and there were times that he teased her when she least expected him to. There had also been the time when she suspected he was jealous because he'd found Kareem at her cabin. She had shrugged off his behavior as male posturing—one male confronting another for dominance—but since her mother's assumption that Salem loved her she wasn't as certain. Eve Sterling liked Salem, and it was apparent Salem had trusted her enough to disclose the circumstances which had led to him losing his family.

A slight smile parted her lips. Eve was fond of Salem, he and Chris were cordial to each other, and her father respected him, while she feared that she had fallen in love with him. He had gained the admiration and respect of the Sterlings. None of that mattered—in only two and a half months she would return to New York City and a lifestyle that included men he had openly disdained as slick, double-talking New York brothers.

Thinking of New York men conjured up the image of John Bohannon. She did not know why, but she felt as if she had been unfaithful to him. It surprised her that she had been content to go out with John only once every two weeks. If a day went by and she did not see Salem she felt a sense of loss she could not explain. Why had it become so important that she see him so often? Why was she permitting herself to become involved with him? She knew everything she would share with Salem Lassiter would have to come to an abrupt end once she boarded her flight to return to the east coast.

She had asked herself a lot of questions, but only needed an answer to one: could she have an affair with Salem, then walk away from him when the time came for her to return to New York?

She could, and she would.

The object of her troubled thoughts returned to the patio, pushing a serving cart. She stared at him, unable to look away as she mumbled a silent prayer for strength.

Her gaze followed his capable hands when he placed a plate of sliced avocado, quartered hard-boiled eggs, large boiled shrimp, and ample pieces of lobster with a serving of piquant salsa in front of her. She stared at the circle of silver with the colorful beads on his left wrist.

"What do the stones on your bracelet represent?" The low timbre of her voice sounded strange, even to her own ears.

Salem placed a bottle of chilled wine on the table before he sat down. "My late grandmother gave it to me after I broke my wrist. She claimed the stones had mystical powers that would protect me from all harm if I was faithful to the way of the Navajo."

"Have you been faithful, Salem?"

He shrugged a broad shoulder under his silk shirt. "Somewhat. She wanted me to become a medicine man, because since the beginning of history the well-being of the Navajo has been entrusted to the medicine man."

"Do you regard yourself as a medicine man?"

He shook his head. "No. I am African American, Navajo and a veterinary surgeon. How about you, Sara? How do you regard yourself?"

She hesitated, then replied, "African American, female, daughter, sister and attorney."

Salem studied her intently for a moment. "A most winning combination."

"I'd like to think it is."

"There's no need to think about it. It is."

Their gazes met across the table, Salem's seemingly
challenging her to refute him. Sara could feel the invisible magnetism that made him so confident, and it was a
full minute before she was able to glance away.

"Wine?"

She nodded, unable to speak. Salem had lied to her. He
was a medicine man, a shaman. He had touched her and
healed her—freeing her from the chains that made it impossible for her to acknowledge she had been born female.
He had healed her so that she was now willing to open her
heart, to love a man completely.

Between sips of the cool, semisweet white wine, she
thoroughly enjoyed the piquant flavor of the salsa with the
avocado, shrimp, egg and lobster.

The salad was followed by the appearance of large
broiled lobsters surrounded by roasted garlic and herb
potatoes and a side dish of creamy coleslaw.

Sara swallowed a forkful of slaw. "You're an excellent
cook, Salem."

"It's not much fun cooking for one person."

The flickering candles cast long and short shadows over
his lean dark face. The sun had set behind the mountains,
and a reddish haze settled on every light surface.

"You can always cook for me." Her voice was low, inviting.

Salem put down his fork, crossing his arms over his
chest. Tilting his head at an angle, he studied her thought-
fully.

"How often would you want me to cook for you?"

She drew in a deep breath, causing the tops of her

breasts to rise above the revealing bodice of her dress. "You could begin with dinner one or two nights a week."

A slight smile played at the corners of his mobile mouth. "How about breakfast?"

"I'll take care of breakfast."

"Dinner at my place," he confirmed.

"And breakfast at mine," she countered.

"Do you think there will come a time when we will share breakfast and dinner under the same roof?"

Lowering her gaze, she focused on the fingers of her left hand toying with the stem of the wineglass. Without warning, her head came up, and she gave him a haughty stare.

"I'm certain there will."

His expression did not change. "I'm looking forward to that time."

"But that can't happen—yet."

Leaning forward on his chair, he impaled her with his penetrating stare. "Why not?"

"There's something I have to know even before I can consider spending the night under your roof."

"You want to know about my late wife?" he asked perceptively.

"Yes."

Closing his eyes, Salem shook his head. "Not tonight." He opened his eyes, unable to hide the pain he had carried for the past two years. "Please don't ask me to talk about her tonight."

"When, Salem?" She spoke in a soft whisper.

"Tomorrow or the next day. Any other time but tonight."

He did not want to tell Sara that tonight would have been his son's fourth birthday. He had brought her to his home for a very selfish purpose; he did not want to be alone— alone to wallow in the past. Grace and Jacob were a part of his past, and Sara represented what he could look forward to in his future.

When she had asked him why her father had asked him to come to Sterling Farms, he had told her a half-truth. Matt had invited him for dinner, but he had also wanted to discuss his relationship with his daughter.

They had spoken in private, and the instant the question was presented to him Salem realized he had fallen in love with Sara. She had captivated him with her intelligence, beauty, independence and repressed sensuality. What had surprised him was that he hadn't realized how much he was in love with her. Matt had asked him to protect her. And he hadn't lied to Sara when he told her he would forfeit his own life to keep her safe.

Matt seemed satisfied with his response, then quietly revealed what he had been involved in before he had become the owner of Sterling Farms. His shock must have been apparent, because Matt reassured him that he had closed that chapter of his life, not wanting to reopen it again.

Matt stated that he was responsible for his wife's safety and well-being, but would willingly relinquish his obligation for his daughter's to Salem.

Salem had accepted the honor before they returned to the room where Christopher and Joshua waited for them. The four men took a solemn pledge to protect their women while hoisting snifters filled with a superior imported brandy. Seconds before he felt the smooth warmth of the liquor spread throughout his chest, he had whispered a solemn plea to the departed spirits of his African and Navajo ancestors to protect Sara Sterling—the woman who had become a part of him without her even knowing it.

He forced a tight smile. "Would you like dessert before or after the movie?"

"Will it keep for another time?"

"Yes. Why?"

She flashed a sheepish grin. "I'm afraid I ate too much. I can hardly move. If I sit here another minute I'm going to fall asleep."

He glanced at his watch. If they left now they would be able to make the next showing in a series of foreign films. Rising to his feet, Salem rounded the table and curved a hand under her elbow, pulling her gently from the chair. He reached for her small purse and handed it to her.

"Let's go, kitten. You can sleep in the car."

"Where are we going?" she questioned, trying unsuccessfully to conceal a yawn.

"Downtown. But first I have to lock up the house."

Chapter 17

The streets of downtown Las Cruces were teeming with tourists who mingled with the city's natives. The tourists were identifiable by the ubiquitous cameras dangling from their necks and the palm-size video recorders clutched tightly in their fists as they entered and exited shops that displayed souvenirs and artifacts of the region. Many stood in long lines outside eating establishments. Others lingered in small groups, trying to decide what would become their next place of interest to visit.

Sara waited off to the side for Salem to purchase their tickets for the showing of a Merchant/Ivory production. Her admiring gaze caressed the length of his tall body as he leaned down to talk to the young woman in the enclosed booth. His pale gray, raw silk jacket hung elegantly over his broad shoulders, and the startling contrast of his raven-black hair against the lighter fabric had caused several women to turn their heads when they walked past him.

Her gaze drank in the sensuality that made Salem Lassiter so mysterious as he turned and approached her. She lowered her gaze, hoping to conceal what her eyes were certain to reveal.

He took her hand, lacing his fingers through hers. "They've sold out this showing. Do you want to wait?"

She glanced up at him. "What time is the next showing?"

"Ten-thirty. We have at least a two-hour wait."

"How's your schedule for tomorrow?"

"I'm free," he admitted.

"Then we'll wait."

Releasing her hand, Salem curved an arm around her waist. "There's a club not far from here that features live music. We can hang out there for a while."

She offered him a brilliant smile. "Let's go."

"I didn't think it would be this crowded on a weeknight," Salem murmured as he seated Sara at a small table for two.

The minute they'd entered the modern, upscale supper club, they felt the pulsing energy flowing from musicians, diners and the friendly staff.

She ignored the menus on the table, glancing around and admiring the decor and the classic attire of the predominantly thirtysomething African American crowd. Most of the women wore dresses that showed quite a lot of flesh without being vulgar, while their escorts favored tailored slacks, jackets and imported footwear.

An attractive waitress approached the table. "Welcome to Topaz. My name is Racine, and I'll be your server tonight." She had directed her comments to Salem, her gaze lingering appreciatively on his face and hair. "Have you decided what you'd like to order?"

Salem shook his head, while studying the beverage selections. "Not yet. Can you give us a little more time?"

"But of course, sugah."

Sara waited until Racine had walked away to chat with a couple seated at a nearby table, then said quietly, "Should I slap her now or later for flirting with you?"

Pressing his fist to his mouth, Salem closed his eyes and shook his head. Opening his eyes, he tried hiding a smile. "Jealous, kitten?"

"Should I not be, *sugah?* Not only was she openly flirting with you, but she totally ignored me. I'm certain she would've given last week's soiled kitty litter more respect."

His smile slipped away, replaced by a scowl. Leaning closer, he reached over the table and covered her hands with his. "Don't look now, but there's a guy at the table to your right who's been gawking at you ever since we sat down. If you don't know him, then I'm going to be the one doing the slapping tonight. And I can assure you that I can hit a lot harder than you can."

Sara did not know whether he was serious or joking. "Let's not act ugly, Salem," she chided softly.

"You were the one who wanted to slap Racine."

"I wouldn't have actually slapped her."

Salem's frown deepened. "Glance over your shoulder at the pervert and tell me if you know him."

Pulling her hands out of Salem's grip, Sara sat back and glanced casually to her right. Staring back at her was Eric Thompson. He was seated at a table with an attractive woman who seemed more absorbed in the menu than her dining partner.

"Do you know him?"

She heard Salem's voice, but it was as if he was sitting more than twenty feet away instead of two. "Yes, I do. We sort of grew up together."

As soon as the words were out of her mouth she saw Eric whisper something to his dining partner, then rise to his feet. Eric walked over to their table, and Salem stood up.

Eric flashed a polite smile. "Excuse me for intruding," he offered Salem as an apology, "but it's been a long time since I've seen Sara." His dark eyes lingered on her face. "Too long."

She forced a smile. "Salem, this is Eric Thompson. Eric, Salem Lassiter." The two men shook hands, offering what could be interpreted as civil smiles.

"Will you be around next week?"

She shifted an eyebrow. "Yes. Why do you ask?"

"I'd like to come out to see you, so we can catch up on what's been going on in our lives since we last saw each other."

"Call me first." Her voice was flat, showing no emotion.

Eric nodded. "Nice meeting you, Lassiter."

"Same here," Salem countered. He waited until the man Sara had introduced as Eric Thompson returned to his table, then he sat down. He stared at Sara staring back at him, sensing her disquiet.

"Was there ever closure?" he asked perceptively.

Tilting her chin, she glanced away. "Now there is."

"Do you want to talk about it?"

"I can't. Not here."

Rising to his feet, Salem reached into the pocket of his slacks, withdrew several bills and placed them on the table. Reaching for Sara's arm, he pulled her gently to her feet. Lowering his head, he said quietly, "Let's get out of here."

Sara stared out of the window as Salem exceeded the state's speed limit by at least twenty miles. He drove expertly along an unlit road with only the Jaguar's headlights for illumination. He had forgotten about the movie, and so had she when she realized she had come face-to-face with her past.

It hadn't bothered her seeing Eric again, but seeing him dining with a woman was as jolting as an electrical shock. And there was no doubt that he and the woman shared something more than friendship, because when Eric returned to his table he had leaned over and kissed his dining partner on the lips. How many times hadn't he kissed *her* in the same manner? Too many for her to count or remember.

Salem maneuvered into the garage at his house, then came around to assist Sara from the car. Her hands were cool to the touch as he held her fingers protectively within his strong grip.

He deactivated the elaborate computerized security system hidden within one of the carved door handles, then pushed open the front door. Shadow emerged from the secluded darkness at the side of the house. Man and beast regarded each other, then Salem escorted Sara into the foyer while Shadow retreated to the darkness.

Taking her purse from her, he placed it on a table beside a wedding basket his grandmother had woven for his mother when she had accepted Vance Lassiter's proposal. The basket was the same one his mother had given him before he had exchanged vows with Grace.

Sara followed him as if in a trance as he led her to the room where he had taken her the day Blaze had thrown her. It was also the room where he had kissed her for the first time. She sat on the armchair while Salem eased his long frame down to the footstool. Curving his fingers around her calves, he raised her legs, resting her feet on his lap.

"What did he do to you, kitten?"

Pressing her head against the back of the chair, she

closed her eyes, savoring the soothing feel of Salem's fingers massaging her legs. "Eric Thompson was the first and only man I have ever slept with."

Her voice was soft and even as she revealed everything, leaving nothing out. She felt his strong fingers tighten slightly when she repeated Eric's claim that she couldn't please him, that whenever he shared her body he fantasized about someone else. The tears she had tried valiantly to keep in check flowed down her cheeks as her words trailed off into a trembling silence.

Reaching up, Salem gathered Sara in his arms, rocking her gently as he had his son whenever he woke up crying. He let her cry until she was spent. Then he lowered his head and kissed her tears.

"He lied to you, kitten," he crooned. "You are able to please a man. You please me."

Raising her head, she stared up at him through the moisture turning her eyes into shimmering emerald pools. "How would you know that? We haven't slept together."

"Loving someone is not about sex. It's about caring, sharing and sacrifice. It's about me wanting to see you, touch you and kiss you." He pressed his mouth to hers. "It's about taking care of you, seeing you smile and making you happy." He kissed her again. "And it's about making certain you're safe. It's all of these things and more."

Curving her arms around his neck, Sara breathed in the scent that was as exclusive to Salem as his fingerprints. "And I do love you, Salem," she breathed out close to his ear.

Pulling back, he stared at her, unable to tell her that he loved her. How could he bare his soul, then have her walk out of his life when she returned to New York? He would not tell her he loved her, but he knew a way of communicating without words.

He laid his hand along her jaw, his fingers caressing the velvet feel of her skin. "I'm going to offer you a choice, kitten. You can tell me to take you home or—" His words trailed off.

"Or what, Salem?" All traces of gold had disappeared from her eyes, leaving them a dark, smoldering green.

His eyes betrayed his rising passion. "Or you can allow me to take you upstairs and make love to you."

Reaching up, she pulled his hand from her face and placed it over her breast. His fingers tightened over the firm flesh. They both gasped from the rush of arousal as the nipple swelled against the fabric that concealed her nakedness from him.

"Take me upstairs," she whispered hoarsely.

Gathering her in his arms, Salem picked her up and headed for the staircase. Sara had buried her face against his neck, her breathing quickening. He knew it had been a long time for her, and he wanted their coming together to be special—for her and for him. He had not been celibate as long as she had been, but he was glad he had waited— waited for her.

Soft recessed lighting provided illumination along the wide hallway containing rooms he rarely entered. He stopped at the bedroom where he slept and walked in. A bedside lamp cast a warm glow over the bed where he had slept alone for more than two years. This night, all of that would change. Sara Sterling would be the first woman to sleep in the bed he had purchased for himself and his wife. Grace had moved into the house, slept under its roof, but never in his bed.

Bending slightly, he placed Sara down on the bed as if she were a piece of delicate crystal. Her eyes seemed larger when she stared at him looming over her. She looked like a cat startled by a flash of bright light.

He smiled at her while he removed her shoes. Sitting down on the side of the bed, he removed his own shoes and then joined her. Lacing his fingers through hers, he turned on his side to face her. Her hands were icy cold.

"Are you frightened, kitten?"

Her breathing sounded unusually raspy. "I don't think so."

His nose nuzzled her scented neck. "Relax, baby. I won't do anything you don't want me to."

Closing her eyes against his intense stare, Sara nodded, pulling her lower lip between her teeth. "You're going to have to be a little patient with me."

Releasing her hand, Salem curved an arm around her waist and shifted her until she lay on his chest, her legs nestled between his. "Take all the time you need. We have all night."

Sara wiggled until she found a comfortable position, her breasts flattening against the hardness of his chest. Resting her head on his shoulder, she listened to the strong pumping of his heart keeping tempo with her own.

"Salem?"

"What, baby?"

"I can't afford to get pregnant. Not now."

He closed his eyes. "Don't worry. I'll take care of everything."

Grief and loss tore at his heart. Sara did not want children, and he did. He loved her, wanted her as his wife and to be the mother of his children. With Grace it had been another man he had to compete with, but with Sara it was her career—a career that would take her two thousand miles away.

His right hand slipped down her spine, his fingers splaying over the firm roundness of her hips. He managed to swallow back a moan when she moved sensually against his groin. His left hand moved down and he cradled her bottom, squeezing gently each time she shifted her hips. He searched for her mouth, his tongue easing between her parted lips, and he wasn't disappointed when she opened her mouth to receive all he was willing to offer.

First Sara was cold, then she was hot, as Salem's tongue moved in and out of her mouth in a rhythm that sent her pulse racing and her senses spinning out of control. Her hands cradled his face, moving up and tunneling through his long hair. Her mouth and tongue were as busy as his when she caught his upper lip between her teeth, pulling it into her mouth before giving the fuller lower one equal attention.

Her fingers massaged his scalp, his ears, trembling as she felt the fires of desire settle between her thighs, and bring with it a rush of liquid.

"Salem," she breathed when he reversed their positions and straddled her body. His hair had fallen over his forehead, shielding his expression from her.

Closing her eyes, she felt rather than saw Salem undress her. What seemed like long agonizing minutes were only seconds when he divested her of the dress. He went completely still, and she opened her eyes to find him staring at her black lace demi-bra and matching thong.

Supporting his greater weight on his elbows, he lowered his chest to hers. "Why did you even bother to wear anything under your dress? I must admit your undergarments are very pretty, but hardly practical."

Her gentle laugh floated up from her chest. "I can't go around without undergarments."

"Yes, you can," he crooned in her ear. "When you're around me you can do without the bra. Your breasts are too beautiful to cover up."

"They'll sag if I don't wear a bra," she countered.

His hand went to the front clasp, and with a quick motion he released it, baring her chest to his heated gaze. He found her breasts perfect. They were round and firm, with large, dark brown nipples.

"Your breasts will be firm even when you're sixty."

Sara did not acknowledge his prediction, but she had inherited her mother's body, and at age sixty-four Eve Sterling wore a bra only on special occasions. She had grown up with an aversion to what she considered a restricting garment, and her firm breasts had not sagged even after she had given birth to two children or with age.

"What about my panties?"

Hooking his fingers in the narrow bands of elastic, he pushed the tiny triangle of lace off her hips and down her legs. His breathing quickened when he surveyed what had teased him for weeks. Sara Sterling was exquisite; she was perfect.

He dangled the thong from a forefinger, shifting his eyebrows. "You call this a panty?"

Shaking his head, he tossed it on the floor beside the bed. Within seconds the bra followed, leaving her completely naked to his burning, searching gaze.

Curving his hands under her shoulders, he sat her up as he went to his knees. "I undressed you, and now it's your turn, kitten."

The heavy lashes that shadowed her cheeks flew up. "You want me to undress you?"

Running a hand through his hair, he pushed it off his forehead. "I'm not going to make love to you, and you're not going to make love to me. We're going to make love to each other." He shrugged out of his jacket and dropped it to the floor beside her dress and underwear. "I've given you a head start by removing my jacket." Beckoning to her with his right hand, he whispered, "Come on, kitten."

Sara rose on shaking knees and placed a hand in the middle of his chest. She wanted to scream at Salem to take her and end her frustration, but didn't. She knew what he was trying to do. He wanted no barriers between when they came together—no baggage from their pasts.

The heat from his body nearly overpowered her as she undid the buttons on his silk shirt. Even though her gaze was lowered she could still feel the heat from his obsidian eyes as he watched her every move. Pulling the hem of his shirt from the waistband of his slacks, she pushed it off his broad shoulders.

Her eyes widened when she saw the tattoo of a gray wolf over his left breast. The likeness was so real that she shuddered. She saw the distinct outline of the whiskers growing from the white hair on the muzzle, noted the black nose, and the black fur ringing the golden eyes.

Raising her gaze, she stared up at Salem staring down at her, the nostrils of his delicate nose flaring slightly. "What is it?"

He did not move, not even his eyes. "*Mai-coh.* It means *witch* in Navajo."

"Are you a witch?" The query was a hoarse whisper.

He blinked once before his mouth curved in a semblance of a smile. "I don't know."

Sara collapsed against his chest, trembling. She had asked him whether he was a shaman, soothsayer or warlock, and he had denied it. "You lied to me," she gasped, trying to slow down her runaway pulse.

"You asked me what I called myself, Sara."

"It's the same thing."

"No, it isn't, kitten."

"Must you always be so literal, Salem? I—"

Whatever she was going to say was cut off when his mouth covered hers in an explosive joining that swept away all and any fear she had of him. Soft moans filled the space as his kisses moved from her mouth, down her throat, over her breasts, belly. The harsh, uneven rhythm of her breathing changed, becoming gasps when the heat from his mouth seared the moist triangle of hair at the juncture of her thighs.

Arching off the mattress, Sara forgot that Salem Lassiter had not confessed to being a witch, forgot that she had not felt desire in more than six years, forgot that she had denied her femininity and forgot that any other man existed as she gave herself up to the fiery sensations taking her higher than she had ever been before.

Passion catapulted the blood through her head, chest and legs, making it impossible for her to think. The pleasure Salem offered her was a sweet agony that teased relentlessly while refusing to release her from the pulsing torment.

His name was locked away at the back of her throat, his tongue sweeping away her inhibitions. He said loving someone was about caring and sharing, and even though he hadn't told her that he loved her, she knew he did.

She felt the first ripple, soft and pulsing, then the second and a third. She lost count after the sixth one, and there was no way she could stop the screams from exploding from the back of her throat as ecstasy shook her uncontrollably until she lay motionless, spent and sobbing.

Sara didn't know when Salem slipped off the bed to remove the rest of his clothes, opened a small packet to protect her against an unplanned pregnancy and returned to the bed. Then she felt his hardness easing into her.

Reveling in the exquisite pleasure of Sara's tight body stretching and closing around his hardened flesh, Salem breathed in and out through his open mouth. He was so light-headed that he felt as if he would pass out before he achieved his own ecstasy in her fragrant softness.

"Oh, baby, oh, baby," he chanted over and over, the words mingling with Navajo. He was any and everything Sara wanted him to be: shaman, warlock, soothsayer, seer. He was *mai-coh* and he was Dream Walker.

He had realized his gift to enter her dreams because she had opened herself to him. She had become a part of him, and he a part of her. Through Sara Sterling he would be able to trace his past, his present and his future.

Her hands slipped down his back, her fingers tightening on the flesh of his buttocks, and he knew he had revived her passion. Slowing his rhythm, he slid in and out of her body with a strong, powerful thrusting of his hips.

A moan of ecstasy slipped through her lips, lingering against his throat. When he first saw Sara after she had tapped his arm at the airport, he had not thought he would succumb to her haunting beauty. He never would have believed she would awaken a response deep enough within him to make him forget his vow not to become involved with another woman. What she did not know was that she was also *mai-coh*.

He slowed his rhythm, hoping to prolong the pleasure taking him beyond himself, but it was not to be. He had been without a woman too long, he had lusted after Sara too long. Burying his head between her shoulder and neck, he closed his eyes tightly and released his dammed-up passions at the same time love flowed from Sara like heated honey.

The throbbing in his lower body continued, leaving him as weak as a newborn. The pleasure Sara had offered him was pure and explosive, and he pressed his face against the pillow which cradled her shoulders to keep him from blurting out how much he loved her.

His head cleared, his respiration slowed, and he returned from his exhilarating free-fall flight. Tightening his grip on Sara's body he reversed their positions, cradling her to his chest.

Placing kisses on the damp strands of her hair, he smiled. "*Ahéhee,* kitten."

"You're welcome," she replied in English.

His hands made stroking motions up and down her spine. "Did I hurt you?"

She chuckled softly. "No, Salem."

"Then why were you crying?"

Raising her head, she rested her chin on his chest and smiled. "Because it was so good."

He shifted his eyebrows. "It was better than good, Sara."

A smile of satisfaction curved her thoroughly kissed mouth as she closed her eyes. It was still in place when she drifted off to sleep.

Sleep took longer to release Salem from the startling events of the day. He had just celebrated what would have been his late son's birthday with a renewal of his spirit with a woman he had fallen in love with.

"You would've loved her, Jacob," he whispered to the silent room before a healing peace permitted him to join Sara in the sated sleep of lovers.

Chapter 18

Sara woke up, rolling over and finding the space where Salem had lain empty. Pressing her nose to the sheets, she inhaled the lingering scent of lime. She wasn't certain of the time, but it was day because streams of light had inched their way through the panels of wall-to-wall, sand-colored silk.

Rolling over, she slipped out of bed and headed for the bathroom. The scene that greeted her rendered her motionless. Salem stood in front of a sink, completely nude, drawing a razor over his lathered cheeks. Her gaze caressed his dark brown body, lingering on the width of his broad shoulders, his flat belly and long, muscled legs. He was a perfect male specimen.

Spying her reflection in the mirrored walls, he turned and smiled at her. "Good morning." His penetrating gaze lingered on her chest before moving lower.

Sara resisted the urge to attempt to cover her nakedness. She returned his smile with a bright one of her own. "Good morning. What time is it?"

He glanced at a clock on a built-in shelf. "It's exactly six." Turning back to the mirror, he drew the razor under his chin. "Did you sleep well?"

"Yes, thank you."

She knew their conversation sounded stilted, but it wasn't every day she woke up in a man's house or in his bed. "I'm going to need a towel and a toothbrush."

"You'll find everything you'll need on the table near the shower stall."

Still self-conscious about walking around in the nude in front of him, Sara made her way across the bathroom. She discovered not only a new toothbrush and the same brand of toothpaste she used, her bath gel, her favorite cologne and body lotion, but also a change of underwear, a T-shirt, socks and jeans. A pair of her boots sat on the floor beside the table.

"How did you get my things?"

Leaning over the sink, Salem splashed water on his cheeks, washing away the soap and lather. He picked up a towel and blotted the moisture from his face.

"I took your keys from your purse and went to your cabin. I didn't think you'd want to walk around in the altogether, not that I'd mind." He wiggled his eyebrows at her.

She wanted to reprimand him for going to her cabin without first seeking her permission, but realized he was right. What she had shared with him was still too new for her to feel comfortable.

Her smile was dazzling. "Thank you."

Picking up her clothes, she walked through the connecting passage to the other bathroom. That one was decorated in white marble with accents of black, while the one Salem used was the reverse.

She turned on the water in the large sunken tub and added the gel. The soothing fragrance permeated the room with the rising bubbles. While the tub filled, Sara brushed her teeth and washed her face. She had just settled down into the warm, scented water when Salem walked into the bathroom, stepped into the tub and sat down opposite her.

"A gentleman usually asks a lady if he can share her bath."

Resting his arms along the ledge of the tub, Salem threw back his head and laughed. "How soon you forget, kitten. I'm not a gentleman, but a *mai-coh.*"

Her expression changed, growing pensive. "Do you Navajo revere the wolf?"

He shook his head, the strands of his unbound hair sweeping over his bare shoulders. "No. In fact, the Navajo's fear of the wolf is similar to that of many Europeans. The Native American belief is that it could be called upon and used by humans for good or evil. Both the Navajo and Hopi believed that human witches used or abused the wolf's powers to harm people."

"What do you believe, Salem?"

"I believe we should put aside the legends and learn to live with the wolf and all wildlife. The wolf, like the African American and Native American, is a survivor. We have proven ourselves to be survivors. But for the wolf, I wonder for how long. If the wolf is to avoid extinction, we—as caretakers of the earth—must let go of our fears. Man must strive to understand that God created every living creature for a purpose and value, and we must learn to recognize the balance and beauty of nature. If we don't, then the wolf will disappear, along with thousands of other living organisms."

"What made you select the wolf as your totem?"

"He came to me in a vision."

Vertical lines formed between her eyes as she squinted at him. "Don't you mean a dream?"

"No, Sara. It was a vision. You may dream, but I have visions."

"What's your Navajo name?"

He told her in Navajo, then translated it into English. "Dream Walker."

Sinking down lower in the water to cover her breasts, she felt herself withdrawing from him. "You...you can enter someone's dream?" she asked, the expression on her face mirroring her obvious skepticism.

His gaze widened, drawing her to him when all she wanted to do was flee the tub and his house. "Yes."

"That's preposterous." Half of her wanted to believe him, while the other half couldn't. She had read about most of the Southwest tribes, attended some of their ritual celebrations, but had remained detached from most because she had been excluded from their most sacred ceremonies.

Salem shrugged a broad shoulder. "Believe whatever you want to believe." He floated across the tub and curved an arm around her waist. Lowering his head, he brushed a light kiss over her lips. "Can you believe that I want you again?"

Sara gasped when his hand swept up her inner thigh. "Salem!" she whispered.

He smiled down at her. "That's my name, kitten." A finger replaced his hand, searching between the delicate folds to find her ready and pulsing. She shuddered violently with his touch. His hand worked its magic, and after a while she collapsed against his wet, naked body, whispering his name over and over.

She hadn't fully recovered from sharing her bath with

Salem when he picked her up and retreated to the bedroom, pressing their wet bodies down on the twisted sheets where they had made love only hours before.

After making certain to protect her, he entered her with an unbridled force that literally took her breath away. Once her flesh closed around his turgid hardness, all semblance of control disintegrated—for both.

She challenged—he accepted the challenge. He challenged—she accepted in kind. He withdrew, his mouth sampling every inch of her body, leaving her moaning in ecstasy. She reciprocated, his chest rising and falling as he labored for every breath. It all ended when he again joined their bodies and found the perfect tempo and harmony before they exploded in a shower of fiery sensations. Afterward they lay side by side, gasping in surrendering moans of complete sexual gratification.

It was minutes before noon when Sara walked into the main house at Sterling Farms. She did not see anyone, though she heard the sound of voices coming from the family room. She peered in and saw Chris sprawled out on the sofa, his left leg elevated on a stool, channel surfing.

"Hey, bro."

Turning his head, he smiled at her. The skin around his dark eyes crinkled as he motioned to her. "Welcome home, sis. Come in and talk to me."

She walked in and sat down next to him. Taking the remote from his hand, she pushed a button and turned off the large-screened television. Staring at him, she noted changes in her brother she hadn't seen before. His face was leaner than it had been in the past, and there were tiny lines around his large, slanting dark eyes that hadn't been there, either. Her gaze lowered to his straight nose, strong mouth and attractive dimpled chin before reversing itself. Even though he was only thirty-three, there was a sprinkling of silver in his wavy black hair. Like his mother before him, he was graying prematurely.

"Where's everybody?"

"Mom and Dad went down to La Mesa Park for a few days. They plan to stay the weekend to see the thoroughbreds race. Miss Marisa left to go into town, and Joe went with her."

"So, they left you all alone."

Dropping an arm over her shoulders, he pulled her head to his shoulder. "I wouldn't be alone if I could drive. If I don't get this damned cast off my leg, I'm going to lose my mind."

"You still have four weeks before it can be removed."

"Four weeks seems as long to me as four months or four years," he mumbled angrily, staring at a small red mark between her neck and shoulder. "You and Salem must really be going at it hot and heavy."

Sara pulled away from him, her body stiffening in shock. "Why would you say that?"

He touched the area on her neck with his forefinger. "He left his brand on you. Tell him to start a little lower next time."

Placing her hand over her neck, she blushed furiously. "Chris!"

"Hey, sis, I call 'em as I see 'em. When are you guys going to tie the knot?"

Her embarrassment vanished quickly. "Don't go there, Christopher Delgado. Two days after Labor Day I'm out of here."

He gave her the cold, lethal stare that always had the power to chill her. "When did you start having flings?"

"Flings?" she repeated.

"I could use another word, Sara, but I won't because you're my sister. Do you or don't you like the man?"

"Of course I like him. Why?"

"Because I'd hate to see you do what Grace did to him."

"What did she do?"

Chris stared at Sara, complete surprise on his handsome face. "You're sleeping with the guy and you didn't ask him?"

Heat flared in her face, and she averted her head to avoid her brother's cold stare. "I did ask him, but he wouldn't tell me at the time. Then I forgot to ask him later."

"Hot damn! The brother probably made you forget your name, too."

She slapped him playfully on the shoulder. "Somebody needs to make you forget yours."

"Wrong, Sara." His expression sobered. "There's no room in my life for a woman—at least not on a full-time basis."

"Is political life so gratifying that it can take the place of a warm body in your bed? Or does it make you laugh enough to make you forget that you're lonely? Does it, Chris?"

"Mind your business, Sara." His words were laced with an icy warning.

"I'll mind my business when you stay out of mine," she countered angrily.

His eyebrows met in a frown. "Wrong, Sara. You're my business because you're my sister. And you will remain my business as long as there is some deranged asshole running around using your car for target practice."

She leaned over, rolled up the right leg of her jeans, and pulled the small automatic handgun out of her boot. "The only time I don't carry this little baby is when I'm with

Dad or Salem. And you should know that I know how to use it."

He mumbled a savage curse under his breath. "What the hell do you think you're doing carrying a gun?"

She placed it back in her boot, pulling down her jeans. "Taking care of myself."

Shaking his head from side to side, Chris closed his eyes, and when he opened them Sara saw fear in the jet-black pools. "What's going on with you?"

Forcing a smile, she touched his hand. "Nothing."

"You sure?"

Her gaze did not waver. "Of course I'm sure." Her answer seemed to satisfy him, and he smiled.

Curving his hand around the back of her head, he kissed her forehead. "Love you, sis."

She smiled at him. "Love you, too, bro."

"Are you really going back after Labor Day?"

"Yes."

He gave her a long, penetrating look. "I never thought I'd say it, but you're a fool, Sara Sterling."

"Why?"

"Because everything you're looking for in New York is right here under your nose."

She looked down her nose at him. "Are you talking about Salem Lassiter?" Chris nodded. "I could say the same thing about you."

He affected a frown. "What are you talking about?"

Rising to her feet, she stared at him for a long moment. "Try Emily Kirkland."

An inexplicable look of withdrawal came over his face. Then he said, "I know." The two words were barely audible.

Sara recognized her brother's vulnerability for the first

time, and she wondered whether he had kept most women at a distance because he was in love with Emily.

An expression of satisfaction brightened her eyes. Emily had waited sixteen years for Chris, and it appeared her patience might bear fruit.

"I'm going to Salem's house for dinner tonight," she said. "Do you want to come with me?"

"No thanks. I have to hang around here for a phone call. I'm not sure whether I'll by flying up to Santa Fe in the morning."

"For what?" Her brother had an apartment in the capital city, but he wasn't scheduled to return to the next scheduled session of the state senate until after Labor Day.

"A few of us want to get together and form a caucus for people of color. There are a lot of complaints that the state has not been addressing the needs of New Mexico's African, Native and Latin Americans."

"That's not only a New Mexican problem, but a national one. Are you sure you'll be able to get around using the cane?"

"I'll survive. Besides, if I need help I'll call Emily Kirkland," he said glibly.

"Don't mess over her, Chris."

He gave her a direct stare. "Have you ever known me to mess over any woman?"

A smile softened her lush mouth. "No. I'm sorry." She turned to walk out of the room but he called her name, stopping her retreat.

She did not turn around. "Yes, Chris?"

"I want you to be careful."

Glancing at him over her shoulder, she flashed a wide grin. "I will."

Chapter 19

Sara preceded Salem through the atrium, staring back over her shoulder at Shadow, who had crept silently from his secluded spot at the side of the large house.

"Does he ever come in?"

"No," Salem replied, deactivating the sophisticated security system.

"Not even in the rain?"

"Not even in the rain," he echoed, pushing open the door. "Shadow is a wolf-dog, a hybrid, which means he has retained the predatory nature of the wolf. If I don't allow him the opportunity to pursue natural prey, he'll kill livestock, pets and even children."

Sara stepped into the foyer and stared up at the man she had fallen in love with. "Aren't you afraid that one day he will kill someone's pet or livestock?"

"I've thought about it on occasion. Most wolf-dog hybrids are not aggressive by nature. But if they're placed in confined areas or in situations where they feel trapped or threatened, they can lash out unexpectedly."

She knew the wolf-dog had the entire run of Salem's property, which was a little less than four square miles. Shadow was used to seeing her and Salem together, but she had never made the attempt to touch him.

"How much does he weigh?"

"He's close to one-fifty."

Sara exhaled. "He weighs more than I do."

Curving his arms around her waist, Salem picked Sara up and spun her around. "Anyone can weigh more than you. What are you? One-ten?"

She managed to look insulted. "Of course not. I'm one-nineteen."

"And how tall are you?"

"Five-eight."

"There's still not much of you," he crooned, dropping a light kiss on her parted lips.

Curving her arms around his neck, Sara pressed her forehead to his. "When are you going to play the cello for me?"

He flashed a wide grin. "I'll play only if you accompany me."

"That's not fair. I haven't played the piano in years."

He lowered her feet to the highly polished wood floor. "You read music, don't you?"

"Yes, I can. But—"

"No buts," he interrupted. "Come with me."

Sara felt as if she had put her foot in her mouth as she followed Salem into the living room. He touched a panel on the wall and the enormous space was flooded with soft golden light from recessed fixtures. He pushed a button, and a shaft of light spilled over the magnificent black concert piano like a spotlight.

Grasping her hand, he led her to the piano bench and seated her. "You can warm up while I get the cello."

She spread her fingers out over the keys and struck a chord. She gasped in surprise. The sound floated up and lingered like an echo. The acoustics in the room were fantastic.

Her fingers literally caressed the keys as she went through a series of scales; her mother's insistence that she study the piano had not gone to waste. All she had learned after the years of music instruction and theory returned with vivid clarity.

She glanced up when Salem handed her a book of music with Beethoven's complete sonatas for piano and cello. "Do you really expect me to play these?"

He nodded. "I do." Lowering his head, he pressed his mouth to the side of her neck, eliciting a shiver from her. "I heard you warming up, kitten. You're very good."

She shot him a skeptical look. "Yeah, right."

Opening the book to the first sonata, she fingered the right hand, then the left, while Salem set up a chair less than five feet away from the piano. It wasn't until he had removed a magnificent cello from its case and sat down with it between his knees that she glanced at him. She watched, transfixed, as he adjusted the tension on the bow, applied a coating of rosin to the hair, then drew it over the strings, tightening them until he was satisfied with the tone.

Her breath caught in her throat when he closed his eyes and warmed up, the fingers of his left hand moving with incredible speed as he went through the scales. Her gaze was glued to the silver bracelet with the colored beads. Salem's hands, like the rest of him, were perfect. They were large and long fingered, with square-cut nails. He had removed his watch, and a lighter band was clearly visible where the sun had not darkened his skin on his left wrist.

Listening to the deep, rich sounds coming from the instrument made her wonder if their paths would have crossed if he hadn't broken his wrist and had gone on to have a musical career instead of becoming a veterinarian.

Now, it did not matter. Fate had brought them together, and she would enjoy the time given them until she returned to New York.

Opening his eyes, Salem smiled at Sara. "Are you ready?"

"Don't you need music?"

"No. I've memorized every note." And he had. It had been years since he had played the sonatas. However, since becoming a widower he had practiced for hours, losing himself in the music until he tired or the tightness in his left wrist forced him to stop.

"You can begin, Sara."

Taking a deep breath, she peered at the notes and began playing. She faltered a few times, but she became more confident by the time the haunting notes of Salem's cello joined the lilting sound of her piano playing.

Salem's playing was as hypnotic as he was—it drew her in and would not let her go. She didn't know when she stopped playing, because after a while she was consumed by the music filling the space. She moved off the bench like someone in a trance, sat down on a plush rug covering the wood floor and closed her eyes.

Sara did not know how long he played or how long she lay on the floor, but when the music ended the last note lingered like a soulful moan rising from the floor of a canyon. She was not aware that she'd been holding her breath until Salem sat down beside her and pulled her onto his lap.

Burying his face in her hair, he whispered to her in Navajo, asking, "Are you all right, baby?"

She nodded, not trusting herself to speak and shatter the mood.

"Why did you stop?"

"I couldn't continue. Not with you playing. I'm sorry you broke your wrist, because you are truly gifted."

Turning her to face him, he cradled her face in his hands. "I'm not sorry. Because if I hadn't become a veterinarian I never would've met you."

Her mind refused to register the significance of his statement. "What do you mean?"

His eyes widened until she could see into the depths of the shimmering black pools. "I don't want you to go back to New York."

"You don't know what you're saying."

"I know exactly what I'm saying, Sara."

She shook her head. "No. I can't."

"Why?"

"I told you before, my career is in New York, not here."

"Can't you have a career here?"

Pulling away from him, she stood up and wrapped her arms around her body. He was asking the impossible. He didn't want her to leave, but what was he prepared to offer her?

"My *life* is in New York, Salem," she repeated, the statement as definitive as an opening sentence in an obituary.

He rose to his feet in one smooth motion and stared at her back, and for the first time since he had come to know Sara Sterling he cursed her and the stubbornness that would not permit her to consider relocating to New Mexico.

He took two steps and came up behind her, his chest pressing against her back. "Last night you asked me about my wife. I couldn't talk about her, because if my son had lived he would have celebrated his fourth birthday yesterday."

A noticeable shudder shook Sara when she heard the words, which seemed to come from deep within Salem's soul.

Turning around, she stared up at him, seeing the lingering pain in his midnight gaze. "I had no right to pry."

"You couldn't have known."

The fingers that had produced the most hauntingly beautiful music she had ever heard curled around her upper arms, and with a minimum of effort pulled her closer.

"We're sleeping together, which means you have every right to know." Lowering his head, Salem rested his chin on the top of her head. "Grace Clark and I met on a New York to San Francisco flight about eight years ago. She was a model at the time, and she had just completed a shoot in New York. She told me she was going home for the first time in more than six months. I was returning from a symposium at Tufts, and we both had layovers in New Orleans. She was friendly, outgoing and very flirtatious. Even though we exchanged telephone numbers before she left to catch her connecting flight to California, I didn't think she would ever call me, so I gave her the number to a veterinary hospital in Santa Fe."

"But she did call you," Sara stated softly.

"Yes." His voice seemed to come from a long way off. "She waited a month, then called and said she was coming to Santa Fe for a magazine layout shoot. Once she arrived she admitted there was no shoot, so we spent the week together touring the city, going to the ballet and the symphony. I couldn't remember when I had enjoyed a woman's company that much, so I promised to come to San Francisco to visit her. The encounters continued for a year until I asked her to marry me, and six months later we exchanged vows."

"Did she give up her modeling career?"

"Not at first. We had managed to see more of each other when we were dating. Then we began to argue. She argued about my being on call at the hospital, and I argued about her accepting assignments that kept her away from home for weeks. We finally compromised, and she took a six-month leave. I felt married for the first time in two years. What I didn't know was that Grace had begun seeing another man."

Sara's breath caught in her throat when her heart lurched in her chest. She chose her words carefully. "How did you find out?"

"I saw them together when they were coming out of a hotel in downtown Santa Fe."

"Did she know you saw her?"

"No, and when I confronted her she laughed in my face. I'll never forget her challenge. She said, 'If I continue to see him, what are you going to do about it, Dr. Lassiter?'"

"What did you do?"

"I left her, commuting between Santa Fe and the reservation to see after my elderly grandmother. Then Grace came to me with the news that she was pregnant. And before you ask, Sara, I have to admit that I didn't know who had gotten her pregnant. After my grandmother died I took Grace back, because I realized I was still in love with her despite her infidelity. She delivered a boy, and when I saw Jacob I knew the child was mine.

"We managed a semblance of what could be called a family for about six months. Then Grace began straying again. The arguments escalated. Her major complaints were that our two-bedroom apartment was too small, and that I spent too much time away from home. I resigned my position at the hospital to set up a private partnership with another vet. Grace became bolder with her liaisons, and after a while I realized I was spending less and less time at home. And whenever I came home it was to be with my son.

"After one hostile exchange, I decided to compromise. I withdrew the monies my parents had put aside for my education and invested it, built this house, then dissolved my partnership to become an on-call vet to local ranchers and to zoos all over the state. Grace never came to see the house while it was under construction, complaining bitterly that Las Cruces was too far from Santa Fe. What she did not say was that it was too far from her philandering lover. We moved in, and our first night under this roof as a family Grace told me that she would not share my bed.

"I lost it, Sara. She was my wife, and even though we'd shared a bed it had been months since we had made love. Any and all love I had for her up until that time died. Despite her infidelity I'd still loved her because she was the mother of my child. We argued for the last time, and I told her that I wanted a divorce. I called my attorney and told him to draw up the papers. A month later Grace was gone… Even if she had wanted to take her own life, there was no reason to murder Jacob."

Sara swallowed to relieve the dryness in her throat. "Did she leave a note explaining why she had planned to commit suicide?"

He shook his head. "She didn't. After the autopsy I found out that she was pregnant again." Salem registered Sara's soft gasp. "And I knew *that* baby wasn't mine."

As she shook her head, Sara's gaze mirrored disbelief. "Oh, sweet heaven. She was responsible for taking three lives."

Salem sighed heavily. "She knew that if I left her, her lover wouldn't marry her, so she felt she had no way out."

"Was it because he was married?"

"No, kitten. He's not married. He's a very ambitious man who finds married women easy prey because they're unable to make too many demands, demands which might interfere with his political aspirations."

Pulling back, Sara's eyes widened until they were the size of silver dollars. "Who is he?" The query came out in slow motion.

Salem's gaze caught and held hers for a full thirty seconds. "William Savoy."

Her lids fluttered wildly. "Governor Savoy's son?" Closing his eyes, Salem nodded. She repeated the name over and over to herself. It would be another two years, but it was certain that her brother would challenge William Savoy in the next gubernatorial election.

"Does Chris know that William was sleeping with your wife?"

"I'm afraid he does."

"Do you think he'll ever expose him?"

Salem managed a wry smile. "I doubt it. I've found your brother to be very ethical. If he's going to defeat Savoy, then it will be because of political issues, not because he's going to expose Savoy's private life."

Curving her arms around his neck, Sara rose on tiptoe, brushing a soft kiss across his mouth. Her mouth caressed his in a dreamy intimacy that told him wordlessly that she was offering him the opportunity to trust and heal.

Her fingers went to the buttons on his shirt, baring his chest. Lowering her head, she let her tongue trace the outline of the wolf over his heart, becoming one with him. His hand cradled the back of her head, his respiration quickening when her warm, moist breath feathered over his flesh.

Her tongue circled one breast, then the other, her teeth teasing the nipples until the tiny buds stood up around the flat surface. Her mouth and hands grew bolder, causing Salem to groan as if he were in pain. She unbuckled his belt, unbuttoned his waistband and slipped her hand between the fabric of his slacks and cotton briefs. It was her turn to shudder when his maleness swelled in her hand.

Closing her eyes, she laid her head against his chest and alternately squeezed and caressed his hardened sex. As he became more aroused, so did she. The fire she had lit in him spread to her, preparing her for his possession.

Salem stood as motionless as a statue, eyes closed, hands curled into tight fists at his sides.

He couldn't move, did not want to move, because he knew if he did he would take Sara on the rug like a stallion mounting a mare in heat.

She was a witch—*mai-coh,* working her magic and taking his strength. He tried concentrating on something—anything except her hands and mouth on his body.

Then she touched him without the barrier of fabric between his flesh and her magic fingers, and without warning he swept her up in his arms and headed for the staircase, taking the stairs two at a time. The sounds of clothing being pushed aside competed with the harsh whispers and labored breathing when Salem and Sara fell across the king-size bed, mouths joined, limbs intertwined.

Salem smothered Sara's lips with a demanding mastery that ignited a fire which threatened to consume both. Forcing her lips open with his thrusting tongue, he simulated what she could expect once he entered her.

Sara felt the heat—everywhere. A heat that left her moaning and panting for fulfillment. A heat that clouded her mind and left her writhing and seeking out the one thing that would end the erotic torment.

Moaning in protest when Salem pulled away, she lay waiting for him to protect her. The seconds of sacrifice were assuaged once he entered her with a powerful thrust that had become a raw act of possession.

He called—she answered. He pleaded—she acquiesced. She demanded—he obeyed. She loved and he returned the love.

Salem made her his prisoner, sliding down the length of her body and drinking deeply from the well of flavorful carnal libation, and after he drank his fill she took him into her mouth, branding his flesh. He cried out to her in Navajo, English and Spanish.

He forced her head up, reversing their positions, and joined their damp bodies. They ended their dance of desire with an explosion of fiery pleasure that left both shaking uncontrollably. They lay together, waiting for their breathing to slow to a normal rate, then made their way to the bathroom.

Sara shared a shower with Salem, enjoying his touch all over again when he washed away the essence of their lovemaking. They lingered under the soothing flow of pulsating water, holding each other. There was no need for words. Their hearts had spoken, their destinies inexorably linked by a power greater than they were, or ever would become.

Chapter 20

Sara woke sometime just before dawn when Salem leaned over and kissed her cheek. "Go back to sleep, kitten. I have to go to assist a foaling."

She sat up, trying to make out his face in the darkened room. "Where?"

"One of the Stoddard's mares is experiencing dystocia. I'm going to deactivate the alarm in case you want to leave the house. You'll be okay because Shadow will be around." He kissed her again, then he was gone.

She lay down on the mound of pillows cradling her back and closed her eyes. The Stoddards were twenty miles north of Sterling Farms, and she prayed Salem would reach the mare in time. The risk of a foal being born with his forelimbs first was an extreme danger to mare and foal. Closing her eyes, she whispered a silent prayer that the foaling would be successful.

* * *

Sara completed her morning ablution and had covered her nakedness with one of Salem's T-shirts when he returned three hours later. She sat on the patio watching the sun rise and paint the sky with shades of pink, mauve and blue.

She could not understand how Grace Lassiter could not have loved the house Salem had built for her. But then, she could not understand why the woman had chosen William Savoy as her lover. She remembered seeing news footage of him. She had found him attractive enough, but she would never forget his eyes. They were a cold, pale blue-gray— cold and cruel.

A gentle smile crinkled her eyes when Salem moved toward her. She noticed the dark stains on his shirt and jeans, knowing it was blood. Rising to her feet, she saw his expression. The foaling had not gone well.

He held up a hand, stopping her. "Don't touch me, Sara. I have to shower and change my clothes."

She blinked once. "Which one did you lose?"

"The foal." His voice was flat, emotionless.

Swallowing noticeably, she nodded. "Are you hungry?"

He managed a half smile. "Starved."

Neither had eaten much when they went to a local restaurant the night before. Sara had ordered a salad, then proceeded to pick at it until he asked for the check. Something had been bothering her, but when Salem asked her she had given him a bright smile and said nothing.

"That's good, because I made up a batch of Miss Marisa's fabulous honey biscuits. All I have to do is pop them in the oven."

His smile brightened. "Now I know I can't let you go. You're beautiful, brilliant, sexy and a wonderful cook."

The gentle eagerness in her gaze vanished, replaced by a lethal calmness that chilled Salem. It was a look he had seen in her half brother's eyes when Christopher Delgado talked to him about his political opponent's proclivity for having affairs with married women.

"You can't let me go, Salem, because you don't have me."

He schooled his features to not show how much she had wounded him. What he was feeling at that moment was as painful as the telephone call asking that he come down to the railroad crossing to identify the bodies in the car registered in his name. Sara did not know it, but she had ripped out his heart, allowing him to hemorrhage unchecked.

"You're right about that, Sara." His voice was low, controlled. "But even if I *never* have you I will always love you."

Sara stared at Salem, her mouth gaping, watching as he turned and walked toward the house. Shadow ambled over to her, sniffed her legs and pressed his moist nose to the back of her hand.

Her fingers grazed the gray fur behind the wolf-dog's ears. Salem's confession was branded on her brain. His life had become an instant rerun. He'd fallen in love with Grace Clark and claimed her as his wife. But he'd never had her, because Grace had given her love to another man.

Shadow whined softly, and she smiled at him when he looked up at her. "I love your master, Shadow. I love him more than I've ever loved any man. But that love isn't enough to make me stay. He has to offer me more."

And she knew that the more had to be a commitment to spend the rest of their lives together. All Salem Lassiter had to do was ask her to marry him, and she would give up everything she had worked for in New York—and stay.

Salem's declaration of love changed them—especially Sara. She waited, waited for more from her lover, but when none was forthcoming she felt herself withdrawing from him. They continued to share dinner and a bed, but there were times when they lay side by side, holding hands rather than making love, and she welcomed the silence. It made it easier for her not to blurt out how much she had come to love him, how much she wanted to become a part of his future.

She did not look forward to the time when she would turn her back on everything she had shared with him to return to a lifestyle that had been as essential to her as breathing.

She had been in Las Cruces for six weeks, and she hadn't realized how much she missed the masses of humanity jockeying for their own personal space, towering buildings blotting out the brilliance of the sun, the noise, pollution and the nonstop excitement that was New York City. She did miss it, yet she was willing to give it up for the love of a man.

Turning her back to Salem, she closed her eyes and feigned sleep. She had lain motionless for ten minutes when his voice punctuated the silence.

"I'm going away Sunday."

Her breathing stopped, then started up again. "Where are you going?"

"Massachusetts. I'm scheduled to go to Tufts as a visiting lecturer for two weeks."

"Do you have a backup vet?"

"Yes."

"I'm going to miss you." Her voice was soft, almost breathless.

"Not as much as I'm going to miss you, kitten. I promise to call you every night."

This elicited a smile from Sara. "I'll try to be home."

Salem moved closer, pressing his naked body against hers. "Thanks. After I return I plan to go up to Taos to see my parents. I'd like you to come with me."

Her eyes opened in the darkened room. "Why?"

He moved closer. "Because I'd like them to meet you."

"Why?" she repeated.

Salem chuckled softly. "You sound like a little child, with all of these whys."

Turning, she tried making out his expression in the soft darkness. The only light in the expansive space came from strategically placed light sensors in electrical outlets.

"You haven't answered my question."

"I told my mother about you." His moist breath whispered over her ear. "And she said she would like to meet you. She and my father will be hosting a show for a local artist who is rumored to be the most talented, contemporary, Native American jewelry designer in the Southwest."

Sara did not want to read more into the invitation than necessary. "I told Emily Kirkland that I would be coming up to Santa Fe at the end of the month. Maybe I'll see her the two weeks you're away."

He thought about her driving to Santa Fe alone. "Can't you see her on the way back from Taos?"

Salem knew he sounded selfish, but he could not retract his query. He was afraid for her, and he did not want to tell her that leaving her for two weeks had nagged at him since they had begun sleeping together, that it reminded him of the time when he and Grace were apart—times when she strayed, but he had reminded himself that Sara wasn't Grace. Even though they would be separated by thousands of miles he wanted to be able to reconnect with her by phone. However, he did not know Emily Kirkland well enough to call her home every night to talk to Sara.

"I'll let you know," Sara replied.

Those were the last four words she uttered before she snuggled against his bare chest and fell asleep. Salem held her gently, his lips pressed to her hair. He loved her, loved her more than he had ever loved any woman, but Sara made it so hard for him. She did not fight with him, yet there was something about her that would not allow her to lower the barrier she had erected and trust him completely.

She never denied him her body, and he had come to look for the passion she offered so selflessly. It was her total commitment that she was not willing to share with him. She confessed to loving him, but that had not solved his dilemma. He had asked her to stay, and she'd refused.

He did not want to make the same mistake with Sara that he had made with Grace. His late wife had given up a career before she was ready to, and he had compromised himself when he resigned his coveted position on a highly skilled surgical team at Santa Fe's largest veterinary teaching hospital. He had asked Sara to stay in Las Cruces, but he would never ask that she give up her career.

Sara walked into the kitchen, surprised to find her mother sitting at the table. "Good morning, Mom."

Eve Sterling glanced up from the newspaper spread out on the table, removed her reading glasses and returned her daughter's smile. "Good morning."

"You're up early."

"Your father got up, and once I was awake I decided to get up."

Sara headed for the counter and poured herself a cup

of coffee from the carafe resting on a warmer, added milk and a teaspoon of sugar, then joined her mother.

"Where did Daddy go?"

"He had a breakfast meeting with a breeder who's looking for mares to increase his stock."

"I hope he's not thinking of selling Blaze."

Her gaze narrowed when she surveyed her mother. Eve Blackwell-Sterling always reminded her of a sleek, graceful cat. Her trim, tight body, slender face, high cheekbones, large, slanting eyes and full, pouting mouth still turned heads whenever she entered a room.

Eve's gaze did not waver. "You know she'll never race competitively."

Shaking her head, Sara swallowed back the sob in her throat. "No, Mama. He can't sell her."

Reaching across the table, Eve captured Sara's hands, holding them tightly. "The horse is four years old, has foaled once, and she won't let anyone ride her but you."

"But she's my horse."

"She's not your horse, Sara," Eve argued softly.

"Daddy gave her to me."

Eve's jaw tightened. "Blaze belongs to Sterling Farms. Just like the other two dozen horses. You talk about Blaze being your horse, but you haven't seen her in over two years. Your father has sacrificed thirty years of his life to make this horse farm a success because he wanted something to leave to his children—a legacy. But his children don't seem the least bit interested in his legacy. So what does it matter if he sells anything that has to do with Sterling Farms? And that includes the land and everything with four hooves. In two years he will turn seventy, and the very next day we will begin selling off land and livestock and terminating all employees."

Sara's lids fluttered wildly. "What?" The word exploded from her mouth.

"We're retiring, Sara. We plan to buy a smaller house closer to the city, then we're going to take an around-the-world cruise. In other words, we're leaving all of this."

"You can't."

"Why not?"

"Because you and Daddy have sacrificed so much to make Sterling Farms a success."

"Does it matter, Sara?"

"It *does*, Mama."

Eve arched an eyebrow. "To *whom*, daughter? You're as obsessed with the law as Chris is with politics. So obsessed and selfish that neither of you want to see anything else. How long will the two of you sacrifice personal happiness for your obsessions?"

Wresting her hands from Eve's grip, Sara stood up and walked to the cooking island. "I know what's in front of my eyes, Mama." She closed her eyes and folded her arms around her body.

Eve leaned back on her chair, crossed her arms under her breasts and tilted her head at an angle. "What?"

"I don't remember taking the witness stand."

Eve managed to look sheepish. "*Touché*, Sara."

She returned to the table and sat down. "I love Salem, Mama."

"How much?"

"More than I ever thought I could love a man." It was Sara's turn to hold her mother's hands when they talked candidly over the next hour, each woman baring her soul.

Sara walked out of the main house toward the stables. Her step was slow and deliberate as she squinted through the lenses of her sunglasses. She was glad she and her mother had talked. There were times in the past when they had talked for hours, she asking Eve Sterling questions most daughters would never ask their mothers.

Before she had reached a decision to offer Eric her virginity, she had asked Eve what she could expect, and her mother had been forthcoming with her answers. That interchange signaled a change in their relationship. They were still mother and daughter, but they were also adult women who respected each other.

Walking into the stable, she noted the empty stalls. She glanced up at the well-lit, well-ventilated structure. Everything in the stable was constructed with the well-being of the housed horses in mind. Her father had spent a small fortune making certain that the health and safety of the animals at Sterling Farms were given top priority, because he was aware that living in a stable was not natural for a horse. He made certain that the horses were let out of their stalls for long periods of time for exercise and social interaction.

Matthew Sterling paid top dollar for the very best bedding materials, nutritional supplies and veterinary care. His employees included a trainer, assistant trainer, groomer and his assistants, and several others to keep the stables and barns clean.

He had worked unceasingly to make the horse farm one of the best and most profitable enterprises of its kind in the Southwest, and now everything he'd worked for would come to an end in two years.

What does he expect me to do? Sara asked herself as she walked out of the stable and headed toward the paddocks. Did her father expect her to give up practicing law and become a horse breeder? What about Chris? Did he want his stepson to turn his back on what was certain to become a celebrated political career to take over Sterling Farms?

The whys still attacked her when she climbed up on a fence post and watched Joe Russell put a stallion through his pacing exercises. The intensifying heat of the sun burned the back of her neck, forcing her to retreat to the hay barn.

She stood in the coolness of the barn, waiting for her eyes to adjust to the shadowy interior. The distinctive smell of sweet hay lingered in her nostrils, and a slight smile curved her lush mouth when she realized how much she savored the redolent smell of hay, the leather of a saddle and the distinctive scent of horse flesh.

She heard a noise and glanced up. Her smile widened. Standing in the loft above her was Kareem Daniels, his thick arms folded over his wide, muscled chest. A bale of hay rested at his feet.

"Good morning." Her greeting was soft and friendly.

Kareem nodded, moving closer to the edge of the loft. "Mornin', Miss Sterling."

Before she could blink, the bale toppled off the loft. It landed with a dull thud, knocking her to the floor and pinning the left side of her body under two hundred pounds of solidly packed dried grass.

She felt a sharp, blinding pain at the back of her head as it hit the floor, then the pressure on her chest over her heart. Her eyes widened when she saw that Kareem hadn't moved.

"Help me," she gasped, trying unsuccessfully to push the hay off her chest and leg with her free hand. He still did not move, and her temper flared. "Get this damn thing off me!"

Kareem turned and made his way down the ladder. He stood less than three feet away from where she lay captive. There was something in his eyes that made Sara more frightened of him than the crushing weight on her chest.

Drawing her right leg up as far as she could bring it, her fingers searched under the leg of her jeans until they closed on the grooved grip of the small automatic in her boot.

The feral gleam in Kareem's gaze vanished, quickly replaced by fear as he stared down into the bore of her silver .32 automatic handgun.

"Get this off me, or there will be two of us dead this morning." There was no mistaking the coldness in her threat.

Kareem closed his eyes, swaying. "I can't," he mumbled.

Releasing the safety with her middle finger, Sara drew her lips back over her clenched teeth. "I'll count to three, and a second after I'm finished I'm going to blow your left ear off."

Kareem closed his eyes and shook his head as if in a trance. The gun Sara Sterling pointed at him was the same caliber his police officer father had put in his mouth to spatter his brains all over the bathroom wall—the same gun that had changed the lives of his mother and sister forever.

His young mother had never recovered from the tragedy. She'd spent the next six years of her life in and out of mental hospitals until she finally swallowed enough tranquilizers to put her demons to sleep—forever. His sister had married and divorced so many times that he had stopped counting.

And his own life was nothing to brag about. He had become involved with a group of criminals who were mixed up in everything from burglaries to stolen cars. Then he hired himself out to anyone who wanted someone eliminated. He had perfected a technique for killing a person with a single blow to the back of the neck. It was clean, bloodless and silent.

Sara's finger squeezed the trigger. "One. Two. Three." Her finger tightened and there was a loud explosion, followed by the smell of cordite, then the sound of a body falling.

Chapter 21

Sara stared at Kareem as he cowered in fear. She had deliberately missed the side of his head by several inches, but she did not release the gun when she tried shifting her body to use her right leg to shove the bale off her chest. She whispered a prayer of gratitude when she registered the sound of voices and running feet. Someone had heard the gunshot.

Matt Sterling raced into the barn, gun drawn, his gaze taking in the scene within seconds. He saw his daughter pinned down by a bale of hay, the gun in her right hand and the figure of Kareem Daniels moaning on the floor with his arms over his head. Slipping his gun in the waistband of his jeans, Matt snatched Kareem up by the back of his shirt and flung him several feet, ignoring the man's howl of pain when his head met a wall.

Moving quickly, he bent over and lifted the bale of hay off his daughter as if it weighed two pounds instead of two hundred. He curved an arm around her waist and pulled her to her feet. She swayed against his side, her fingers clutching the front of his shirt to steady herself. Reaching for the cellular phone attached to the belt around his waist, Matt turned and glared at Kareem.

"If he moves, baby, I want you to shoot him between the eyes."

Sara could not ignore the throbbing ache in her left shoulder. That area had taken the full force of the falling bale. Raising her right hand, she trained the weapon on Kareem, who continued to moan even though she hadn't wounded him.

Matt punched in several numbers on the cell phone. "This is Matt Sterling. I need somebody to come out to Sterling Farms." His gold-green eyes narrowed as he watched Kareem. The man had curled into a fetal position. "I'll be waiting for him."

He ended the call, shifting his gaze from Kareem to his daughter. "Are you all right?"

She nodded, offering a brave smile. "I'm certain I'm going to have a few bruises, but probably no more than Mr. Daniels." Her father had flung Kareem so savagely against the wall that he had literally bounced before landing on the floor.

"What happened?"

It was only when she had to recall the incident that she started to shake, shake so hard that she handed her gun to her father. "I don't know if it was an accident, because it happened so quickly. One minute the hay was on the edge, then it came crashing down."

"Do you think he pushed it?"

"I don't know, Daddy."

"Why didn't he help you?"

"I don't know," she repeated.

Less than ten minutes after Matt placed the call, a sheriff's deputy sped across the property. He stopped his cruiser at a barn where a small crowd had gathered.

He pulled out his notebook and took Sara Sterling's statement before he retreated to the corner where a young man cowered in fear. He could not make sense of his babble, and called the local hospital for medical assistance to assess the man's mental state.

Sara sat on a love seat in the family room, the fingers of her right hand massaging the muscles in her left shoulder. Her parents glared at her, and she knew they wanted answers, answers to why she had been carrying a concealed weapon—especially her mother.

Eve arched questioning eyebrows. "Well, Sara?"

She gave her mother a direct stare. "I started carrying it after the incident when someone shot at the Volkswagen."

"Do you think it was Kareem?"

She shook her head. "I doubt it. As soon as I pulled out the gun he froze as if someone had given him a paralyzing drug. I think he's too frightened of guns to even attempt to touch one."

Matt's heavy lids lowered over his brilliantly colored eyes. "I think Sara's right. Deputy McMillan said he kept mumbling 'don't let her shoot me' over and over." A deep frown creased his lined forehead. "I don't care whether he's responsible or not for that hay falling on Sara. He's fired. I'll send him his check with a warning that if he ever comes around here again I'm going to be the one who'll shoot him. And I'll make certain not to miss."

"Are you certain you don't want me to call the doctor to examine you?" Eve asked.

"I'm okay, Mom," Sara replied. And she was. She was bruised and sore where her body had taken the full impact of the falling bundle. Rising to her feet, she walked over to the sofa, kissed her mother, then her father. "I'm going to lie down and relax. I've had enough excitement for one morning."

The soft ringing of the telephone awoke Sara at ten, Mountain Time. Blinking, she reached for the receiver.

"Hello." Her voice was a sensual contralto.

"Sara."

She came awake immediately. It was Salem. Why was he calling her so early? He had been away for a week, and had established a pattern of calling her every night at nine o'clock—her time.

"Salem! What's wrong? Why are you calling me at this hour?"

There was a heartbeat of silence before his voice came through the receiver again. "What's going on?"

"What do you mean?"

"What's happening with you?"

"Nothing."

"Don't lie to me!"

Her temper flared. "Don't you dare yell at me, Salem Lassiter."

"I won't if you don't lie to me."

"I'm not lying."

"Something happened to you this morning," he continued, this time in a softer tone. "I felt it."

She went completely still, shaking as a cold chill swept over her body. "What did you feel?" Her voice was barely a whisper.

Again there was a pause. "I felt death."

Closing her eyes, Sara realized she couldn't hide anything from Salem—not when he felt her fear thousands of miles away. Taking a deep breath, she related everything that had happened in the barn. She ended with the news that her father had discharged Kareem Daniels.

"Good. I'll be home in a couple of days."

"Don't you have another week?"

"I have to go," he replied, not answering her query. "I love you, kitten."

"Salem!"

There was only the sound of a dial tone. He had hung up. Replacing the receiver in its cradle, Sara slid down to the pillows and closed her eyes.

Who is he? she asked herself for what seemed the hundredth time. What powers did Salem Lassiter possess that enabled him to connect with her across thousands of miles? And what other powers did he claim? Was he able to read her mind, to know what she was willing to sacrifice to spend the rest of her life with him?

Sara finally fell asleep. She had stayed up later than usual, waiting for Salem's call, and it was now after midnight. It seemed as if she had just fallen asleep when something woke her.

Sitting up on her bed, she stared at the window. The light of a full moon silvered the rug on the floor and the outline of the upholstered armchair. She smiled, her pulse racing with excitement.

"Salem."

Swinging her legs over the side of the bed, she reached for a white eyelet robe to cover her nakedness. Her bare feet were silent as she raced out of her bedroom, down the wide hallway and to a door leading to the wing of the house where she slept.

She unlocked the door and stepped into cool, dry, nighttime desert air. A wide smile parted her lips when she saw him. He stood in the shadows, leaning against a column, legs crossed at the ankles, arms folded over his chest. Quickening her pace, she raced to him, arms outstretched.

Salem straightened, pulling her against his body. He inhaled her sensual perfume, felt the velvety softness of her arms around his neck, and registered the firm fullness of her breasts against his chest.

He lowered his head and his mouth swooped down to capture hers, stealing her breath from her lungs. He moaned when her hands searched under the hem of his T-shirt, her fingertips sweeping over his breasts.

He ached for her, burned for her. He hadn't thought he would miss her so much, but he had. The telephone calls weren't enough. He had to see her, touch her, love her.

Sara pressed her open mouth to his, wanting to absorb him into herself—making them one. Her hands moved from under his shirt to his hair. Her fingers made quick work as she pulled the elastic band from the thick strands, leaving them to spill over his wide shoulders like a cascading veil of black silk.

"Take me home with you," she whispered against his lips.

His right hand moved down her spine, cradling a slim hip. "Go get dressed."

Pulling reluctantly out of his embrace, Sara turned and made her way back to her bedroom. She pulled on a change of underwear, jeans, T-shirt and a pair of running shoes. Going over to a desk in the corner of her sitting room, she scribbled a note and left it on a countertop in the kitchen. She didn't want her father calling the sheriff to report her as a missing person.

She left the house and found Salem waiting by his Jaguar. He held the door open for her. He closed the door softly, then rounded the car and took his seat behind the wheel.

"It's a nice night for a moonlight drive." He shifted his eyebrows when she stared at him as if he had taken leave of his senses. "What do you think?"

"I think you're crazy, Salem Lassiter."

He turned the key in the ignition, chuckling softly under his breath. "You've got that right. I'm a little crazy about you."

"Just a little?"

He shrugged his shoulders under the dark-colored T-shirt. "A little bit more than crazy." He drove slowly away from the Sterlings' main house until he reached the road that led to his property.

"I missed you," he stated simply.

Closing her eyes, Sara leaned her head back against the leather seat. "And I you."

They arrived at his house, and soon after they walked into the bedroom he examined her bruised shoulder before they demonstrated silently how much they truly missed each other. They were insatiable, their appetites heightened by the separation, and when Sara finally fell asleep in Salem's embrace pinpoints of light had begun to brighten the eastern sky.

It took him longer to succumb to the tension and exhaustion that had prevented sleep. The specter of death had visited Sara again. He had been thousands of miles from her, helpless and unable to protect her.

A cold chill had washed over him when he was explaining the evolution of the wolf to a group of students who were spending the summer in Grafton, Massachusetts, attending preveterinary courses at Tufts University School of Veterinary Medicine. His words had trailed off, locked in his throat, when he found that he couldn't breathe. He managed to excuse himself and retreat to a restroom, where he splashed cold water on his face. It was another ten minutes before he was able to return to the lecture hall. Throughout the discourse he had watched the clock, praying for the noon hour and the end of morning classes.

It was only after he had spoken to Sara that he was able to relax completely. Knowing she was alive and safe belayed his own apprehension until he saw her again.

Salem made the three hundred and fifty–mile drive from Las Cruces to Taos in under five hours, and when he pulled into the area set aside for parking at the bed-and-breakfast where he had made reservations for two, Sara was more than ready for a leisurely bath before they left to attend the showing of the elder Lassiters' gallery later that evening.

They were shown to their suite of rooms, which claimed a spacious bedroom with a fireplace, bath and a private entrance to a patio and garden. The furnishings were classic and classy, New Mexico fashion.

"Would you like me to order something to drink?" Salem asked, pulling the hem of his shirt from the waistband of his jeans.

"I'll have water, thank you." Sara smiled at him over her shoulder as she headed for the bathroom.

He wiggled his eyebrows at her. "Do you want to share your bath?"

"No, Salem. We'll be late." Whenever they shared a bath they usually wound up touching and kissing each other until the water cooled their unbridled passions.

Glancing down at his watch, he nodded in agreement. It was after five, and the showing at his parents' gallery was scheduled for seven. He had wanted to leave Las Cruces earlier, but Sara had called him and told him that she had to take care of some business. She later told him the *business* was Eric Thompson.

The attorney had come to see her, and she wanted complete closure on what they had once shared. Salem hadn't asked her what she and Thompson had discussed, because whatever they had shared was her past. He only thought of her as it related to his future—a future that was tenuous, because she had given him no indication that she had changed her mind about returning to New York.

He took their luggage to the bedroom, hanging garment bags on the rods in double walk-in closets. His parents had invited him and Sara to stay in their home, but he had declined the offer. He had only slept with Sara in his own home or at her cabin, and he knew he would not feel comfortable sharing her bed under his or her parents' roof unless they were married.

Sara felt the heat of Salem's gaze every time she shifted her attention to listen to Nona Lassiter. She had shocked him when she had emerged from the bathroom at the bed-and-breakfast wearing a *de rigueur* black dress. The sleeveless garment skimmed her curvy body, the hem ending midcalf with a generous slit in the front. He had gasped when she turned, displaying her bare back from nape to waist. Incredibly sheer black hose, a pair of silk sling-black heels and a pair of dramatic diamond studs in her pierced lobes completed her elegant outfit.

She had been equally impressed when she noted the exquisite design of his lightweight wool, pale gray suit with a double-breasted jacket. He had elected to wear a stark white shirt with a wine-colored tie, the first one she had ever seen him wear.

Nona's soft drawl recaptured her attention. Even though Salem was the image of his father, he had inherited his mother's jet-black eyes, dark skin and angular face. Petite and incredibly slender, Nona had recently celebrated her sixty-first birthday, and claimed a liberal sprinkling of gray in her short natural hairstyle. Her infectious smile crinkled her large, sparkling eyes. They reminded Sara of polished onyx.

"Did you see anything that you like?"

Sara pursed her vermilion-colored lips. "Yes—everything."

Nona laughed. "You're a smart woman, Sara Sterling."

Reaching into her purse, Sara withdrew a credit card. "I saw a bracelet that's calling my name."

Long, slender, dark brown fingers plucked the card from her fingertips. "You won't need that," whispered a familiar male voice close to her ear.

Turning, she held out her hand to Salem. "Give that back to me, please."

He slipped the card into the breast pocket of his jacket. "I'll keep this for you until later." He curved his arms around hers and Nona's waists, pressing a kiss to his mother's cheek. "Don't forget to offer Sara a family discount."

Sara felt the heat steal up her neck and flare in her face. "I do not need a discount, Salem," she hissed through clenched teeth.

"Stop teasing her, Salem," Nona warned softly.

His expression sobered, becoming impassive. "I'm not the tease, Mother."

Vertical lines appeared between Nona's dark eyes. "What are you talking about?"

He dropped his arms. Leaning down from his impressive height, he pressed his mouth to his mother's ear. "Ask Sara who's a tease."

Nona's frown deepened as she watched her son turn and walk away. "Just when I think I know who he is, he does it to me again," she remarked in a quiet voice.

"What does he do?" Sara asked.

Nona patted Sara's hand. "I'll tell you tomorrow. I told Salem that I want the two of you to come for brunch. It will give you and me the chance to talk and get to know each other better."

Sara spent the better part of an hour examining the extremely talented artists' pieces, deciding to do her Christmas shopping early. She selected an exquisite squash-blossom necklace for her mother. The sterling silver necklace was set with Montezuma Nevada turquoise and looked as if it had been crafted in a long-ago era. She chose a silver bracelet for Emily Kirkland set with Persian turquoise, and a belt buckle for her father made with gold on silver with a *ketoh*—or bow guard design—overlay and stampwork.

She did not know what to buy for her brother, because Chris did not wear jewelry, except for a watch. Before the night ended she selected a small rug, which could double as a wall hanging, depicting seventy-two birds on a Tree of Life resting in a Navajo wedding basket. It was only after Nona had taken the rug off the dowel that she admitted that she had woven it.

Sara awoke the following morning to the sound of rain and a dull cramping in her lower abdomen. Rolling over, she covered her head with a pillow, willing the pain to go away.

"What's wrong, kitten?"

"Go away, Salem." Her voice was muffled under the mound of feathers.

His fingers grazed her spine. "PMS?"

She threw off the pillow, sat up and stared at him. "How did you know?"

Salem pushed his heavy hair off his forehead, then reached over and pulled her close to his chest. "I know your body, sweetheart. Your breasts are fuller and more sensitive than usual. You let me know that last night."

Sara nodded. Whenever he had touched her breasts, she had literally arched off the mattress, and when his mouth replaced his hands she hadn't waited for him to reach his own sexual completion when she found herself dissolving in an exploding downpour of fiery sensations that left her crying and moaning his name.

"What time are we expected at your parents' house?"

"Anytime before ten-thirty."

"What time is it?"

Salem glanced over at the travel clock on the bedside table. "Nine-thirty."

She moaned softly. "It's time to get up."

"Do you want me to call and cancel? We can always do this another time."

"And have your mother angry with me for keeping her son away from her? I think not, Salem Lassiter."

Salem flashed a slow, sensual smile. "You know that she likes you."

Sara affected a moue. "I know nothing of the sort. But I must confess that I like her. I like her a lot."

Sara had spent a pleasant two hours with the elder Lassiters, sharing brunch under the loggia of their adobe-style house. She had been overwhelmed by the priceless art treasures filling the many rooms. There was evidence of Vance's sculpture and Nona's paintings and weaving on shelves, walls, floors and tables in every room—even the bathrooms.

Vance Lassiter was a quiet, gentle, tall man with handsome features and intelligent dark eyes. His short, steel-gray hair was typical of many who spent entire careers in the military.

Nona smiled at her husband and son. "If you'll excuse Sara and me, we're going for a walk."

Salem gave his father a knowing look, while Vance arched his eyebrows in acknowledgment. It was apparent the ladies wanted to talk—in private.

Vance stood up and pulled back Sara's chair while Salem did the same for Nona. The men stood, arms crossed over their chests, watching the two women walk across the loggia until they disappeared from their range of vision.

A cool mountain breeze feathered across Sara's face as she glanced up at the dark clouds in the sky. The early-morning rain had stopped, but angry clouds lingered.

It had been years since she had been in Taos, and after seeing the western ridge of the Sangre de Cristos mountains she was reminded of what she had liked about the magical little town. It was a microcosm of all that was good about New Mexico. With an elevation of more than six thousand feet, it claimed snow skiing, rafting, fishing, camping, hiking, cycling, a thriving arts and literary community and a slow, laid-back lifestyle that catered to the outdoor enthusiast.

Nona reached for Sara's hand, squeezing her fingers. "I'm only going to ask one thing of you, Sara."

Sara stopped, staring at Nona. "What's that?"

"Don't hurt my son." She closed her eyes, biting down on her lower lip and exhibiting her own vulnerability. She opened her eyes, giving Sara a direct stare. "I don't think he would survive a second time."

"Why would I hurt him?"

"Because he's in love with you."

"And I'm in love with him," Sara stated defensively.

"And Grace Clark stood exactly where you're standing and said the very same words to me. She loved Salem, and she loved another man." Nona wagged her head slowly. "She lied, Sara."

Straightening her shoulders and pulling her hand out of Nona's grip, Sara gave her a long, penetrating stare. "I'm not lying, Mrs. Lassiter. I love Salem."

Nona nodded, seemingly believing her simple statement. "Please call me Nona. Let's walk a little farther."

They made their way over to a stone bench in the middle of a field of colorful wildflowers and sat down.

Sara took a glance at the older woman's delicate profile. "What did you mean last night when you said that you didn't know Salem?"

Folding her hands on her lap, Nona closed her eyes. "I knew he was going to be different when I carried him in my womb. My mother-in-law had predicted it because she had had a dream about him. She said he would walk in two worlds, but he would have to find the one who allowed him to use the gifts that were given him by the Holy People.

"The *Diné* are the Navajo People, and Navajo legend maintains that the *Diné* had to pass through three different worlds before emerging into the world as we now know it—the Fourth World. They also believe that there are Earth People and there are Holy People. The Holy People have the power to help or harm the Earth People. The Earth People must maintain harmony and balance on Mother Earth, since these two are an essential segment of the universe. They call this harmony *Hózóh*.

"My son has been given many gifts by the Holy People. He is a brilliant musician, veterinarian and healer. He also has been given the gift of prophecy. However, it has taken him many, many years to acknowledge and accept these gifts. Why you've come into his life at this time is a mystery to me, because it is only now that Salem has begun to use his gifts."

It was Sara's turn to close her eyes. "He knows when I'm faced with danger."

"That's because your spirits are linked. Even though I see you as two people—individuals—Salem knows you're not. You're a part of him, Sara, as he is a part of you."

"What else do you know?"

Nona smiled, her black eyes sparkling like polished jet. "I know that you're going to give me grandchildren. One to replace the one I lost, and a few more."

Sara's body stiffened in shock, and she was momentarily speechless. "Did Salem tell you that?"

"No," Nona replied glibly. "Not even Salem knows that—at least not yet. Call it wishful thinking."

Throwing back her head, Sara laughed, and much to her surprise Nona's laughter joined hers. Then she sobered.

"Salem told me that you're an attorney. Where do you practice law?"

"I'm what is officially known as an Assistant U.S. Attorney. I'm assigned to a federal courthouse in Brooklyn, New York."

"Would you give it all up to marry my son?"

There was a beat of silence before Sara stated with a quiet firmness, "Yes, I would."

Sara settled down on the leather seat and smiled at Salem smiling back at her. "Your parents are wonderful."

He nodded, starting up the car. He was going to drop her off in Santa Fe before he returned to Las Cruces. Sara told him that she planned to spend a few days with Emily Kirkland, then drive back with her brother.

Reaching over, Sara turned on the radio to an all-music station. Half an hour into the one-hour drive from Taos to

Santa Fe an emergency news bulletin preempted the music. She listened, her heart pumping uncontrollably when the newscaster reported that the Santa Fe police had captured and wounded a man who had tried to force his way into the building where the television station KHRP had its offices. An unconfirmed report stated that the man was armed with a rifle, and that he claimed he wanted to kill Emily Kirkland because she had not responded to his online marriage proposals.

Sara's eyes filled with unshed tears, and she couldn't stop her hands from shaking. "Oh, sweet heaven," she mumbled over and over. "We've got to get to Emily!" she shouted.

Chapter 22

There was a noticeable police presence ringing the private community where Emily Kirkland resided. A uniformed Santa Fe police officer had replaced the development's guard.

Salem drove up to the visitor's checkpoint and gave the officer his name and Sara's. They waited while he called Emily's residence, then waved them through.

"Pull into the driveway with the white Vette," she directed him. He parked alongside the sports car, and Sara was out of the car and racing to the front door before he turned off the ignition.

Sara alternated pounding on the door and ringing the doorbell. She moved back a step when the door was opened by a plainclothes officer who had attached a shield to the pocket of his jacket.

"Name and identification," he barked.

"Sara Sterling," she replied as if in a trance.

"I need a picture ID, miss."

She had left her handbag in the car. Turning, she retreated to the car just as Salem was closing the door. "I need my purse. They won't let us in unless we show them IDs with our photographs."

Salem used the remote on his key ring and retrieved her purse from the console between the front seats. He handed it to her, then reached into the back pocket of his slacks for his driver's license.

They were allowed access to Emily's home after the officer checked and rechecked the photographs on their licenses. Sara hurried into the living room and found Emily sitting next to her mother. Joshua Kirkland stood with his hands clasped behind his back, facing the French doors leading to the patio.

"Emmie."

Emily glanced at her and stood up. Her lower lip trembled as she extended her arms, and she wasn't disappointed when Sara closed the distance between them and held her tightly, offering her strength.

"Thank you for coming," Emily whispered tearfully.

Sara rubbed her back in a comforting gesture. "You're safe now, Emmie."

Pulling back, her clear green eyes awash with unshed tears, Emily nodded. Her curly hair looked as if she had run her fingers through it.

"The crazy fool wanted to kill me because I didn't email him back."

"Don't, Emmie. Don't think about him. He's in police custody. They'll take care of everything."

The telephone rang, and everyone in the room went still. A female detective waited for the third ring, then picked up the receiver. She whispered a greeting, then covered the receiver with her hand.

"There's a Michael Kirkland on the line."

Joshua turned around, Vanessa stood up, and Emily pulled away from Sara to answer the phone.

"Hey, Michael. I guess you heard." She forced a smile. "Can you think of a better way to boost ratings? No, there's no need for you to request an emergency family leave. Yes, Mom and Dad are here with me. Sara and Salem just walked in." A frown distorted her beautiful face. "Stop it, Michael! I don't want to hear a single word about you killing someone." She held the receiver away from her ear as if it had suddenly become a venomous reptile. "Dad, you'd better talk to your son!"

Tall, silver-haired, elegant Joshua Kirkland crossed the room and took the phone from his daughter's outstretched hand. His voice was low, not permitting anyone to over-hear his conversation.

The front door opened again, and two couples walked into the living room, their arms filled with brown sacks, take-out pizza boxes and plastic bags that were straining at the seams.

A short man with thinning blond hair and glasses held his bags aloft. "Hey, Kirkland, what the hell is this—a wake? That idiot messed up our lunch plans, so we decided to hang out here instead."

Emily smiled at the network's assistant news director. "Thanks, Gary. You're the best."

Sara took Salem's hand, pulling him in the direction of the kitchen. "Come. Help me set the table."

They hadn't taken more than two steps when Sara heard her brother's voice. Leaning heavily on a cane, State Senator Christopher Delgado hobbled into the living room.

There was complete silence while everyone watched Emily Kirkland stare at Christopher as if she had never seen him before.

Chris stared back at her, his features deceptively composed. "I had to come to make certain that you were all right," he stated in a formal tone.

Emily nodded. "I…I'm fine."

"Chris."

He turned, noticing his sister and his parents' neighbor for the first time. "Hey, sis, Salem."

She shifted her eyebrows in a questioning manner. "Are you staying to eat?"

"Is there enough for me?"

"If there isn't, then we'll call out for more," Emily said, smiling broadly.

The door of Emily's house opened and closed dozens of times as people came and went over the next six hours. Joshua and Vanessa Kirkland had retreated to their Santa Fe hills home once they realized their daughter was recovering from the frightening ordeal with the help of her friends and colleagues.

Someone had slipped half a dozen CDs on a disc player, and a festival atmosphere ensued. Two of the many bags contained a number of six-packs, and when the tabs were popped the level of noise escalated appreciably.

Emily had one of the detectives call a local restaurant for a delivery of more food from their take-out menu. He shook his head, marveling at how quickly she had forgotten the incident. If the stalker had gained access to the room where she sat preparing copy for an upcoming taping, she would not have been smiling and ordering food for her friends.

An hour later the delivery man was stopped at the gate, his packages examined, given the money for the order along with a sizeable tip and escorted back to his truck.

The familiar strains of a romantic ballad came through

the speakers of a sophisticated stereo unit, and someone dimmed the recessed lights. Chris limped over to Emily, offering her his hand. She smiled up at him, rising to her feet, and permitted him to lead her out to the middle of the living room. A lightweight cast gleamed against his tanned leg under a pair of walking shorts. He leaned on the cane with his right hand, while his left arm circled her waist.

Sara watched Salem make his way across the room and reach for her hand. "Will you dance with me, kitten?"

Her smile gave him his answer as she pressed her body close to his. They danced for what seemed like hours, stopping only to quench their thirst.

It was nearing midnight and only Sara, Emily, Salem and Chris remained in the expansive living room, talking softly. The head of the television station had made a special request to the Santa Fe police to have Emily's property guarded until all of the details were gathered from the alleged stalker.

Emily sat next to Chris, her head resting against his shoulder. "You guys are going to have to hang out here tonight, because there's no way I'm going to clean up this mess by myself."

The remnants of pizza boxes, cans of beer and plates filled with evidence of spicy buffalo wings, corn on the cob, onion rings, spareribs, tossed and Caesar salads, and salad platters of tuna, chicken, seafood and fruit littered the table in the dining area and every flat surface in the living room and kitchen.

"I'll help you in the morning," Sara volunteered.

"I'll stay and help, too," Salem added.

Chris let out an audible sigh. "I guess you can count me in on the cleaning duties."

Emily combed her fingers through her hair. "Chris, you

can sleep down here, unless you're willing to navigate the stairs."

He shook his head. "Down here is fine."

Pulling out of his embrace, Emily stood up, rolling her head on her neck. "Salem, you can take the bedroom at the end of the hall. If you need any grooming supplies you'll find them in the adjoining bathroom."

Salem rose to his feet, smiling at Sara. "I'd better get our bags from the car."

Stretching her arms above her head, Sara smothered a yawn. "I'm sorry to poop out on you guys, but I'm exhausted." She stood up, walked over to the love seat and ruffled her brother's hair. "You need a haircut, bro." Leaning over, she kissed his cheek.

He nodded in agreement. "I'll cut it before I go back to work. Good night, sis."

"Good night."

Sara hugged Emily, the two women holding each other tightly. "Thanks again for being here for me," Emily whispered in her ear.

"That's what friends are for."

"I'll talk to you about Salem in the morning," Emily continued. "But I should let you know that several of my female colleagues want to know if he's available."

Pulling back, Sara looked at Emily from under her lashes. "Hell, no, he's not."

"That's exactly what I told them."

Hell, double no, she fumed, making her way over to the staircase. Her steps were slow and measured as she climbed the stairs and walked into the bedroom where she had slept when she had come to Emily's house for the first time. She kicked off her mules, slipped out of her slacks and blouse and made her way to the bathroom.

She brushed her teeth, washed her face, then took a

shower. When she walked back into the bedroom she found
that Salem had left her luggage by the bed.

Pulling back the blanket on the bed, she slipped between
the crisp sheets, and as soon as her head touched the pillow
she was asleep.

Emily had been given a week's leave, and Sara spent
the week with her even though she missed Salem. They
alternated calling each other, and the conversations always
ended with declarations of love.

She had confessed to Emily that she had fallen in love
with Salem. She admitted she loved him enough to give
up everything she had worked to achieve in New York if
only he would commit to a future with her.

"If he professes to love you, then why hasn't he asked
you to marry him?" Emily argued softly.

Sara shook her head. "I don't know. He's asked me to
stay in Las Cruces, but I told him I couldn't."

"I'd say the same thing. I don't know what's wrong with
men. They expect women to do all of the sacrificing while
they continue with business as usual."

Taking a sip of herbal tea, Sara stared into the flickering flames of the fire burning in the fireplace, nodding.
"Tell me about it, girlfriend."

The summer temperatures had dropped to an unsea-
sonable fifty-five degrees, prompting Emily to light a fire.
Sara had pulled a sweatshirt over her tank top and added
thick cotton socks to her bare feet. Both women, clad in
jeans, had placed oversize throw pillows on the floor in
front of the fireplace.

"Maybe he's frightened," Emily said after a comfortable silence.

Sara gave her a look of disbelief. "Of what?"

"Marriage. After all, his first one was a major disaster.

Anyone with half a brain knew that his wife was sleeping with William Savoy."

"Was she beautiful?"

Emily shrugged her shoulders. "Well, I guess you could say that she was attractive. She photographed very well. She was tall, at least our height, but thin. Too thin. And for a sister, girlfriend, she had no booty."

Sara smiled and took another sip of her tea. "I'm glad I'm not suffering from that affliction."

Turning over on her belly, Emily peered around at her rounded bottom. "Same here."

"I'm going to be pushing off in the morning. Chris has to see his orthopedist on Thursday."

Emily nodded, her gaze fixed on the fire. "I can't believe you only have two weeks left before you have to go back to New York."

It was Sara's turn to nod in agreement. It was the middle of August, and two days after Labor Day she would board a plane that would take her back to New York City. Instead of sleeping in her near-white furnished cabin, in the bedroom where she had grown up, or in the bed she'd shared with Salem Lassiter in the ultramodern expansive structure he had erected in the Mesilla Valley, she would turn back the blankets on a bed in a bedroom in Brooklyn Heights. She would no longer wake up to see the towering peaks of the Organ Mountains, but the impressive span of the Brooklyn Bridge and the familiar Manhattan skyline.

Salem Lassiter had become lover, healer, teacher and for that she would be eternally grateful. She was not certain of her future, but she was certain that a part of her would always love him.

Sara drove her brother back to Las Cruces in his late-model Saab. Chris was anxious to finally be rid of the cast that had covered his leg just below his knee to his ankle. The break had been severe enough for the doctor to recommend that he keep the lightweight cast on an additional two weeks.

She let Chris off at the front of the house, then drove around to the garages. She parked his car next to the blue Volkswagen. The windows had been repaired, and the paint touched up where pieces of flying glass had chipped away the brilliant sapphire-blue color.

And for the first time in weeks, Sara breathed a sigh of relief. The shadow of danger that had cast a cloud over her stay was gone. Emily's stalker had given a full disclosure of his eccentric behavior when he imagined himself in love with her, then finally succumbed to the wounds he'd sustained when he tried to elude capture.

What she refused to think about were the threats that had sent her fleeing the Brooklyn courthouse after her last conviction. She would deal with it when she returned. However, it wasn't the only thing she had to face—there was also her relationship with John Bohannon.

Sara carried her bags into the house and dropped them in the entryway, then made her way to the family room. Her brother and parents were relaxing on overstuffed chairs, talking softly.

"Hello," she intoned cheerfully.

Matt Sterling stood up and pulled her against his chest. "Welcome home, prodigal daughter."

"Daddy," she drawled, kissing his smooth jaw. Easing out of his embrace, she walked over and sat down next to her mother. "Missed you, Mom."

Eve flashed a warm smile. "Missed you, too. A man called here for you last night."

"Who?"

"Someone named Bohannon. He said he was calling from Phoenix."

A slight frown furrowed Sara's smooth forehead. "Phoenix? But John lives in New York. Did he say why he was calling from Arizona?"

Eve shrugged a shoulder. "He said he was there on business. He wanted to know when you'd be home, because he thought he would stop by to see you on his way back east."

"Did he leave a number?"

"I left it on your bedside table."

Sara nodded. "I'll get it later." Her gaze swept from her mother to her father. "What are you guys planning to do tonight?"

Matt stared at his wife. "I was trying to get your mother to go out to dinner with me. She said she wanted to wait for you and Chris."

Chris pushed to his feet. "Well, we're here. Let's go. It's not every day that we all get to go out together."

"Do I have time to shower and change my clothes?" Sara asked.

Matt glanced at his watch. "You have twenty minutes."

"Thanks." She turned and headed for her bedroom.

Chapter 23

Sara could not remember the last time she had shared dinner at a restaurant with her mother, father and brother. Matt Sterling was in rare form, teasing his wife about pleading a headache on an average of four nights each week.

Chris glanced up from his soup, remarking in deadpan, "You guys still do *that?*"

Sara gave her brother a good-natured punch to his shoulder. "Watch your mouth, brother. They're not that old."

Matt glared across the table at his stepson. "I bet I get more than you do."

"I suppose you would, Dad. Having a broken leg can put one at a distinct disadvantage."

"Ask your mother about the time I'd broken my ankle. I never imagined she could be so creative."

"Mateo," Eve admonished softly. "Not here."

The other three diners turned and stared at Eve. It had

been years—many years—since she had addressed him by the Spanish variant. Chris and Sara had grown up hearing their mother address their father as Mateo, but only when she was close to losing her temper.

Matt inclined his head. "Forgive me, *Preciosa.*"

"You're forgiven, my darling." Eve tilted her head, awaiting her husband's kiss. He did not disappoint her when he covered her mouth with his.

Exchanging a knowing glance with her brother, Sara winked. They had grown up in a household filled with love and a lot of passion. Their parents adored each other, and were demonstrative when displaying their affections. She wanted what her parents had—a lifelong love filled with passion—a passion which would continue well into old age.

Salem stood in the shadows on Sara's loggia, waiting for her. She had called him from Santa Fe earlier that morning, informing him of her return. Since the call he had begun counting the hours, days and weeks to when he would no longer see, touch or make love to her.

He had confessed his love to her so many times that he'd lost count. Loving her had stripped him bare, leaving him vulnerable to untold pain and anguish. He'd told himself that Grace would be the last woman in his life, but somehow Sara managed to slip under the barrier. She had become a part of his existence just by being who she was, and he'd found her perfect: face, body, passion, spirit and an inner strength that did not lessen her femininity.

Her stubbornness and unwillingness to compromise frustrated him, making him wonder what he hadn't given her. How much more of himself did she want him to relinquish?

He heard the distinctive sound of a car's engine and he

straightened from his leaning position. Shadow also rose to his feet, ears erect.

"She's back, partner," Salem murmured softly. Shadow wagged his tail in response, while growling deep in his throat. "Sara is very special to me," he continued in a monologue with the wolf-dog, "and I want you to keep her safe."

The sweep of headlights came into view, then the outline of the Volkswagen. Salem wasn't aware that his breathing had accelerated until he watched Sara step out of the car.

Her slender figure was in silhouette until she moved under the glow of the lanterns affixed to the wall of the loggia. Her eyes appeared abnormally large in the diffused light. His gaze lingered on her face, moved leisurely down her body, then reversed itself. Her face looked younger, fresh without makeup, and the pale peach slip dress she wore made her appear virginal, untouched.

"Welcome home." His deep voice vibrated with suppressed passion.

A mysterious smile tilted the corners of Sara's mouth. "Thank you. I'm glad to be home."

Salem took two steps, reached out and eased her into a gentle embrace. "Every time you go away I hold my breath until you return."

"You're going to have to exhale sometime."

Burying his face in her hair, he inhaled the hypnotic fragrance that made him want to strip her naked. He did not know what it was about Sara Sterling that aroused a lust he found difficult to control. He did not feel complete until she writhed beneath him, whispering what she wanted him to do to her. And there was never a time when he did not comply with her wishes.

"I don't want to."

Sara closed her eyes, drew in a deep breath, and let it out slowly. She was certain Salem felt her trembling, trembling with a wanton desire, one that made her want to beg him to make love to her where they stood.

Rising on tiptoe, she pressed her breasts to his hard chest, her parted lips to his hot throat. "Come inside with me, Salem. Let me show you how much I've missed you—missed having you inside me."

Salem's warm blood boiled with her erotic confession, and it was his turn to shudder in arousal. He hadn't realized his hands were shaking until Sara pulled out of his embrace to unlock the door to her cabin.

What happened next became a surrealistic mirage. Neither could remember when they had shed their clothes, which trailed from the front door to the bedroom.

Sara lay facedown on her belly, Salem straddling her trembling form as he became *mai-coh,* his tongue and teeth tasting and branding her flesh from nape to ankles.

Moans of rapture punctuated the sounds of labored breathing as Sara and Salem shed all inhibition to offer each other a passion that swept away lingering remnants of mistrust.

Turning her over effortlessly, Salem supported his greater weight on his arms as he stared down at her flushed face. Passion had turned her eyes into pools of shimmering jade-green—pools deep enough for him to drown in.

Parting her legs with his knee, he eased his hardness into her moist heat, shuddering violently when her legs curved around his waist, allowing for deeper penetration.

Heat rippled under his skin, becoming hotter and more intense each time Sara arched against his powerful thrusts. They had ceased to exist as individuals, separate entities, becoming one with each other. Everything ceased to exist beyond the love and passion they offered.

Waves of ecstasy throbbed through Sara as she felt her defenses weakening. How could she leave New Mexico, leave Salem? Not when she loved him so much. Not when she had also become *mai-coh*. They had cast spells over each other—spells neither was able to break.

Her fingers were entwined in his long hair, increasing the pressure on his scalp as her pleasure intensified. The pulsing ripples began, deepening and escalating in strength when she tried suppressing them. She did not want the pleasure to end—not yet. She wanted it to go on—forever, if possible.

But it did not. A spasm seized her, hurtling her through the universe, her screams exploding and floating up as she arched, convulsed, then shuddered uncontrollably at the same time Salem's dammed-up passions erupted.

Moisture from his body bathed her flesh, seeping onto the delicate cotton sheets, and then she registered an unfamiliar wetness between her thighs. Her eyes opened, her heart racing in a panic she had never known.

"Sweet heaven!" she gasped, pushing against his chest. Salem had collapsed on her smaller frame, and it was impossible to move him. "Salem! What have you done? Get off me!"

He groaned, then rolled off her trembling body. Lying on his back, he threw a muscular arm over his forehead, waiting for his runaway breathing to return to normal.

Sara slipped off the bed; her knees were shaking so much she could hardly stand. The light from the lamp on the bedside table revealed her worst fear. The evidence of their lovemaking was clearly visible along her inner thighs.

Within seconds her passion dissipated, replaced by anger. "I hate you." Her voice was low, vibrating with rage.

Salem sat up, his gaze filled with genuine confusion. "What?" The single word exploded from him.

"I trusted you to protect me." Her breasts shuddered as her chest rose and fell with the fury making it difficult for her to draw a normal breath.

"I told you I did not want to get pregnant." Each word was forced through clenched teeth.

His head cleared, and Salem realized what she was saying, what he had done. She had asked him to protect her, and he had—every time—until now.

He combed his fingers through his hair, pushing the heavy strands off his face. "I...I'm sorry, Sara." His apology sounded trite, even to him.

Turning her back, Sara folded her arms around her body. "Please leave."

Moving off the bed, Salem stood behind her; the imprint of his passion was branded on her velvety flesh. "Sara."

"Go."

He made an attempt to touch her, but pulled his hand away at the last possible moment. "Let's talk about it. If you become pregnant we can—"

"We can do *nothing*. We have nothing. Now, get out now!" she ordered, cutting him off.

Salem gritted his teeth in frustration. He had to explain to her that having a baby—if he had actually gotten her pregnant—wasn't the end of her world, that she would be able to combine motherhood with a career.

"Marry me, Sara."

Closing her eyes, Sara breathed heavily through her open mouth. The words she had longed to hear Salem utter sounded empty, hollow. If he had asked her the day before, a week ago, even a month ago, she would've said yes without hesitating. But not now, not because she might be carrying his child. She didn't want him to want her out of guilt, or because he was feeling noble because he didn't want her to be an unwed mother.

Squaring her shoulders, she tilted her chin, walked across the room, and entered the bathroom. She closed the door and her eyes. Two minutes later she sat on the floor, staring into space with unseeing eyes. Of all of the times they'd made love, Salem had picked the most fertile time in her cycle not to protect her.

A wry smile twisted her mouth as she blinked back tears. She had waited six years for Salem to walk into her life, and she had less than six weeks to ascertain whether she was carrying his child.

Her legs had begun to tingle from sitting on the cool tiles in the same position, so she pushed to her feet and made her way to the bathtub. Leaning over, she turned on the water, stepped in, then sat down to wash away all of the passion she had shared with the man she loved despite his duplicity.

Salem stared at the closed door for a full five minutes before he made an attempt to pick up his clothes off the floor. He didn't remember dressing, or walking back home. He did not remember retreating to the shower stall and turning on the cold water, nor his inability to stop the tears flowing down his face. What he did remember was the pain of losing a woman he loved more than himself.

Sara waited until morning to pick up the telephone and call the number John Bohannon had left with her mother. She punched in the numbers, listening to the measured ringing, waiting for his familiar voice.

"Hello."

She smiled when she heard his authoritative tone. "Hello, John."

"Sara. I'm glad you called. I was planning to check out this morning."

"Are you going back to New York?"

"I was hoping to see you before I left."

"Do you have time to stop in Las Cruces?"

There was a noticeable pause before John's voice came through the wire again. "I can spare a couple of days."

"Please come. I'd like to show you some real Southwestern hospitality before you return to the concrete jungle. When should I expect you?"

"I have to call and reserve a flight to Las Cruces, then book a room at a local hotel."

"Just book the flight, John. You can stay with us."

"Are you sure, Sara?"

"Of course I'm sure." My folks have six bedrooms."

"If that's the case, I'll call you after I touch down."

"I'll pick you up at the airport."

"That's all right, darling. I'll take a cab. Remember, I have an expense account that I hardly ever use."

"Just tell the driver that you want to come to Sterling Farms."

"It's like that?"

She had to smile. "Yes, John, it's like that. I'll see you later."

"Later, beautiful."

She hung up, feeling better than she had in hours. She had spent the night on the sofa in the living room dreaming—dreaming that she cradled a baby to her breasts. A baby with black hair and gold-green eyes—Salem's baby.

The image had haunted her until she walked out of the house and lay in the hammock, watching and waiting for streaks of light to crisscross the night sky.

John Bohannon's coming to Sterling Farms was heaven-sent. Her friend was what she needed to keep her from wallowing in a morass of self-pity. His presence would remind her of what she could look forward to once she returned to New York.

Chapter 24

Sara stood on the loggia with her mother, watching John step out of the taxi. A warm smile softened the tension around her mouth when she waved to him. He nodded in acknowledgment as he waited for the driver to retrieve his luggage.

Eve arched an eyebrow when she noticed his Louis Vuitton carry-on and garment bag, Rolex watch and Gucci loafers. There was no doubt Mr. John Bohannon favored clothes and accessories with recognizable labels.

John flashed his practiced professional smile. "Good afternoon."

Sara slipped her arm through John's. "Welcome to Sterling Farms."

"Thank you for inviting me." He dropped his carry-on and extended his hand to Eve. "John Bohannon."

She took the proffered hand, offering a friendly smile. "Eve Sterling. Welcome. Sara will show you to your room."

He nodded, letting out his breath slowly. Everything was going better than he'd planned. When he had boarded the flight in New York for Phoenix, he hadn't thought he would be given the opportunity to see Sara before she returned to New York. Lady Luck had deserted him for a while, but it appeared that she had returned—and just in time.

Sara led John into the house, down a wide hallway and into the section known unofficially as the guest wing. The room she had chosen for him claimed a view facing the mountains, a massive brass bed covered with an antique quilt and pale yellow-and-white-striped wallpaper on three of the four walls. The room's focal point was a towering fireplace built within a wall of aged bricks. Overstuffed chairs claimed the same pale yellow as the walls, while the color scheme was repeated in an adjoining bathroom.

John turned and smiled at her. "It's perfect." His expression changed, becoming impassive. "You look wonderful, Sara." And she did. Her cheeks had filled out, the slight puffiness under her eyes had disappeared, and the well-worn jeans molded to her slim body turned him on more than many of the body-hugging garments he had seen her wear in the past.

"Thank you. I'll let you settle in. Then I'll take you on a tour. My father and brother are in Albuquerque, so you won't get the chance to meet them until tomorrow."

John's smile widened as his confidence intensified. "What time are they due back? I'd like to meet them before I leave."

He did not say that he had to take care of his business before Sara's father returned, because he doubted whether Matthew Sterling would welcome him under his roof if he knew of his intentions.

"They're scheduled to arrive around six."

John stroked his moustache with a forefinger. "I plan to fly out at six. We'll probably miss one another."

A frown furrowed her forehead. "I thought you said you could hang out here for a couple of days."

"That was before I called my boss. He's having a problem with one of my clients. The man is threatening to take his business to another firm."

Sara slipped her hands into the pockets of her jeans, pulling the fabric taut over her hips. "Well, this means that we'll have to squeeze everything into one day instead of two. I suggest you change into something a little more casual. I don't think you'll want to return to New York smelling like a horse."

Sara closed the door to the bedroom and retreated to the family room where she found Eve sitting at a desk, signing her name on a stack of checks. She sat down on a chair close to the desk.

"Well, Mom, what do you think?"

Eve did not look up as she signed her name with a flourish. "About what?"

"About John?"

"There's nothing to think about. He's handsome, well-dressed and apparently has a lot of money."

Blinking slowly, Sara stared at her mother's delicate profile. "You don't like him?"

Even glanced up, looking at Sara for the first time. "I don't know him, therefore I can't dislike him, Sara. The question should be, do *you* like him?"

She shrugged. "Of course. I like him as a friend."

"So?"

"So, that's it. He's a friend."

"Who are you trying to convince, Sara?"

Rising to her feet, Sara walked over to a window and stared at the mountain peaks in the distance. "No one." Her jaw tightened as she folded her arms under her breasts.

"It's over between Salem and me." There was a suffocating silence, and when Eve did not comment she turned to stare at her. "Do you want to know why?"

Eve gave her a penetrating look, shaking her head. "No, I don't." She replaced the cap of her pen, then stood up. "I don't want to get involved in whatever it is you and Salem can't agree on."

Sara couldn't believe her mother was shutting her out. In the past she had always been willing to listen to her pour out her heart whenever she was hurting emotionally.

"Why not, Mama?"

"Because you're a grown woman, Sara. There are times when you're so hard that it frightens me. Then there are the times when you want to be a little girl and hide from your feelings and from the truth. This is one of those times. You invite one man to stay under your roof while you're sleeping with another one who's less than a mile away. That spells trouble. Big trouble."

"There's not going to be any trouble."

"I hope you're right."

Sara forgot her mother's ominous prediction when she held John's hand, leading him to the paddocks. He had changed into jeans and a pair of low-heeled boots and had shielded his head and eyes from the blazing sun with a baseball cap and sunglasses.

"How many horses do you have?" John questioned.

"Only twenty," she replied. "My father sold off four mares a couple of weeks ago. He's in Albuquerque finalizing the deal. My brother went along to make certain all of the legal documents are in order."

"I forgot you told me that your brother is also an attorney."

"My brother's a state senator."

John stopped suddenly, causing Sara to stumble slightly. She held on to his arm to keep her balance. "He's an elected official?"

"I told you he'd won the election by a very narrow margin."

Cursing under his breath, John managed a tight smile. "I guess I forgot."

And he had forgotten. Just when he thought things were looking up for him, Sara's revelation—that her brother was an elected official—did not bode well.

Sara reached for a straw hat hanging from a post and covered her head with it. Then she climbed up on the top railing, while John stood beside her watching the grazing horses. Joe Russell led a spirited stallion around the track, watching his legs as he established a raking stride.

"He's magnificent," John remarked, unable to pull his gaze away.

"That's Temptation. He's destined to become a winner." There was no mistaking the pride in Sara's voice. "Not only is he fast, but he's strong. It's not often you find a horse with his endurance."

John's gaze narrowed through his dark lenses. "I'm worried about you, Sara."

Turning her head, Sara stared down at him looking up at her. "Why?"

He gave her a direct stare. "Has anyone called you from New York?"

She shook her head. "No. Why?"

"There're still rumors floating around that the last creep you had convicted wants you eliminated."

"That's nothing new, John."

"It doesn't bother you that someone is talking about taking out a contract on your life?"

She turned away from him, feigning indifference. "Of course it bothers me. I wouldn't be normal if it didn't. But there's not much Norman Quinn can do behind bars. You forget he was sentenced to eight to twenty-five."

"And you think he still doesn't have connections?"

"I'm not saying he doesn't, John. But I can't worry about him or his threats."

John placed his hand on her thigh. "Let me take care of you, Sara."

She felt the heat of his touch through the denim fabric. "How?"

"Marry me," he whispered. "I can give you things you've only dreamed of. I can protect you, take care of you."

Her mouth opened in dismay, and she forced herself not to push his hand off her thigh. She swallowed several times before she was able to recover from his startling proposition.

"I don't want you to misconstrue my inviting you here as—"

"I'm not misconstruing anything," he countered angrily, stopping her words. "I make enough money to take care of you. The past three years my salary with bonuses has been over seven figures."

Swinging her leg over the railing, she climbed down and faced him. "When I was born I was worth seven figures, so it's not about money. My father can buy and sell horses that are worth close to seven figures every day if he chooses to."

"Then what is it about, Sara?"

"It's about me not taking advantage of your feelings. It's about me not leading you on."

Rage nearly blinded him, and John wanted to slap her until she begged him to stop. Did she not know who he was? How important he had become? How everyone praised his intelligence, his intuitiveness? How when he walked into a room all heads turned in his direction? Everyone recognized and acknowledged John Harry Bohannon—except Sara Sterling.

He no longer wanted or needed her acceptance, because he intended to kill her.

The idiot he had paid to eliminate her was now locked away in a padded cell babbling to himself. He had given Kareem a small fortune, money he could now ill-afford to spend, to make certain Sara Sterling never returned to New York. He did not blame Kareem as much as he blamed himself. The adage about never sending a boy to do a man's job was certainly true in this case.

Alan, the other idiot who had given him insider information that he had passed along to his clients, refused to see him or accept his phone calls after he'd threatened his sister. Suddenly everything he had worked for was coming down around him like an avalanche.

John did not have to worry about Kareem talking to the authorities, because he had been diagnosed as delusional, and Alan, his former friend and coconspirator, had disappeared. But he suspected that Alan was waiting for Sara to return before he resurfaced with enough information to send him to jail for stock fraud.

Sara did not know that he had flown to Phoenix to meet someone who purchased a small, powerful handgun for him. And she also did not know that he hadn't flown from Phoenix to Las Cruces—because he never would have made it past airport security with the gun—but had hired a car service to make the seven hundred and fifty–mile trip. It had taken the driver more than ten hours to deliver him to the Las Cruces airport, where he picked up a taxi.

He had less than twenty-four hours to eliminate Sara

before he returned to the Las Cruces airport. His flight might not be to New York, but to a South American country whose extradition policies with the United States were usually ignored—if the price was right.

If he killed Sara without getting implicated he would use the New York ticket, but if he failed he would be forced to learn another language.

John forced a smile he did not feel. "Thank you for being honest."

Nodding, Sara closed her eyes briefly. When she opened them she met his direct stare. "It's not you, John."

"Who is it, Sara?"

"It's me."

He arched an eyebrow with her admission. "So, I suppose what everyone says is true."

She frowned. "And what is that?"

"That you don't like men."

A wave of heat rushed to her face, and it had nothing to do with the summer sun. "That's not true." Turning away from him, she braced her hands on the upper rail. "There's someone else."

John moved closer to her, pinning her between his body and the fence. "Are you involved with someone?"

Nodding, she drew in a deep breath. "I was."

He took another step, his chest grazing her back. His gaze lingered on the expanse of skin between the collar of her blouse and the nape of her neck. From his greater height he recognized several faint red marks. He had been with enough women to recognize the signs of a passionate session of lovemaking.

"*Was,* Sara?"

"We broke up last night." Her voice was soft, breathless.

"Before or after you made love?"

She tried turning around, but discovered she couldn't. "Move back, please." He took a step back, and she shifted to face him.

John's right hand came up and cradled her cheek. "Do you want to tell me about it?"

Sara blinked back tears, grateful that her sunglasses shielded her eyes. "Not now."

"How about over dinner? We can go somewhere quiet and talk. Even though I'll never claim you as my wife, I'd like to think we still can be friends."

Curving her arms around his waist, Sara laid her head on his shoulder. "Of course. We'll have dinner at my place tonight."

Pulling back, he stared at her, complete surprise on his face. "Your place?"

"I have a cabin about a mile from the main house."

A powerful relief surged through John, and he was hard-pressed not to laugh aloud. "I'm looking forward to it."

What he didn't say was that it was perfect—better than any plan he could have formulated. Now, all he had to do was plan his escape from Sterling Farms—undetected.

Chapter 25

Salem felt the tightness in his wrist, but he refused to stop. He'd lost count of the number of hours he had sat at the piano, playing everything from Beethoven to Wagner. The wild, loud unrestrained notes mirrored his moods: anger, frustration, futility.

After returning home, he had called his service and directed them to forward all of his calls to the backup vet, then switched on his answering machine. He didn't want to see or talk to anyone until he sorted out the fiasco he had made of his life.

He had berated himself over and over about why he hadn't protected Sara, and could not come up with a plausible excuse. She trusted him, and he had given her his word that he would always take care of contraception, but he had failed her and himself.

The speculation of her becoming pregnant with his child was as frightening to him as it was to her. She'd never had a child, unlike him—a child he'd loved and lost. He hadn't dismissed the notion that if Sara were pregnant he would lose another child and its mother. He knew she would return to New York to raise the child—unless he fought her on her terms and in her arena—the court.

Welcoming the pain in his left hand, Salem segued into Wagner's overture to *Tannhäuser,* pounding the keys like a man pursued by demons. If he were going mad, then he welcomed it, because he would prefer living in a world of madness to existing without Sara—his *mai-coh.*

He slowed his playing when he thought of how his going mad would affect Sara. The Holy People had given him the gifts of music, healing and prophecy, and if his spirit *was* linked to Sara's, his madness would become her madness. His fingers stilled, resting limply on the keys.

Then he felt it—the rush of cold sweeping over his body, temporarily paralyzing him.

Closing his eyes, he felt her fear, saw her tears and heard her whisper his name.

Springing to his feet, he knocked over the piano bench as he raced out of the living room, making his way to the rear of the house. He shouted for Shadow in Navajo, and the wolf-dog appeared from the blackness of the night.

Salem opened the door of the Navigator and Shadow jumped up into the truck. He managed to close the door and turn the key in the ignition in one smooth, continuous motion. His heart slammed against his ribs, but his hands were steady. He couldn't afford to lose control, not when Sara was in danger.

He maneuvered over a rise and saw her cabin ablaze with light before he made out the distinctive shape of her Volkswagen parked alongside the north side of the building. Shifting into park, he applied the brake and turned off the engine.

Moving silently out of the truck, he and Shadow made their way toward the cabin. It was a moonless night, but Salem had come to Sara's cabin enough times to know the terrain in the dark.

Shadow loped alongside him, his tail held high like an alpha wolf. When they were less than two hundred feet from the front door Salem motioned to the wolf-dog to stop. Going down on one knee, he wrapped an arm around the thick neck, whispering softly in his ear. Shadow trotted around to the side of the house, disappearing into the darkness.

Salem stood up, walked to the front door and knocked softly. Pressing his ear to the door, he heard voices—male and female. He knocked again, then waited.

The door opened and he saw Sara staring up at him as if he were a stranger. "I want to talk to you," he said without preamble.

She shook her head. "Not now, Salem."

His impassive expression did not change. "When?"

As she opened her mouth to reply, the figure of a man moved into the doorway. "Apparently, you did not understand the lady. She said not now."

Salem recognized the New York accent immediately. However, he did not want to believe that Sara had called one of her Big Apple buppies to console her.

Crossing his arms over his chest, Salem stared at the man, who had curved his left arm under Sara's breasts. "If your name is Sara, then I'll permit you to address me. If it isn't, then I suggest you shut the hell up."

"Back it up!" John shouted, raising his right hand and pressing the barrel of a small gun to Sara's temple. "You picked the wrong time to come visiting, *my brother,* because now you're going to have to see me blow your girlfriend's brains out before I take care of you. Now do as I said, and back it up."

Salem backed off the loggia, his gaze trained on the gun pressed to the side of Sara's head. He didn't want to believe what he was witnessing. Grace had planned to take her own life, and now someone was planning to take Sara's.

"You don't want to do this," he stated softly.

"Oh, yes I do," John drawled.

"John, please," Sara pleaded.

"It's too late for begging, Sara," John snarled, tightening his grip around her ribs. "I know you wouldn't show any mercy in your courtroom. You've said so tonight. You wouldn't help me. Why should I show you any mercy now?"

Salem wanted to distract the man Sara called John—distract him enough to try to disarm him. "Do you actually think I'm going to stand here and let you murder the woman I love?"

"Shut up!" John shouted. He forced Sara out of the doorway and onto the loggia.

"Sara and I have made plans," Salem continued, his voice lowering to a soft whisper.

"He's right," Sara concurred quickly. "Salem and I are going to be married. I might be carrying his—"

John's arm moved up around her throat, tightening, stopping her words. "I thought I told you to shut up! That goes for both of you."

"You're a fool, city boy," Salem taunted. "If you hurt her you'll never make it more than a hundred yards before you find yourself without a throat."

John waved the gun. "Remember, I'm the one with the gun. So, who's a fool?"

Before the words were out of his mouth, Salem raised his right hand and a blur of gray fur flew through the air like a missile. Shadow's canine teeth sank into the flesh behind John's thigh, causing him to drop his gun and his victim.

His screams reverberated in the stillness of the night as Shadow held him captive. Sara fell to the floor of the loggia, crawling on all fours as Salem rushed forward, shouting at Shadow in Navajo.

The wolf-dog released John seconds before Salem's left hand grabbed his shirt, pulling him up savagely. Drawing back his right arm, he slammed his fist into the moaning man's face. Blood spurted from his nose and mouth when he hit him a second time.

Sara picked up the gun, then stood up. "Don't kill him, Salem!" she screamed when he hit John a third time. Holding the gun with both hands, she pointed it skyward and fired.

Salem's arm halted in midair as he turned and stared at her. "Let him go, Salem." Her voice was soft, coaxing. He obeyed, and John fell to the floor of the loggia in a crumpled, moaning heap. Shadow stood over the fallen man, growling deep in his throat.

She lowered the gun and handed it to Salem, butt first. "I'm going inside to call the sheriff. Try not to kill him."

He applied the safety, tucking the automatic into the waistband of his jeans. "I'll think about it."

Sara smiled a sad, tired smile, then turned and walked back into the house. Salem opened and closed the fingers of his bruised and aching right hand.

He walked over and sat down on a chair, staring out into the night. He had made it in time. He had saved Sara's life.

The sheriff arrived with two deputies, read John his Miranda rights and then loaded him into one of the cruisers. He deliberately ignored his plea for medical attention for his broken nose and missing teeth.

Salem sat on the love seat next to Sara, holding her hand while she told the sheriff that John had wanted to kill her to keep her from investigating a stock fraud. She hadn't known he was involved in a scheme in which he had misused confidential information obtained from a securities company to purchase stock for an electronic giant in advance of a cash purchase offer for that entity by a major communications firm. John Bohannon had instructed his clients to purchase securities for the company before the acquisition was finalized, resulting in his earning more than half a million dollars in commissions. She had refused to help him that evening, and he had pulled a gun.

She also revealed that John had confessed to hiring Kareem Daniels, and that Kareem had been too traumatized by her gun to complete his assignment.

The sheriff closed his notebook, shaking his head. "It's going to be up to your boss to request extradition. But that's only after we charge him with attempted murder."

Sara let out her breath in a weary sigh. "I won't push too hard for the extradition. He'd probably cop a plea, pay a hefty fine and receive probation. A New Mexico state prison will be a far different scene from the federal country clubs most white-collar criminals check into."

The sheriff nodded to Salem. "You'd better take care of your hand, Doc. From the looks of Bohannon's face, I'd say you have a nasty right jab."

Salem stared at his bruised knuckles. He had hit John Bohannon almost hard enough to break his hand. "If he had a choice, I'm sure Bohannon would welcome a jab to Shadow's canines."

Rising to his feet, the sheriff picked up his hat. He

smiled at the couple. "I'll let you know if I need anything else. Try to get some sleep tonight."

"Thank you." Salem and Sara had spoken in unison.

She rose and walked the sheriff to the door, waiting on the loggia and watching the taillights of his car until they disappeared into the night.

She stiffened when she felt the warmth of Salem's body behind her. Closing her eyes, she bit down hard on her lower lip. He had come to her. He had saved her life.

"How can I thank you?"

His fingers circled her neck as he lowed his head and pressed a kiss on her nape. "Marry me, Sara."

A slight shudder shook her. "Why?"

"Because I love you."

"Not because I might be pregnant?"

He pressed a kiss along the side of her neck. "No."

"What if I am pregnant?"

"Then nine months from now we'll celebrate the birth of our son or daughter."

She opened her eyes and turned to stare at him. "You want me to marry you. What if I want something in return?"

His gaze narrowed. "What do you want?"

"Will you relocate to New York?"

The seconds ticked off slowly, becoming minutes, as they stared at each other. He wanted something, and she wanted something. She had challenged, and he would accept the challenge.

"Yes." The single word was firm and final. "I would relocate anywhere to be with you."

Sara collapsed against his chest, her arms circling his neck. He loved her; he loved her enough to give up everything he had worked for to follow her. He was willing to give up his practice, his home and his pet for her, while all she had to give up was a job—a job she could get in any state in the union.

"And I you, Salem," she whispered against the warmth of his throat. Raising her head, she smiled up at him. "Can you wait for me to go back to New York and turn over my cases to another attorney?"

Curving his arms around her waist, Salem picked her up and kissed her soundly on her mouth. "I'll try, kitten."

"It won't take long."

He smiled at her. "You promise?"

She combed her fingers through his hair, holding it back off his face. "I promise."

Sara picked up a folder and placed it on a mounting pile on the left side of her desk: *U.S. v. Stratton.* She held a small microcassette recorder in her left hand. The task of recording the status of the cases was monotonous, and there were times when she held the recorder, not saying anything, and stared into space.

She had been back two weeks. Her return had disrupted the normal flow of business in the busy courthouse when she walked in two days after Labor Day and handed her boss her letter of resignation. The contents of the letter thanked him for his confidence and trust, and his willingness to allow her to gain a vast array of knowledge and experience in her field.

There were rumors about giving her a farewell party at a local club, but she declined their offer. She did not want to go back to the place where she had met John Bohannon. She still found it hard to believe that she had trusted him as a friend and that he had wanted to kill her to protect his reputation and his career.

A knock on the open door garnered her attention. She smiled at a legal secretary. "Yes, Tanya?"

"There's a guy in the lobby who wants to see you."

"Who is he?"

Tanya ran her tongue over her wet-look lipcolor. "Tall, about six-two, maybe three. Drop-dead gorgeous. The suit's Armani, shirt and tie look like Ralph Lauren. I couldn't quite make out the shoes."

Sara shook her head in amazement. Tanya described men in terms of designer labels. "That not telling me much."

"Hair, Sara. Black shiny ponytail."

She stood up, dropping the recorder on the desk. "Salem." His name came out in a breathless whisper. He had come to New York.

Tanya nodded. "Yeah, that's it. He said his name was Salem. Should I show him in?"

Reaching in the lower drawer for her handbag, Sara shook her head. "No. I'm leaving now. Can you put the files away? I'll finish these up on Monday."

She plucked her suit jacket from the coat rack, pushed her arms into it, then composed herself and walked down the corridor to the waiting area.

A sensual smile curved her mouth when she saw Salem leaning against a massive marble column, arms crossed over the front of a navy blue, double-breasted jacket, feet in loafers and crossed at the ankles. The silver bracelet with the colorful beads was visible on his left wrist below the French cuff of his startlingly white shirt. A leather carry-on bag rested next to his feet.

He straightened when he saw her, his gaze fusing with hers as she closed the distance between them. He counted the steps until she was standing only inches away, then reached for her.

"What are you doing here?" Her voice had a breathless quality.

Angling his head, he looked her up and down. "I've come for you."

Her gaze was fixed on his strong mouth. "I told you when I'd be back. I still have another week."

"Remember when we talked about my being your man?"

She nodded. "Yes, I remember."

"Well, I'm your man, Sara, and I told you that I would come after you if I felt you'd stayed away too long. This is one of those times."

"We've only been apart two weeks."

He arched an eyebrow. "That's one week too long," he stated quietly as he leaned over and picked up his luggage.

Winding her arm through his, she led him across the marble floor and out of the courthouse. The cool autumn air whispered over their faces as they made their way down the steps.

A mysterious smile curved her mouth. "I'm glad you came, Salem."

"Are you?"

"Very."

They walked to a corner, and Sara raised her arm to hail an oncoming taxi. Salem opened the door and helped her in before he moved in beside her.

She gave the driver her address, then leaned back and placed her hand over Salem's. There was no need for conversation. They had said everything before she left Las Cruces.

They had set a date for their wedding, and Eve Sterling had contacted Nona Lassiter for a listing of guests for their children's nuptials. Sara had selected Emily Kirkland to be her maid of honor, and Salem had asked Christopher Delgado to be his best man.

He'd called her every night, consoling her long-distance when she told him that she wasn't pregnant. She had changed her mind about becoming a mother—she wanted a child, his child.

The driver pulled up in front of the brownstone building and Salem paid the fare on the meter. Five minutes later he followed Sara up three flights of stairs and walked into her small, neat one-bedroom apartment. He noticed the outlines of pictures that had hung on the walls, empty bookshelves and labeled cartons containing articles she planned to ship to Las Cruces.

Salem placed his carry-on on the floor near the door, removed his suit jacket, hanging it on a nearby coatrack, then held out his arms. He wasn't disappointed when Sara moved into his embrace.

He pressed a light kiss on her eyelids, on the tip of her nose, then searched for her moist mouth. "I've missed you, kitten," he whispered against her lips.

"Show me how much, my darling," she murmured.

"Where's your bedroom?"

Holding his left hand, while his right was busy undoing his tie, she led him to the bedroom.

It was later, much later, that they lay in bed holding hands and talking softly about what they wanted for their future. They left the bed to eat, then returned to make love a second time. It wasn't until just before dawn that they took a vow to love each other—forever.

Epilogue

Three months later—Christmas Eve...

Sara Sterling-Lassiter stood in the middle of the living room, her green-gold gaze sweeping slowly around the room. Everything looked perfect.

She and Salem were celebrating their first Christmas together as husband and wife, and they were also hosting their first dinner party. The invited guests included in-laws, the Kirklands, her brother and Marisa Hall and Joseph Russell.

Salem walked into the living room, a satisfied smile curving his strong mouth. "You look beautiful." The timbre of his soft voice reflected the peace and joy radiating from his dark eyes.

Sara glanced down at the revealing neckline of her dark green dress. "You don't think it's too risqué?" A soft swell of her golden-brown breasts was visible each time she inhaled.

Moving closer to his wife, Salem curved an arm around her narrow waist. "The dress isn't risqué at all, Mrs. Lassiter, but you are."

A rush of heat darkened her skin as she lowered her lashes in a demure gesture. Her left hand moved up the front of his crisp white shirt, resting over his heart. The gold band on her third finger matched the one on Salem's. She hadn't known when they attended the showing at the elder Lassiter's gallery, but Salem had purchased the rings bearing the images of flute players a month before proposing marriage.

He had also bought her a gold-on-silver Navajo story bracelet with a Monument Valley scene in overlay and stampwork. His parents had offered them half a dozen pieces of artwork or sculpture as wedding gifts, and it had taken Sara three days to make her selections. The additional pieces were magnificent additions to the collection in the foyer.

"Everything looks beautiful," he crooned against her ear.

And it did. Sara had decorated the house with dozens of clay pots filled with white poinsettia plants. Red and white candles were positioned around the outdoor patio, the scene reminiscent of stars in the desert.

She had decided to host the cocktail hour on the patio before their guests moved indoors to the formal dining room for a sit-down dinner.

Salem found it hard to believe how much joy Sara offered him. She had decided not to seek employment with a law firm for the first six months of their marriage, declaring that she wanted to get used to being a wife before she combined marriage with a career. He was pleased with her decision, because it permitted her to spend more time with her mother and father.

Pulling back, he stared down at her upturned face. "Is there something you want to tell me?"

Dark green lights shimmered in her brilliant eyes as she affected a sensual moue. "Do you always have to read my mind, my darling?"

He arched an eyebrow. "I can't read your mind, kitten. But I do know you're hiding something from me."

Curving her smooth, bare arms around his neck, she pressed her breasts to his chest. "I won't be able to hide it too much longer. We're going to have a baby."

His gaze widened, his heart pounding painfully in his chest; he tightened his hold on her waist. "Are you sure?"

"Of course. It was confirmed yesterday."

Closing his eyes, Salem whispered a silent prayer of thanks. He had been given a woman he loved selflessly, and was now offered the opportunity to experience the joy of fatherhood one more time.

Sara stared at the perplexed look on her husband's face. "You didn't know?"

He shook his head. "No."

"But you have the gift of prophecy."

Salem nodded slowly. "I do, and I had a dream that you were whispering something in my ear. But I never thought…imagined *this*."

A slight frown appeared on her face. "You're not pleased?"

Pulling her closer to his body, Salem buried his face in her hair. "Oh, kitten, how can you say that? I'm pleased, stunned, happy, ecstatic, all of the above. But most of all—I love you."

"And I you, Salem."

The sound of the doorbell chimed throughout the expansive structure in the Mesilla Valley.

Sara and Salem walked through the living room to the grand foyer to welcome their guests into their home for what was certain to become a very special night for everyone.

* * * * *

REQUEST YOUR FREE BOOKS!

2 FREE NOVELS
PLUS 2 FREE GIFTS!

KIMANI ™
ROMANCE

Love's ultimate destination!

KROM11B

The third title
in the
Hopewell General
miniseries...

*ROMANCING
THE M.D.*

Fan Favorite Author
MAUREEN
SMITH

**Hopewell General:
A prescription for
passion.**

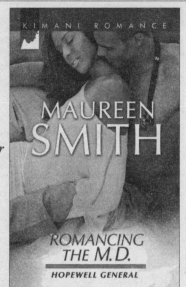

An internship at prestigious Hopewell General is a dream come true for Tamara St. John—and she isn't about to risk it for Victor Aguilar. The sinfully seductive doctor is driving her crazy with desire, but Victor refuses to keep their love behind closed doors. It's time to stake his claim on Tamara's heart—with a passionate dose of forever!

Coming in October 2011 wherever books are sold.

**In November, look for
CASE OF DESIRE by** *Jacquelin Thomas,*

**the exciting conclusion
to the Hopewell General miniseries!**

www.kimanipress.com

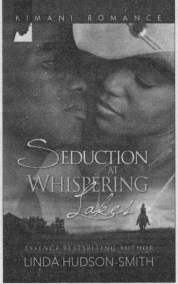